W9-DIU-324

"HIGGINS IS A WONDERFUL STORYTELLER!"
—*The New York Times Book Review*

"UNDERSTATED VIOLENCE, UNDERSTATED SEX, AND ENOUGH PLOT TWISTS TO KEEP YOU GUESSING UNTIL THE FINAL SHOWDOWN." —*Playboy*

Two brilliant men and a beautiful woman are drawn into a chilling triangle of passion and danger . . . racing toward the moment of truth that will force each of them to stand alone, to live or die . . .

SOLO

"A PAGE-TURNER . . . A TERRIFIC YARN."
—*The Philadelphia Inquirer*

"HIGGINS KEEPS THINGS MOVING."

—*Time*

"HIGGINS IS BACK IN FINE FORM. . . . EASILY HIS MOST EXCITING AND COMPELLING THRILLER SINCE *THE EAGLE HAS LANDED*. . . . THE ULTIMATE CONFRONTATIONS . . . KEEP YOU IN SUSPENSE EVERY STEP OF THE WAY."
—*Publishers Weekly*

BY THE SAME AUTHOR:

(As Jack Higgins)
East of Desolation
Night Judgement at Sinos
The Eagle Has Landed
Storm Warning
Day of Judgment
Luciano's Luck
Touch the Devil
Exocet
Confessional
Night of the Fox

(As Harry Patterson)
The Valhalla Exchange
To Catch a King
Dillinger

(As James Graham)
The Wrath of God
The Khufra Run
A Game for Heroes

SOLO

Jack Higgins

A DELL BOOK

Published by
Dell Publishing Co., Inc.
1 Dag Hammarskjold Plaza
New York, New York 10017

Dell ® TM 681510, Dell Publishing Co., Inc.

ISBN: 0-440-18078-3

Reprinted by arrangement with Stein and Day Publishers

Printed in the United States of America

One Previous Edition

December 1987

10 9 8 7 6 5 4 3 2 1

KRI

For my daughter Ruth Patterson,
who thinks it's about time

Revenge is a kind of wild justice.

—FRANCIS BACON

PROLOGUE

The man from Crete walked in through the gate in the high, brick wall surrounding the house near Regent's Park, stepped into the shrubbery, merging with the darkness. He glanced at the luminous dial of his watch. Ten minutes to seven, which meant he had a little time to spare.

He was wearing a dark anorak, from one pocket of which he produced a Mauser with a bulbous silencer on the end of the barrel. He checked the action and slipped it back into his pocket.

The house was imposing enough, which was only to be expected, for it was owned by Maxwell Joseph Cohen—Max Cohen to his friends. Among other things, chairman of the largest clothing manufacturing firm in the world, one of the most influential Jews in British society. A man loved and respected by everyone who knew him.

Unfortunately, he was also an ardent Zionist, a considerable disadvantage in the eyes of certain people. Not that it bothered the man from Crete. Politics was a waste of time. Games for children. He never queried important targets, only the details, and in this case he'd checked them thoroughly. There was

Cohen, his wife, and the maid—no one else. The rest of the servants lived out.

He took a ski mask from his pocket, which he pulled over his head, leaving only his eyes, nose, and mouth exposed. Then he pulled up the hood of the anorak, stepped out of the shrubbery, and moved toward the house.

Maria, the Cohens' Spanish maid, was in the living room when the doorbell rang. When she opened it, she received the shock of her life. The phantom before her held a pistol in his right hand. When the lips moved in the obscene slash in the woolen helmet, he spoke somewhat hoarsely in English with a heavy foreign accent.

"Take me to Mr. Cohen."

Maria opened her mouth to protest. The pistol was extended menacingly as the Cretan stepped inside and closed the door behind him. "Quickly now, if you want to live."

The girl turned to go up the stairs, and the Cretan followed. As they moved along the landing, the bedroom door opened, and Mrs. Cohen appeared. She had lived with the fear of this kind of thing for some years now, saw Maria, the hooded man, the gun, and in a reflex action jumped back instantly into the bedroom. She slammed and locked the door, then ran to the telephone and dialed nine-nine-nine.

The Cretan pushed Maria on. The maid stumbled, losing a shoe, then paused at the door of her master's study. She hesitated, then knocked.

Max Cohen answered with some surprise, for it was a strict house rule that he must never be disturbed in his study before eight in the evening. He was aware

of Maria standing there, one shoe off, terror on
her face, and then she was pulled to one side and the
Cretan appeared, the silenced gun in his hand. It
coughed once.

Max Cohen had been a boxer in his youth, and for
a moment it was like being back in the ring. A good
solid punch in the face that knocked him clean off
his feet. And then he was on his back in the study.

His lips tried to form the words of that most common of Hebrew prayers recited three or four times a
day by any Orthodox Jew, the last prayer he utters
on the verge of death. *Hear, O Israel. The Lord our
God, the Lord is one.* But the words refused to come,
and the light was fading very fast now, and then there
was only darkness.

As the Cretan ran out of the front door, the first
police car to answer the call turned in at the end of
the street, and he could hear others approaching fast.
He darted across the garden into the darkness and
clambered over a wall into another garden. Finally
he opened a gate to let himself out into a narrow
lane. He pulled down his hood, removed the ski
mask, and hurried away.

His description, he assumed, had already been ob-
tained from the maid by the crew of the first police
car on the scene and was being transmitted over the
radio. Not that it mattered. A couple of hundred
yards and he would be lost in the darkness of Regent's
Park. Straight across to the underground station on
the other side, change at Oxford Circus.

He started to cross the road. There was a squeal
of brakes. A voice called, "Hey, you!"

It was a police car, one quick glance told him that,

and then he dodged into the nearest side street and started to run. His luck, as always, was good, for as he ran along the line of parked cars, he saw a man up ahead getting into one. The door slammed, the engine started.

The Cretan wrenched the door open, dragged the driver out head first, and jumped behind the wheel. He gunned the motor, swinging the wheel, crumpling the nearside fender of the car parked in front, and drove away quickly as the police car roared up the street after him.

He cut across Vale Road into Paddington. He didn't have long if he was to lose them; he knew that in seconds every police car in that part of London would be converging on the area, sealing it tight.

There was a road works sign, an arrow pointing to the right which didn't give him much choice. A one-way street between warehouses, narrow and dark, leading down to Paddington Goods Station.

The police car was close now—too close. He increased speed and saw that he was entering a long narrow tunnel under the railway line, and then his lights picked out a figure up ahead.

It was a girl on a bicycle. A young girl, in a brown coat, a striped scarf around her neck. He was conscious of her white frightened face as she glanced over her shoulder. Her bicycle wobbled.

He swung the wheel, scraping the nearside fender against the tunnel wall so the sparks flew. It was no good. There just wasn't the room. There was a dull thud—no more than that—and then she bounced to one side off the front of the car.

The police car braked to a halt sharply. The Cretan kept on going, straight out of the end of the tunnel into Bishops Bridge Road.

Five minutes later he ditched the car in a side street in Bayswater, crossed the Bayswater Road, and walked briskly through the darkness across Kensington Gardens, emerging at Queens Gate.

There was quite a crowd when he crossed to the Albert Hall and a queue up the steps to the box office, for there was an important concert that night. The Vienna Philharmonic doing the *St. Anthony Chorale* by Brahms with John Mikali playing Rachmaninov's *Concerto No. 2 in C minor*.

July 21, 1972. The Cretan lit a cigarette and examined the picture of Mikali on the poster—the famous one with the dark, curly hair, the pale face, the eyes like clear black glass.

He walked around to the rear of the building. One of the doors had an illuminated sign over it that said *Artists*. He entered. The doorkeeper in his booth glanced up from the sports news and smiled.

"Evening, sir, cold tonight."

"I've known worse," the Cretan said.

He descended to the corridor leading to the back of the stage. There was a door marked *Green Room*. He opened it and switched on the light. It was surprisingly spacious as dressing rooms went and reasonably furnished. The only thing that had visibly seen better days was the practice piano against the wall, an old upright Chappell that looked in imminent danger of collapse.

He took the Mauser from his pocket, opened a makeup case, removed the base panel, and stuffed the Mauser inside out of sight. Then he took off his anorak, tossed it into the corner, and sat down in front of the dressing mirror.

There was a knock on the door, and the stage manager looked in. "You've got forty-five minutes, Mr. Mikali. Can I get them to bring you some coffee?"

"No, thank you," John Mikali said. "Coffee and I don't agree. Some chemical thing, my doctor tells me. But if you could manage a pot of tea, I'd be most grateful."

"Certainly, sir." The stage manager, on his way out again, paused. "By the way, if you're interested, there's just been a newsflash on the radio. Someone's shot Maxwell Cohen at his house near Regent's Park. Hooded man. Got clean away."

"Good god," Mikali said.

"The police think it's political, Mr. Cohen being such a well-known Zionist. He only escaped death by a miracle last year, from that letter bomb someone sent him." He shook his head. "It's a funny kind of world we live in, Mr. Mikali. What kind of man would do a thing like that?"

He went out and Mikali turned and looked in the mirror. He smiled slightly, and his reflection smiled back.

"Well?" he said.

ONE

Some forty sea miles south from Athens, and less than five from the coast of the Peleponnese, lies the island of Hydra, once one of the most formidable maritime powers in the Mediterranean.

From the middle of the eighteenth century many ships' captains amassed huge fortunes trading as far as America, and Venetian architects were brought in to build large mansions which may be seen to this day in the most beautiful of all ports.

Later, as Greece suffered under the harsh regime of the Ottoman Empire and the island became a haven for mainland refugees, it was the sailors of Hydra who challenged the might of the Turkish Navy in the War of Independence that finally brought national freedom.

To a Greek, the names of those great Hydriot sea captains—Votzis, Tombazis, Boudouris—have the same magic as John Paul Jones to Americans, Raleigh and Drake to the English.

Among those names none had a more honorable place than Mikali. The family had prospered as blockade runners when Nelson commanded in the Eastern Mediterranean, had provided four ships for the allied fleet that had crushed the might of the Turkish Em-

pire once and for all at the Battle of Navarino in
1827.

The fortune that was the result of the piracy and
the blockade running of the Turkish wars, shrewdly
invested in a number of newly-developing shipping
lines, meant that by the end of the nineteenth century, the Mikalis were one of the wealthiest families
in Greece.

As individuals, the men were all seafarers by nature,
except for Dimitri, born in 1892, who showed an un-
healthy interest in books, attended Oxford and the
Sorbonne, and came home only to take up a post as
Lecturer in Moral Philosophy at the University of
Athens.

His son, George, soon restored the family honor.
He opted to attend the School of Merchant Marine at
Hydra, the oldest of its kind in Greece. A brilliant
and gifted seaman, he held his first command at the
age of twenty-two. In 1938, restless for fresh horizons,
he moved to California to take command of a new
passenger cargo ship for the Pacific Star line, working the San Francisco–Tokyo run.

Money meant nothing to him. His father had deposited one hundred thousand dollars to his account
in a San Francisco bank, a considerable sum in those
days. What he did, he did because he wanted to do
it. He had his ship and the sea. Only one thing was
lacking, and he found that in Mary Fuller, whom he
met at a dance in Oakland in July, 1939. She was the
daughter of a high-school music teacher, a widow
named Agnes Fuller.

His father came over for the wedding, bought the
young couple a house by the sea in Pescadero, and

returned to a Europe where gunfire already rumbled like thunder on the horizon.

George Mikali was halfway to Japan when the Italians invaded Greece. By the time his ship had made the round trip and docked in San Francisco again, the German Army had taken a hand. By May 1, 1941, Hitler, by intervening to save Mussolini's face, had overrun Yugoslavia and Greece and driven out the British Army, all in twenty-five days and with the loss of fewer than five thousand casualties.

For George Mikali, there was no way home. At least he had his ship. He could fight the war in his own way by helping to maintain the supply routes. In February, while his ship was taking on supplies in San Diego, George Mikali had word that his wife, after three years of ill-health and miscarriages, had given birth to a son. Yes, he agreed on the phone, he should be named John. Yes, he would come to San Francisco at once.

Mikali could be spared from his duties for only three days.

In that time he persuaded his mother-in-law, now a high-school principal, to move into his home on a permanent basis and tracked down the widow of a Greek seaman who had served under him and had lost his life in a typhoon off the Japanese coast. She was aged forty, a solid, heavily-built woman named Katina Pavlo, from Crete. She had been working as a maid in a waterfront hotel.

He took her home to meet his wife and his mother-in-law. In her black dress and headscarf she had seemed to them an alien figure, this short, stocky peasant woman, and yet Agnes Fuller had found herself strangely drawn to her.

As for Katina Pavlo, barren through eighteen years of marriage, her prayers and several thousand candles lit in desperate supplication to the Virgin unanswered, what was happening seemed like a miracle when she looked into the cot at the side of the bed and saw the sleeping child. She gently touched her finger to one tiny hand. He made a fist, held on as if he would never let go.

It was as if a stone dissolved inside Agnes Fuller. What she saw in Katina's dark face made her content. She had Katina return to the hotel for her few things and move into the house that night.

George Mikali went to war, sailing to the islands again and again, one milk run after another, until the early evening of June 3, 1945, en route to Okinawa, when his ship was attacked and sunk with all hands by the Japanese submarine I–367 commanded by Lieutenant Taketomo.

His wife, always in ailing health, never recovered from the shock and died two months later.

Katina Pavlo and the boy's grandmother continued to raise him between them. The two women had an extraordinary instinctive understanding that drew them together where the boy was concerned, for there was little doubt that both loved him deeply.

Although Agnes Fuller's duties as principal of Howell Street High left her little time for teaching, she was still a pianist of no mean order. She was therefore able to appreciate the importance of the fact that her grandson had perfect pitch at the age of three.

She started to teach John piano herself when he was four, and it soon became apparent that he had a rare and unique talent.

It was 1948 before Dimitri Mikali, now a widower, was able to make the trip to America again, and what he found astounded him. A six-year-old American grandson who spoke fluent Greek with a Cretan accent and played the piano like an angel.

He sat the boy gently on his knee, kissed him, and said to Agnes, "They'll be turning in their graves in the cemetery back there in Hydra, those old sea captains. First me—a philosopher. Now a piano player. A piano player with a Cretan accent. Such a talent is from God himself. It must be nurtured. I lost a great deal in the war, but I'm still rich enough to see he gets everything he needs. For the moment, he stays here with you. Later, when he's a little older, we'll see."

From then on, the boy had the best in schooling and in music teachers. When he was fourteen, Agnes Fuller sold the house and, with Katina, moved to New York so that he could continue to get the level of teaching he needed.

One Sunday evening, just before his seventeenth birthday, Agnes Fuller collapsed before supper with a heart attack. She was dead before the ambulance reached the hospital.

Dimitri Mikali was by now Professor of Moral Philosophy at the University of Athens. Over the years, his grandson had visited him for holidays on many occasions, and they had grown close. He flew to New York the moment he received the news and was shocked by what he found.

Katina opened the door to him and put a finger

to her mouth. "We buried her this morning. They wouldn't let us wait any longer."

"Where is he?" the professor asked.

"Can't you hear him?"

The piano sounded faintly through the closed doors of the sitting room. "How is he?"

"Like a stone," she said. "The life gone from him. He loved her," she added simply.

When the professor opened the door, he found his grandson seated at the piano in a dark suit playing a strange, haunting piece like leaves blown through a forest at evening. For some reason, it filled Dimitri Mikali with a desperate unease.

"John?" He spoke in Greek and put his hand on the boy's shoulder. "What's that you're playing?"

"*Le Pastour* by Gabriel Grovlez. It was her favorite piece." The boy turned to look up at him, the eyes like black holes in the pale face.

"Will you come to Athens with me?" the professor said. "You and Katina. Stay with me for a while? Work this thing out?"

"Yes," John Mikali said. "I think I'd like that."

For a while he did. There was Athens itself to enjoy, that noisy, most cheerful of cities, that seemed to keep going day and night without stop. Into the big apartment in the fashionable area near the Royal Palace, where his grandfather held open house most nights, writers, artists, musicians—they all came. And also politicians, for the professor was much involved with the Democratic Front Party, indeed provided most of the finances for their newspaper.

And there was always Hydra, where they had two houses; one in the narrow back streets of the little port itself, another on a remote peninsula along the coast beyond Molos. John began staying there for lengthy periods with Katina to look after him. Katina reported to his grandfather on the telephone that John seemed morose. His grandfather immediately had a Bluthner concert grand shipped out at considerable expense. From what Katina told him, it was never played.

In the end, John came back to Athens to stand against the wall at parties, watchful, polite, immensely attractive with the black curling hair, the pale face, the eyes like dark glass, totally without expression. And he was never seen to smile, a fact the ladies found most intriguing.

One evening, to his grandfather's astonishment, when one of them asked him to play, the boy had agreed without hesitation, sitting at the piano and playing Bach's *Prelude and Fugue in E flat,* mirror-brilliant, ice-cold stuff, that reduced everyone present to astonished silence.

Later, after the applause, after they had left, the professor had gone out to his grandson, standing on the balcony, listening to the roar of the early morning traffic which never seemed to stop.

"So, you've decided to join the living again? What now?"

"Paris, I think," John Mikali said. "The Conservatoire."

"I see. The concert platform? Is this your intention?"

"If you agree."

Dimitri Mikali embraced him gently. "You are everything to me, you must know this now. What you want, I want. I'll tell Katina to pack."

* * *

He found an apartment near the Sorbonne in a narrow street not far from the river, one of those village areas so common to the French capital with its own shops, cafes, and bars, the sort of neighborhood where everyone knew everyone else.

Mikali attended the Conservatoire, practiced between eight and ten hours each day, and dedicated himself solely to the piano to the exclusion of all else, even girls. Katina, as always, cooked and kept house and fussed over him.

On February 22, 1960, two days before his eighteenth birthday, he had an important examination at the Conservatoire, the chance of a gold medal. He had practiced for most of the night, and, at six o'clock in the morning, Katina had gone out to get fresh rolls from the bakery and milk.

He had just emerged from the shower, was fastening the belt of his robe, when he heard the screech of brakes in the street outside, a dull thud. Mikali rushed to the window and looked down. Katina lay sprawled in the gutter, the rolls scattered across the pavement. The Citroën truck that had hit her reversed quickly. Mikali had a brief glimpse of the driver's face and recognized him. Then the truck was around the corner and away.

Katina took several hours to die. John sat in the hospital beside her bed, holding her hand, never letting go, even when her fingers loosened in death. The police were subdued and apologetic. Unfortunately, they said, there had been no witnesses, which made matters difficult, but they would keep investigating, of course.

Not that it was necessary, for Mikali knew the

driver of the Citroën truck well enough—Claud Galley, a coarse brute of a man who ran a small garage close to the river, with the aid of two mechanics.

He could have given the police the information. He did not. This was personal. Something he had to handle for himself. His ancestors would have understood perfectly, for in Hydra, for centuries, the code of the vendetta had been absolute. The man who did not take vengeance for the wrong done to his own was himself cursed.

And yet there was more to it than that. A strange, cold excitement filled his entire being as he waited in the shadows opposite the garage at six o'clock that evening.

At half-past, the two mechanics left. Mikali waited another five minutes, then crossed the road to the entrance. The double doors stood open to the night, the Citroën parked pointing toward the street. Behind the truck a concrete ramp sloped steeply down to the basement.

Galley was working at a bench against the basement wall. Mikali's right hand slipped into the pocket of his raincoat and tightened on the handle of the kitchen knife he carried there, and then he saw there was an easier way that carried with it a considerable measure of poetic justice.

He leaned into the cab of the Citroën, pushed the gear lever into neutral with one gloved hand, then released the handbrake. The vehicle gathered momentum, started to roll faster. Galley, half-drunk as usual, became aware of the movement only at the last moment and turned, screaming, as the three-ton truck squashed him against the wall.

But there was no satisfaction in it at all, for Katina was gone, just like the father he had never known, the mother who was only a vague memory, and his grandmother, Agnes Fuller.

He walked for hours in the rain in a kind of daze and was finally accosted by a prostitute on the embankment, close to midnight.

She was forty and looked older, which was why she didn't turn the light up too high when they reached her apartment. Not that it mattered, for at that particular moment in time, John Mikali was not sure what was real and what was not. In any case, he had never been with a woman in his life.

A fact that his inexpert fumblings soon disclosed, and with the amused tenderness such women often show in these circumstances, she initiated him into the mysteries as quickly as anyone could.

He learned fast, riding her in a controlled fury, once, twice, making her, who did not know pleasure from the men who bought her, beg for more. Afterward, when she slept, he lay in the dark, marveling at this power he possessed that could make a woman act as she had. Strange, because it had little meaning for him at all, this thing that he had always understood was so important.

Afterward, walking the streets again toward dawn, he had never felt so alone in his life. When he finally came to the central market it was a bustle of activity as porters unloaded heavy wagons with produce from the country. Yet they seemed to move in slow motion as if under water; it was as if he existed on a separate plane.

He ordered tea in an all-night cafe and sat by the

window smoking a cigarette, then became aware of a face staring out at him from the cover of a magazine on the stand beside him. A slim, wiry figure in camouflage uniform, sun-blackened face, expressionless eyes, a rifle crooked in one arm.

The article inside, when he took the magazine down, discussed the role of the Foreign Legion in the war in Algiers, which was then at its height. Men who only a year or two before had been stoned by dock workers in Marseilles on their return from Indochina and the Viet prison camps were fighting France's battle again in a dirty and senseless war. Men with no hope, the writer called them. Men who had nowhere else to go. On the next page, there was a photo of another legionnaire, half raised on a stretcher, chest bandaged, blood soaking through. The head was shaven, the cheeks hollow, the face sunken beyond pain, and the eyes staring into an abyss of loneliness. To Mikali it was like staring at his own mirror image. He closed the magazine. He placed it carefully on the stand, then took a deep breath to stop his hands from shaking. Something clicked in his head. Sounds came up to the surface again. He was aware of the early morning bustle around him. The world had come back to life, though he was no longer a part of it, nor had he ever been.

God, but he was cold. He stood up, went out, and walked quickly through the streets, hands thrust deep into his pockets.

It was six o'clock in the morning when he returned to the apartment. It seemed gray and empty, devoid of all life. The piano lid was open, music still on the stand as he had left it. He had missed the examination; not that it mattered now. He sat down and

started to play slowly and with great feeling that
haunting piece, *Le Pastour* by Grovlez, that he had
been playing on the day of his grandmother's funeral
in New Year when Dimitri Mikali had arrived.

As the last notes died away, he closed the lid of the
piano, stood up, crossed to a bureau, and found his
passports, both Greek and American, for he had dual
nationality. He looked around the apartment for the
last time, then let himself out.

At seven o'clock, he was on the Metro on his way
to Vincennes. Once there, he walked briskly through
the streets to the Old Fort, the recruiting center for
the Foreign Legion.

By noon, he had handed over his passports as proof
of identity and age, passed a stringent medical, and
signed a contract binding him to serve for a period of
five years in the most famous regiment of any army in
the world.

At three o'clock the following day, in company with
three Spaniards, a Belgian, and eight Germans, he
was on his way by train to Marseilles, to Fort Saint
Nicholas, the last staging post before North Africa.
He had crossed a line now. There could be no going
back.

Ten days later, together with a hundred and fifty
recruits and a number of other French soldiers then
serving in Algiers and Morocco, Mikali left Marseilles on a troopship bound for Oran.

And on March 20, he finally arrived at his ultimate
destination: Sidi-bel-Abbés, still, as it had been for
almost a century, the center of all Legion activity.

The discipline was absolute, the training brutal in
its efficiency and designed with only one aim. To

produce the most ruthlessly efficient fighting men in
the world. Mikali flung himself into it with the same
fierce energy he had brought to his music. He earned
the attention of his superiors from the beginning.

When he had been at Sidi-bel-Abbés for a few weeks,
he was taken, one day, to the *Deuxième Bureau.* In
the presence of a captain, he was presented with a
letter from his grandfather, who had been informed
of his whereabouts, asking him to reconsider the decision he had taken.

Mikali assured the captain that he was perfectly
happy where he was and was requested to write a letter to his grandfather saying so, which he did in the
captain's presence.

During the six months that followed, he made
twenty-four parachute jumps, was trained in the use
of every form of modern weaponry, was drilled to a
peak of physical fitness he would never have dreamed
possible. He proved to be a remarkable shot with
both rifle and handgun, and his grading in unarmed
combat was the highest in his class, a circumstance
that caused him to be treated with considerable respect by his comrades.

He drank little and visited the town brothel only
occasionally, yet the women there vied for his attention, which amused him, since he was interested solely
in his performance and didn't care which of them
he ended up with.

He was a junior corporal before he saw his first action in October, 1960, when the regiment moved into
the Raki Mountains to attack a large force of *fellagha*
that had been in control of the entire area for some
months.

There were some eighty rebels on top of a hill that

was virtually impregnable. The regiment made a frontal attack that was only apparently suicidal: At the crucial point in the battle, the 3d Company, which included Mikali, was dropped in on top of the hill by helicopter.

The fight that followed was a bloody, hand-to-hand affair, and Mikali distinguished himself by knocking out a machine-gun post that had accounted for more than two dozen legionnaires' ruin.

Afterward, as he was sitting on a rock tying a field service dressing to a flesh wound in his right arm, a Spaniard had stumbled past him laughing insanely, holding two heads in one hand by the hair.

A shot rang out, and the Spaniard went forward onto his face, crying out. Mikali was already turning, clutching his submachine gun, firing with one hand at the two *fellagha* who had risen from a pile of corpses nearby. He got them both.

He stood there for a while waiting, to see if anyone else moved. After a while, he sat down, tightened the bandage on his arm with his teeth, and lit a cigarette.

Within the twelve months that followed, he fought in the alleys of Algiers itself, dropped three times by parachute at night into mountainous country to attack rebel forces by surprise, and survived ambush on numerous occasions.

He had a wound stripe and the *Medaille Militaire*, was a senior corporal by March, 1962. He was an *ancien*, which is to say the kind of legionnaire who could survive for a month on four hours sleep a night and force march thirty miles in a day in full kit if necessary. He had killed men, he had learned

that killing women and children, too, was sometimes
an inevitable part of guerrilla fighting. Finally, the
fact of the death of others meant nothing to him.

After the decoration, he was pulled out of active
service for a while and sent to the guerrilla warfare
school at Kefi, where he learned everything there was
to know about explosives. About dynamite and TNT
and plastics and how to make an efficient booby trap
in dozens of different ways. And always to carry a hid-
den second weapon for emergencies. To that end, he
procured on the black market a Smith & Wesson magnum, which he learned to fire with extraordinary
accuracy and came to consider his ace in the hole.

On July 1, he returned to the regiment after finishing the course and hitched a ride in a supply truck.
It was a beautiful day, the sun high in a sky the most
vivid blue he had ever seen. Women in black robes
picked yellow lemons in the groves on either side of
the asphalt road, helped by children from the small,
whitewashed farmhouse. This was the coastal belt,
safe country, and yet as he lit a cigarette, sitting there
on a packing case on the back of the rocking truck, a
wave of grayness passed over him, a kind of dark pre-
monition, an animal instinct that told him all was
far from well.

His hand moved inside his blouse, feeling for the
butt of the Smith & Wesson. And then there was
suddenly a strange emptiness, no sound at all, and he
felt under water again as he had in Paris that morning, only now he felt hurled out as if he were flying
through the air itself and miraculously found himself
on his hands and knees in the village square.

The truck had been blown apart by a charge of
dynamite detonated by some form of remote control.

Mikali tried to get up. As he struggled to his feet, he heard the rattle of a machine pistol, and he knew that the bullets that knocked him back off his feet had smashed into his chest.

As he lay there, numb but conscious, he could see the driver of the truck twitching feebly on the other side of the burning wreck. Four armed men came forward, stood over the driver, laughing. Mikali couldn't see clearly what they were doing, but the man started to scream. Then there was a shot and the man twitched no longer.

The four turned their attention to Mikali, who had dragged himself into a sitting position against the village well, his hand inside his camouflage jacket where the blood oozed through.

"Not too good, eh?" the leader of the little group said in excellent French. Mikali saw that the knife in the man's left hand was wet with blood.

Mikali smiled for the first time since Katina's death. "Oh, it could be worse."

His hand came out of the blouse clutching his ace in the hole, the Smith & Wesson magnum. His first shot fragmented the top of the man's skull, his second took the one behind him between the eyes. The third man was still trying to get his rifle up when Mikali shot him twice in the belly. The fourth dropped his weapon in horror and turned to run. Mikali's final two shots shattered his spine, driving him headlong into the burning wreckage of the truck.

Beyond, through the smoke, villagers moved fearfully from their houses. Mikali removed the empty shells from the Smith & Wesson, took a handful of rounds from his pocket with difficulty, and reloaded very deliberately. The man he had hit in the stomach groaned and tried to get up. Mikali shot him in the head.

He took off his beret and held it against his wounds to stem the flow of blood and sat there against the well, the revolver ready, daring the villagers to come near him.

He was still there, conscious, surrounded only by the dead, when a Legion patrol found him an hour later.

Which was all rather ironic, for the following day, July 2, was Independence Day, and seven years of fighting were over. Mikali was flown to France to the military hospital in Paris for specialist chest surgery. On July 27, he was awarded the *Croix de la Valeur Militaire*. The following day, his grandfather arrived.

Though the old man was seventy now, he still looked fit. He sat by the bed looking at the medal for quite a while, then said gently, "I've had a word with the Legion headquarters. As you're still not twenty-one, it appears that with the right pressure, I could obtain your discharge."

"Yes, I know."

And his grandfather, using the phrase he had used on that summer evening in Athens nearly three years earlier, said, "You've decided to join the living again, it would seem?"

"Why not?" John Mikali answered. "It beats dying every time, and I should know."

He received an impressive certificate of good conduct, which stated that senior corporal John Mikali had served for two years with *honneur et fidelité* and was discharged before his time for medical reasons.

There was more than a little truth in that. The two bullets in the chest had severely damaged the left lung, and he entered the London Clinic for chest surgery. Afterward, he returned to Greece—not to Athens, but to Hydra. To the villa beyond Molos on the promontory above the sea with only the mountains behind, the pine forests. Wild, savage country, accessible only on foot or by mule on land.

To look after him, he kept an old peasant couple who lived in a cottage by the jetty in the bay below. Old Constantine ran the boat, brought supplies from Hydra town when necessary, saw to the upkeep of the grounds, the water supply, the generator. Constantine's wife acted as housekeeper and cook.

Mostly Mikali was alone except when his grandfather came over to stay. They would sit in the evenings with pine logs blazing on the hearth and talk for hours about everything under the sun. Art, literature, music, even politics, in spite of the fact that this was a subject to which Mikali was totally indifferent.

One thing they never discussed was Algeria. The old man didn't ask, and Mikali never spoke of it. It was like a stone sinking to the bottom of a pond. What Mikali had done there had sunk beneath the surface, apparently without a trace, as if it had never happened.

He had not touched the piano once during those two years, but now he started to play again. His fingers were stiff at first. But all the years of training quickly came back. It took him nine months to regain his health, by which time he had long regained his mastery of the piano.

One calm summer evening in July, 1963, during one

of his grandfather's visits, he played after dinner the Bach *Prelude and Fugue in E flat* that he had played that evening in Athens—the evening he had decided to go to Paris.

It was very quiet. Through the open windows to the terrace, the sky was orange and flame as the sun set behind the island of Dokos a mile out to sea.

His grandfather sighed. "So, you are ready again, I think?"

"Yes," John Mikali said and flexed his fingers. "Time to find out, once and for all."

He chose London, the Royal College of Music. He leased an apartment in Upper Grosvenor Street off Park Lane, which was convenient to Hyde Park, where he ran seven miles every morning, wet or fine, always pushing until it hurt. Old habits died hard. Three times a week he worked out at a well-known city gym.

The Legion had branded him clear to the bone, could never be shaken off entirely. He realized that just before twelve one rainy night when he was mugged by two youths as he turned into a side street coming out of Grosvenor Square.

One took him from behind, an arm around his neck, and the other appeared from the entrance beside some railings to the basement area of a house.

Mikali's right foot flicked expertly into the crotch of the one in front of him, then as his head came down in agony, Mikali's knee smashed into his face. The youth screamed and keeled over. The second assailant was so shocked that he slackened his grip. Mikali broke free, swinging his right elbow back in a short arc. There was a distinct crack as a bone frac-

tured. The boy cried out and fell to his knees. Mikali
simply stepped over him and walked quickly away
through the heavy rain.

At the college his reputation grew over three hard
years. He was good—better than that. They knew it;
so did he. He formed no close friendships. It was not
that people disliked him. On the contrary, they found
him immensely attractive, but there was a remoteness
to him. A barrier that no one seemed to be able to
penetrate.

There were women in plenty, but not one who
could succeed in arousing the slightest personal feeling in him. His relations with women were genuinely
a matter of complete indifference to him. He was a
performer. Like a professional's pride in bringing
Bach to life with his fingers on the keyboard, it
pleased him to turn in as excellent a performance in
bed as on the concert stage. His reputation as a lover
had reached almost legendary proportions by the end
of his final year.

For his music he was awarded the Railden gold
medal, which was not enough. Not for the man he
had become. So, he went to Vienna to put himself
under Hoffman for a year. The final polish. Then,
in the summer of 1967, he was ready.

There is an old joke among musicians that to get
onto a concert platform in the first place is even
more difficult than to succeed once you are there.

To a certain extent, Mikali could have bought his
way in. Paid an agent to hire a hall in London or
Paris, arrange a recital, but his pride would never
stand for that. He had to seize the world by the

throat. Make it listen. There was only one way to do that.

After a short holiday in Greece, he returned to England, to Yorkshire as an entrant in the triennial Leeds Festival, one of the most important pianoforte competitions in the world. To win that was to ensure instant fame, a guarantee of a concert tour.

He placed third and received immediate offers from three major agencies. He turned them all down, practiced fourteen hours a day for a month at the London flat, then went to Salzburg the following January. There, in the competition, he took first prize, beating forty-eight other competitors from all over the world, playing Rachmaninov's *Fourth Piano Concerto,* a work he was to make peculiarly his own in the years to come.

His grandfather stayed for all seven days of the festival. Afterward, when everyone else had left, he took two glasses of champagne onto the balcony where Mikali stood looking out over the city.

"The world is your oyster now. They'll all want you. How do you feel?"

"Nothing," John Mikali said. He sipped a little of the ice-cold champagne and suddenly, and for no accountable reason, saw the four *fellagha* walking around the burning truck and coming toward him laughing. "I feel nothing."

In the two years that followed the dark eyes stared out from the pale, handsome face on posters in London, Paris, Rome, New York, and his fame grew. The newspapers and magazines made much of his two years in the Legion, his decorations for gallantry. In

Greece, he became something of a folk hero, so that his concerts in Athens were always considerable events.

But things had changed in Greece now that the Colonels were in charge after the military coup of April, 1967, and King Constantine was exiled to Rome.

Dimitri Mikali was seventy-six and looked it. Although he still kept open house in the evening, few people attended. His activities on behalf of the Democratic Front Party had made him increasingly unpopular with the government, and his newspaper had already been banned on several occasions.

"Politics," Mikali said to him on one of his visits. "It's a nonsense. Games for children. Why make trouble for yourself?"

"Oh, I'm doing very well really." His grandfather smiled. "What you might call a privileged position, having a grandson who is an international celebrity."

"All right," Mikali said. "So you've got a military junta in power, and they don't like the mini-skirt. So what? I've been in worse places than Greece as it is today, believe me."

"Political prisoners by the thousand, the educational system used to indoctrinate little children, the Left almost stamped out of existence. Does this sound like the cradle of democracy?"

None of which had the slightest effect on Mikali. The following day he flew to Paris and gave a Chopin recital that same night, a charitable affair in aid of international cancer research.

There was a letter waiting for him from his London agent, Bruno Fischer, about the itinerary for a tour of England, Wales, and Scotland in the autumn.

He was spending some time going over it in his dressing room after the recital when there was a knock on the door and the stage-doorkeeper looked in.

"A gentleman to see you, Monsieur Mikali."

He was pushed out of the way, and a large, burly individual with thinning hair and a heavy black moustache appeared. He wore a shabby raincoat over a crumpled tweed suit.

"Hey, Johnny. Good to see you. Claud Jarrot—staff sergeant, Third Company, Second R.E.P. We did that night drop at El Kebir together."

"I remember," Mikali said. "You broke an ankle."

"And you stayed with me when the *fellagha* broke through the line." Jarrot stuck out a hand. "I've read about you in the papers, and when I saw you were giving this concert tonight, I thought I'd come along. Not for the music. It doesn't mean a damn thing to me." He grinned. "I couldn't pass up the chance of greeting another old Sidi-bel-Abbés hand."

It could be he was after a touch, he was certainly shabby enough, but his presence brought back the old days. For some reason, Mikali warmed to him.

"I'm glad you did. I was just leaving. What about a drink? There must be a bar near here."

"Actually I have a garage only a block away," Jarrot said. "I've got a small apartment above it. I've got some good stuff in at the moment. Real Napoleon."

"Lead on," Mikali said. "Why not?"

The walls of the living room were crowded with photos cataloguing Jarrot's career in the Legion, and there were mementos everywhere including his white kepi and dress epaulettes on the sideboard.

The Napoleon brandy was real enough, and Jarrot drank it too fast.

"I thought they kicked you out in the putsch?" Mikali said. "Weren't you up to your neck in the OAS?"

"Sure I was," Jarrot said belligerently. "All those years in Indochina. I was at Dien Bien Phu, you know that? Those little yellow bastards had me for six months in a prison camp. We were treated like pigs. Then the Algeria fiasco when the old man went and did us dirt. Every self-respecting Frenchman should have been OAS, not just mugs like me."

"Not much future in it now, surely?" Mikali said. "The old boy showed he meant business when he had Bastien-Thiry shot. How many attempts to knock him off and not one of them succeeded."

"You're right," Jarrot said, drinking. "Oh, I played my part. Here, take a look."

He removed a rug from a wooden chest in the corner, fumbled for a key and unlocked it with difficulty. Inside there was a considerable assortment of weapons. Several machine pistols, an assortment of handguns and grenades.

"I've had this stuff here four years," he said, "but the network's busted. We've had it. A man has to make out other ways these days."

"The garage?"

Jarrot placed a finger against his nose. "Come on, I'll show you. This damn bottle's near empty anyway."

He unlocked a door at the rear of the garage and disclosed a room piled with cartons and packing cases of every description. He opened one and extracted another bottle of Napoleon brandy.

"Told you there was more." He waved an arm. "More of everything here. Any kind of booze you want. Cigarettes, canned food. Be cleared out by the end of the week."

"Where does it all come from?" Mikali asked.

"You might say off the back of a passing truck." Jarrot laughed drunkenly. "No questions, no pack drill as we used to say in the Legion. Just remember this, *mon ami*. Anything you ever need—anything. Just come to old Claud. I've got connections. I can get you anything, and that's a promise. Not only because you're an old Bel-Abbés hand. If it hadn't been for you that time, the *fellagha* would probably have cut my balls off, among other things."

He was quite drunk by now, and Mikali humored him, slapping him on the shoulder. "I'll remember that."

Jarrot pulled the cork with his teeth. "To the Legion," he said. "The most exclusive club in the world."

He drank from the bottle and passed it across.

Mikali was on tour in Japan when he received bad news. His grandfather, increasingly infirm with advancing years and arthritic in one hip, had needed canes to walk with for some time. He had lost his balance on the tiled floor of the balcony of the apartment and fallen to the street below. The fall had killed him.

Mikali canceled what concerts he could and flew home, but it was a week before he got to Athens. In his absence, the coroner had ordered the funeral to take place, cremation according to Dimitri Mikali's wishes as conveyed in a letter of instructions to his lawyer.

Mikali fled to Hydra as he had done before, to the villa on the peninsula beyond Molos. He crossed from Athens on the hydrofoil and found Constantine waiting to pick him up in the launch. When he went on board, the old man handed him an envelope without a word, started the engines, and took the boat out of the harbor.

Mikali recognized his grandfather's writing at once. His fingers shook slightly as he opened the envelope. The contents were brief.

> If you read this it means I am dead. Sooner—later, it comes to us all. So, no sad songs. No more of my stupid politics to bore you with either because, in the end, the end is perhaps always the same. I know only one thing with total certainty. You have lightened the last years of my life with pride and with joy, but most of all with your love. I leave you mine and my blessing with it.

Mikali's eyes burned, he experienced difficulty in breathing. When they reached the villa, he changed into climbing boots and rough clothes and took to the mountains, walking for hours, exhausting himself.

He spent the night in a deserted farmhouse and could not sleep. The following day, he continued to climb, spending another night like the first.

On the third day, he staggered back to the villa where he was put to bed by Constantine and his wife. The old woman gave him some herbal potion.

He slept for twenty hours and awakened calm and in control of himself again. It was enough. He phoned through to Fischer in London, and told him he wanted to get back to work.

At the apartment in Upper Grosvenor Street there was a mountain of mail waiting. He skimmed through quickly and paused. There was one with a Greek postage stamp marked personal. It had been sent to his agent and readdressed. He put the other letters down and opened it. The message was typed on a plain sheet of paper. No address. No name.

Dimitri Mikali's death was not an accident—it was murder. The circumstances are as follows. For some time, he had been under pressure from certain sections of the government because of his activities for the Democratic Front. Various freedom-loving Greeks had together compiled a dossier for presenting to the United Nations including details of political prisoners held without trial, atrocities of every description, torture, and murder. It was believed that Dimitri Mikali knew the whereabouts of this dossier. On the evening of the 16th June, he was visited at his apartment by Colonel George Vassilikos who bears special responsibility for the work of the political branch of Military Intelligence, together with his bodyguards Sergeant Andreas Aleko and Sergeant Nikos Petrakis. In an effort to make Mikali disclose the whereabouts of the dossier he was beaten severely and burned about the face and the private parts of his body with cigarette lighters. When he finally died because of this

treatment, Vassilikos ordered his body to be
thrown from the balcony to make the death look
like an accident. The coroner was under orders
to produce the report he did and never actually
saw the body, which was cremated so that the
signs of ill-treatment and torture would be erased.
Both Sergeants Aleko and Petrakis have boasted
of these facts while drunk, in the hearing of several people friendly to our cause.

The rage in Mikali was a living thing. The physical
pain which gripped his body was like nothing he had
ever known in this life before. He doubled over in
spasm, fell to his knees, then curled up in a fetal
position.

How long he stayed there he had no means of
knowing, but toward evening he found himself wan-
dering through one street after another as darkness
fell, with no idea where he was. Finally, he went into
a small cafe, ordered coffee, and sat down at one of
the stained tables.

Someone had left a copy of the London *Times*. He
picked it up, his eyes roaming over the news items
mechanically without really taking them in, and then
he stiffened as he saw a small headline halfway down
the second page.

Greek Army Delegation visits Paris for NATO
consultations.

In his heart, he knew whose name he was going to
find even before he read the rest of the news item.

* * *

After that, the whole thing fell into place with total certainty, as if it were a sign from God Himself, when the phone rang. It was Bruno Fischer.

"John? I was hoping you'd arrived. I can get you two immediate concerts, Wednesday and Friday, if you want them. Hoffer was due to play the *Schumann A minor* with the London Symphony. He's broken his wrist."

"Wednesday?" Mikali said automatically. "That only gives me three days."

"Come on, you've recorded the damn thing twice. One rehearsal should be enough. You could be a sensation."

"Where?" Mikali asked. "The Festival Hall?"

"Good God, no. Paris, Johnny. I know it means climbing right back onto another airplane, but do you mind?"

"No," John Mikali said calmly. "Paris will be fine."

He replaced the phone. Breathing deeply, his hands gripping the ledge, he felt filled with an excitement he had never known in his life, in the grip of some tremendous force. Fate was taking him to Paris.

The military coup planned by the Colonels who seized power in Greece in the early hours of April 27, 1967, had been expertly planned in total secrecy, which to a great extent explained its success. Newspaper coverage in the days that followed had been extensive. Mikali spent the afternoon before his evening flight to Paris at the British Museum, checking through every available newspaper and magazine published in the period following the coup.

It was not as difficult as it might have been, mainly because it was photos only that he was after. He found two. One was in *Time* magazine and showed Colonel George Vassilikos, a tall, handsome man of forty-five with a heavy, black moustache, standing beside Colonel Papadopoulos, the man who was, to all intents and purposes, dictator of Greece.

The second photo was in a periodical published by Greek exiles in London. It showed Vassilikos flanked by his two sergeants. The caption underneath read: The butcher and his henchmen. Mikali removed the page carefully and left.

He called at the Greek Embassy when he reached Paris the following morning, and he was received with delight by the cultural attaché, Dr. Melos.

"My dear Mikali, what a pleasure. I'd no idea you were due in Paris."

Mikali explained the circumstances. "Naturally they'll get a few quick announcements out in the Paris papers to let the fans know it's me and not Hoffer who'll be playing, but I thought I'd like to make sure you knew here at the Embassy."

"I can't thank you enough. The Ambassador would have been furious if he'd missed it. Let me get you a drink."

"I'll be happy to arrange tickets," Mikali told him, "for the Ambassador and anyone else he cares to bring. Didn't I read somewhere that you have some brass staying here from Athens?"

Melos made a face as he brought him a glass of sherry. "Not exactly culture oriented. Colonel Vassilikos, Intelligence, which is a polite way of saying. . . ."

"I can imagine," Mikali said.

Melos glanced at his watch. "I'll show you."

He moved to the window. A black Mercedes stood in the courtyard, a chauffeur beside it. A moment later, Colonel Vassilikos came down the steps from the main entrance, flanked by those same two sergeants, Aleko and Petrakis, who went everywhere with him. One of them got in front with the chauffeur, the second with the Colonel in the rear. As the Mercedes moved away, Mikali memorized the number, although the car was recognizable enough because of the Greek pennant on the front.

"Ten o'clock on the dot," Melos said. "Exactly the same when he was here the last time. If his bowels are as regular, he must be a healthy man. Out to the military academy at St. Cyr for the day's work, through the Bois de Meudon and Versailles. He likes the scenery that way, so the chauffeur tells me."

"No time for play?" Mikali said. "He sounds a dull dog."

"I'm told he likes boys, but that could be hearsay. One thing is certain. Music figures very low on his list of priorities."

Mikali smiled. "Well, you can't win them all. But you and the Ambassador, perhaps?"

Melos went down to the front entrance with him. "I was desolated to hear of your grandfather's unfortunate death. It must have come as a terrible shock. To have returned to the concert platform so soon after. . . . I can only say, your courage fills me with admiration."

"It's quite simple," Mikali said. "He was the most remarkable man I ever knew."

"And immensely proud of you?"

"Of course. Not to continue now, if only for his sake, would be the greatest betrayal imaginable. You

could say this Paris trip is my way of lighting a candle
to his memory."

He turned and went down the steps to his rented
car.

At five-thirty that evening, Mikali waited in an old
Citroën stopped at the side of the Versailles road not
far from the Chateau itself. Jarrot was at the wheel.

"If you'd only tell me what this was all about," the
Frenchman grumbled.

"Later." Mikali offered him a cigarette. "You said
if I ever wanted anything to come to you, didn't you?"

"Yes, but. . . ."

At that moment the black Mercedes with the Greek
pennant cruised by, and Mikali said urgently, "Go
after that car. No need to rush. He's not doing more
than forty."

"That doesn't make sense," Jarrot said as he drove
off. "Not in a heap like that."

"It's simple really," Mikali said. "The Colonel likes
the scenery."

"The Colonel?"

"Just keep driving."

The Mercedes took the road across the Bois de
Meudon, the park at that time in the evening quiet
and deserted. It started to draw away. At that moment, a motorcyclist swept past them at high speed,
flashers going, a sinister figure in crash helmet and
goggles and dark, caped coat, a submachine carbine
slung across his back.

He disappeared down the road passing the Mercedes. "Bastard," Jarrot spat out of the window.
"There's been a lot of these CRS swine riding around
on those flashy motor bikes recently. I thought they
were only supposed to be riot police."

Mikali smiled softly, lit another cigarette. "You can slow down. I know how to do it now."

"Do what, for Christ's sake?"

So Mikali told him. The Citroën swerved violently as Jarrot braked hard and pulled it in to the side of the road.

"You're crazy. You must be. You'll never get away with it."

"Oh, yes I will, with your help. You can supply me with everything I need."

"Like hell I will. Listen, you madman, a voice on the phone is all the Sûreté would need."

"What a fat, stupid man you are," Mikali said calmly. "I'm John Mikali. I play in Rome, London, Paris, New York. Does it make any kind of sense that I could be contemplating such a crazy idea? Why would I do such a thing? My grandfather fell to his death from that balcony by accident. The court said so."

"No!"

"Whereas you, old stick, are not only a cheap crook, as became painfully clear when you showed me all that loot at your garage that night. You were also heavily involved with the OAS."

"No one can prove that," Jarrot said wildly.

"Oh, yes they can. Just your name and even a hint of an OAS connection, and it's Service Five, isn't that what they call the strong arm squad—the *barbouzes*? Half of them old pals of yours from Algiers, so you know what to expect. They'll spread you on the table, wire up your privates, then press the switch. You'll be telling them everything down to the finest detail within half an hour, only they won't believe you. They'll keep on, just to see if they've got it all. In the end you'll be dead or a drooling idiot."

"All right," Jarrot groaned. "Don't go on. I'll do it."

"But of course. You see, Claud, all you have to do is live right. Now let's get out of here."

He wound down the window and let the evening air cool his face. He hadn't felt so truly alive in years, every nerve in him strung to perfect tune. It was like that last final moment in the wings before walking out into the light toward the piano and then the applause rising, lifting in great waves. . . .

It was just after six o'clock on the following evening as Paros, the Embassy chauffeur at the wheel of the Mercedes, turned, Versailles on his left, and entered the Bois de Meudon. One of the sergeants sat beside him. The other was in the back on the occasional seat, facing Colonel Vassilikos, who was studying a file. The glass panel was closed.

It had rained heavily all afternoon, and the park was deserted. Paros was taking his time as usual and became aware, in the rapidly falling dusk, of lights close behind him. A CRS man in dark uniform raincoat and helmet pulled alongside and waved him down. With the collar turned up against the rain, the dark goggles, Paros could see nothing of his face at all.

"CRS," Aleko said.

The glass panel opened. Colonel Vassilikos said, "Find out what he wants."

As the Mercedes braked to a halt, the CRS man pulled in front, got off his heavy BMW machine and pushed it on its stand. He walked toward them. His raincoat was very wet, and he carried a MAT 49 machine carbine across his chest.

The sergeant in the front seat opened the door and got out. "What's the trouble?" he demanded in bad French.

The CRS man's hand came out of his pocket holding a .45 Colt automatic of the type issued to the American Army during the Second World War.

He shot the sergeant twice in the chest, slamming him back against the Mercedes. The man fell into the gutter on his face.

The other sergeant sitting in the occasional seat, his back to the glass panel, took the third bullet in the base of his skull. He fell forward, dead instantly, bowed as if in prayer on the seat beside the Colonel who cowered back, frozen in shock, his uniform spattered with blood.

Paros gripped the wheel tightly, his entire body trembling as the barrel of the Colt swung toward him. "No—please no!"

Over the years Mikali had learned to speak Greek of a kind to meet even the most exacting demands of Athenian society, but now he reverted to the accent of the Cretan peasant as taught to him by Katina so many years ago.

He pulled Paros from behind the wheel. "Who are you?" he demanded, keeping his eyes on Vassilikos.

"Paros—Dimitri Paros. I'm just an embassy driver. A married man with children."

"You should choose a better class of employment instead of working for fascist bastards like these," Mikali said. "Now run like hell across the park."

Paros stumbled away, and Vassilikos croaked, "For God's sake."

"What's He got to do with it?" Mikali dropped the Cretan accent and pushed up his goggles. An expression of total astonishment appeared on the Colonel's face. "You? But it isn't possible."

"For my grandfather," Mikali said. "I wish I could make it slower, but there isn't time. At least you'll go to hell knowing who it's from."

As Vassilikos opened his mouth to speak again, Mikali leaned in and shot him between the eyes.

A second later Mikali was pushing the BMW off its stand and riding away. A car passed him, going toward Versailles. In his mirror he saw it slow as it approached the Mercedes, then stop. Not that it mattered now. He turned off the road into one of the footpaths and vanished into the trees.

In a secluded parking area on the other side of the park, deserted at that time of the evening, Jarrot waited fearfully beside the old Citroën truck. The tailgate was down, forming a ramp, and he was pretending to tinker with one of the rear wheels.

There was the sound of the BMW approaching through the trees. Mikali appeared and took the motorcycle straight up the ramp into the back of the truck. Jarrot quickly raised the tailgate, then rushed around to the cab and climbed behind the wheel. As he drove away, he could hear police sirens over to his left in the far distance.

Mikali stood at the open furnace door in the garage and fed the CRS uniform in, piece by piece, even the plastic helmet. The BMW stood in the corner beside the Citroën truck, stripped of the false police signs and number plates which, being mainly plastic, burned nicely.

When he went upstairs he found Jarrot sitting at

the table, a bottle of the Napoleon and a glass in front of him.

"All three," he said. "My god, what kind of man are you?"

Mikali produced an envelope which he dropped on the table. "Fifteen thousand francs as agreed." He took the Colt from his pocket. "I'll hang on to this. I prefer to get rid of it myself."

He turned to the door. Jarrot said, "Where are you going?"

"I have a concert in exactly thirty minutes," Mikali told him. "Had you forgotten?" He glanced at his watch. "I'll have to get moving."

"Jesus Christ," Jarrot said and then added violently, "What if something goes wrong? What if they trace you?"

"You'd better hope they don't. For your own sake as much as mine. I'll come back after the concert. Say eleven o'clock. Okay?"

"Sure," Jarrot said wearily. "I got no place to go."

Mikali got into his rented car and drove away. He felt calm and relaxed, no fear at all, but it seemed obvious that Claud Jarrot's attitude left a great deal to be desired. He was certainly not the man he had been in the old days in Algeria. It was unfortunate, but it seemed painfully apparent that he was going to have to do something about Jarrot. For the moment, there was the concert.

He reached the Opera House with only fifteen minutes to spare, barely time enough to change. But he made it and stood watching in the wings, as the conductor went on stage.

He followed him to a storm of applause. There

was a full house and he noticed Melos and the Greek Ambassador and his wife in the third row, Melos sitting in the aisle seat.

The *Concerto in A minor* was written by Schumann originally as a one-movement phantasie for piano and orchestra for his wife Clara, herself a concert pianist. Later, he expanded it into a three-movement concerto which the music critic of the London *Times* once described as a labored and ambitious work and praised Madame Schumann's attempts to pass her husband's rhapsody off as music.

In Mikali's hands that night, it sparkled, came alive in a way that totally electrified the audience. Which was why there was considerable surprise, to say the least, when halfway through the *intermezzo*, in response to a message brought by a footman, the Greek Ambassador, his wife, and the cultural attaché got up and left.

Jarrot watched the news on television. The killing was obviously political, according to the commentator, which was proved by the fact that the assassin, who had allowed the chauffeur to go free, had referred to the victims as fascists. Probably a member of one of the many disaffected political groups of Greeks living in exile in Paris. In this case, the police had an excellent lead. The man they were seeking was a Cretan—a Cretan peasant. The chauffeur was definite about the accent.

The pictures of the bodies, particularly in the rear of the Mercedes, were graphic to say the least and made Jarrot remember some of Mikali's exploits from the old days. And he had said he was coming back after the concert. Why? There could really only be one reason.

He had to get out while there was still time, but who could he turn to? Certainly not to the police and not to any of his criminal associates. Quite suddenly, in spite of his half-drunken state, he thought of the obvious answer. The one person. Maître Deville, his lawyer. The best criminal lawyer in the business, everyone knew that. He'd saved him from prison twice now. Deville would know what to do.

He wouldn't be at his office now, of course, but at the apartment where he lived alone since his wife had died of cancer three years previously, Rue de Nanterre, off the Avenue Victor Hugo. Jarrot found the number and dialed it quickly.

There was a slight delay then a voice said, "Deville here."

"Maître? It's me, Jarrot. I must see you."

"In trouble again, eh, Claud?" Deville laughed good-humoredly. "I'll see you at the office first thing. Let's say nine o'clock."

"It can't wait, Maître."

"My dear man, it will have to. I'm going out to dinner."

"Maître, have you heard the news tonight? About what happened in the Bois de Meudon."

"The assassinations?" Deville's voice had changed. "Yes."

"That's what I've got to see you about."

"Are you at the garage?"

"Yes."

"Then I'll expect you here in fifteen minutes."

* * *

Deville poured Jarrot another brandy. "Go on, drink up, I can see you need it. An amazing story."

"I can trust you, Maître, can't I?" Jarrot demanded wildly. "I mean, if the flics got even a hint of this."

"My dear fellow," Deville said soothingly. "Haven't I told you before? The relationship between a lawyer and his client is like that between a priest and penitent. After all, if I'd disclosed what I knew of your OAS connection to the SDECE. . . ."

"You're the best, Maître, everybody knows that," Jarrot said.

He was right. Jean Paul Deville was fifty-five years of age and one of the most successful lawyers practicing at the criminal bar in Paris. In spite of this, his relations with the police were excellent. Although he used every trick in the book on behalf of his clients, he was fair and just and scrupulously correct in his dealings. A gentleman in the old-fashioned sense of the word, who had cooperated to the advantage of the Sûreté on more than one occasion, which made him a popular figure in that quarter.

His family had all been killed when Stuka dive bombers had pounded Calais in 1940. Deville himself had not served in the army because of bad eyesight. A clerk in a lawyer's office, he had been shifted to eastern Germany and Poland along with thousands of his fellow countrymen as a slave laborer.

Like many Frenchmen caught behind the Iron Curtain at the end of the war, he had not reached France again until 1947. His family in Calais having all died, he had decided to make a new life for himself in Paris, going to the Sorbonne on a special government grant for Frenchmen who had been displaced, and taking a law degree.

Over the years, he acquired a considerable reputation. He had married his secretary in 1955, but there had been no children. Her health had always been poor, and with cancer of the stomach she had taken two painful years to die.

All of which had occasioned nothing but sympathy for him, not only with the police and his own profession, but among the criminal fraternity as well.

It was really rather ironic when one considered that this benign and handsome Frenchman was, in reality, Colonel Nikolay Ashimov, a Ukrainian who had not seen his homeland for something like twenty-five years. Probably the single most important Russian intelligence agent in Western Europe. An agent, not of the KGB, but of its bitter rival, the intelligence section of the Red Army known as the GRU.

The Russians, even before the end of the war, had spy schools at various places in the Soviet Union, each with a distinctive national flavor, like Glacyna, where agents were trained to work in English-speaking countries, living exactly as they would in the West, in a replica of an English town.

Ashimov spent two long years preparing in a similar way at Grosnia, where the emphasis was on everything French, environment, culture, cooking, and dress being faithfully replicated.

He had a distinct advantage over the other trainees as his mother was French. His progress was rapid, and he was finally sent to join a group of French slave workers in Poland in 1946, enduring the hardships of their existence, assuming the role of the Jean Paul Deville, who had died of pneumonia in a Siberian coalmine in 1945. And then, in 1947, he had been sent home to France.

* * *

"But what do I do?" Jarrot demanded of Deville. "If you saw the news on television, you know what he's capable of."

"Fantastic," Deville said. "I've heard him play, of course. He's quite brilliant, and I remember vaguely reading in some magazine that he'd served in the Legion for a couple of years as a boy."

Jarrot said, "He was never a boy, that one. If I told you some of the things he pulled off in Algiers in the old days. Why, at Kasfa, he took two bullets in the lung and still managed to kill four *fellagha* with a handgun. A handgun, for Christ's sake."

Deville poured him another brandy. "Tell me more."

Which Jarrot did. By the time he was finished, he had, as usual, drunk too much. "So what do I do?"

"Eleven o'clock, I think he said he'd return." Deville glanced at his watch. "It's ten now. I'll get my coat, and we'll go back to the garage. I'd better drive. You're in no fit state to cross the street on your own."

"The garage?" Jarrot's speech was slow and heavy. "Why the garage?"

"Because I want to meet him. Reason with him on your behalf." He slapped Jarrot on the shoulder. "Trust me, Claud, to help you. After all, that is the reason you came to see me, isn't it?"

He went into his bedroom, pulled on a dark overcoat, and took down the black Homburg hat he always wore. He opened the drawer in his bedside bureau and took out an automatic pistol. He was, after all, going to confront a man who, if everything he had heard tonight was true, was a psychopathic killer of the first order.

He weighed the pistol in his hand, then, on impulse and hunch alone, taking the biggest chance of his life, he put it back in the drawer.

In the other room, he found Jarrot at the brandy again.

"All right, Claud," he said cheerfully. "Let us go."

The concert was a total success, of course. Mikali was called back again and again, with many members of the audience clamoring for an encore. Finally, he obliged. There was an excited murmur, then complete stillness as he seated himself at the piano. A pause and then he started to play *Le Pastour* by Gabriel Grovlez.

He parked the rented car some distance from the garage and walked the rest of the way on foot through the heavy rain, quietly letting himself in through the judas in the main gate. He still had the Colt in the right-hand pocket of his raincoat. He felt for the butt as he stood there in the darkness listening to music faintly playing in the apartment above.

He went upstairs quietly and opened the door. The living room was in half-darkness, the only light the lamp on the table at which Jarrot snored gently in a drunken sleep.

One bottle of Napoleon beside him was empty, another already a quarter down. A portable radio played music softly, and then the announcer's voice interrupted with more details on the massive police hunt for the assassin of Vassilikos and his men.

He reached over and switched it off, then took the Colt from his pocket. A soft voice said in excellent English with a slight French accent, "If that's the gun

I think it is, it would be an error of the first magnitude to kill him with it."

Deville stepped from the shadows at the back of the room. He still wore his dark overcoat and carried a walking stick in one hand, his Homburg in the other.

"They would extract the bullet from his corpse, forensic tests would show it had come from the same gun that was used on Vassilikos and his men. I am right, am I not? It is the same gun?" He shrugged. "Which still doesn't mean they would stand much chance of tracing you, but silly to spoil such a brilliant operation with even a single act of stupidity."

Mikali waited, the Colt against his thigh. "Who are you?"

"Jean Paul Deville. By profession, criminal lawyer. This creature here is a client of mine. He came to me earlier tonight in considerable agitation and told me everything. You see, we have a special relationship. I am, you might say, his father confessor. He'd been a naughty boy with the OAS a year or two back. I got him off the hook."

He reached inside his coat; the Colt swung up instantly. "A cigarette only, I assure you." Deville produced a silver case. "I haven't fired a gun in years. No blunt instruments. Nothing up my sleeve at all. This whole affair is between you and me and this poor drunken swine here. He hasn't spoken to another living soul."

"And you believe him?"

"Who could he run to? Like a scared rabbit, he came to the only safe burrow he knew."

"To tell you?"

"He was afraid that you intended to kill him.

Quite terrified. He told me everything about you. Algeria, the Legion. Kasfa, for example. That little affair made a deep impression on him. He gave me the reason for the whole thing as well. The fact that Vassilikos had tortured and murdered your grandfather."

"So?" Makali waited patiently.

"I could have written a letter detailing all these acts before leaving my apartment tonight. Posted it with a covering note to my secretary asking for it to be passed on to the right people at SDECE."

"But you didn't."

"No."

"Why not?"

Deville walked over to the window and opened it. Rain poured down relentlessly. There was the sound of traffic in the night.

"Tell me something—do you usually speak Greek with a Cretan accent like you did in the park?"

"No."

"I thought not. A brilliant stroke that, coupled with your reference to Vassilikos and his men as fascists, to the chauffeur. Of course it does mean that all over Greece tonight, they'll be hauling in every communist, every agitator, every member of the Democratic Front they can lay their hands on."

"That's their hard luck," Mikali said. "Politics bores me, so could you kindly get to the point."

"It's really quite simple, Mr. Mikali. I have a vested interest in chaos. The disorder, fear, and uncertainty you have created in Athens is also happening tonight in Paris. There isn't a left-wing agitator in the city who won't be either under cover or in police hands by morning. Not only communists, but socialists. The

Socialist Party won't like that, and very soon the workers won't like it either, which makes things rather difficult for the government with an election coming up."

Mikali said softly, "Who are you?"

"Does that matter?"

"Like I said, politics bores me."

"An excellent basis for the sort of relationship I'm seeking."

"So what do you want?"

"Perhaps, my friend, for you to repeat your performance in the Bois de Meudon when I require it. Very special occasions only. A unique and totally private arrangement between the two of us."

Mikali said softly, "Blackmail, is that it?"

"Don't be stupid. You could kill me now and Jarrot. Walk away from here with an excellent chance of no one ever being the wiser. Who on earth would ever suspect you? Good god, you even played for the Queen of England at a special reception at Buckingham Palace last year, isn't it so? When you're in London, passing through Heathrow, what happens to you?"

"They take me to the VIP lounge."

"Exactly. Can you remember when customs anywhere in the world last checked your baggage?"

Which was true. Mikali put the Colt on the window ledge and took out a cigarette. Deville gave him a light. There was a strange disturbing intimacy between them now, standing together at the window, the smell of the rain on the night air.

Deville said, "I've often felt sorry for creative artists. Musicians, painters, writers. It's over, particularly in the performing arts, so soon; the briefest of high points. Afterward, down you go. Like sex."

His voice was soft and eminently reasonable. Patient, civilized in tone. For a moment, Mikali might have been back at the villa in Hydra, sitting in front of the pine log fire, listening to his grandfather.

"But this evening—that was different. You enjoyed it. Every dangerous moment. I'll make you a prophecy. Tomorrow, the music critics will say that tonight you gave one of your greatest performances."

"Yes," Mikali said simply. "I was good. The house manager said they won't have an empty seat in the place on Friday."

"Back in Algeria you killed everyone, isn't that so? Whole villages—women, children—it was that kind of war. This afternoon, you killed pigs."

Mikali stared out of the window into the night and saw the *fellagha* turning from the burning truck at Kasfa, drifting toward him in slow motion as he waited, stubbornly refusing to die, the red beret crushed against his wounds.

He had beaten death then at his own game four times over. He felt again the same breathless excitement. The affair at the Bois de Meudon had been the same, he knew that now. A debt for his grandfather, yes, but afterward. . . .

He raised his hands. "Give me a piano score, any concerto you care to name, and with these I will try to give you perfection."

"Much more," Deville said softly.

The breath went out of Mikali in a long sigh. "And who exactly would you have in mind in the future?"

"Does that matter?"

Mikali smiled slightly. "Perhaps not."

"Good—but to start, I'll give you what my Jewish friends would call a *mitzvah*. A good deed for which I expect nothing in return. Something for you. Your touring schedule. Is it likely to take you to Berlin during the first week of November?"

"I can name my own dates in Berlin. I have an open invitation there always."

"Good. General Stephanakis will be visiting the city on the first of November for three days. He was, if you're interested, Vassiliko's direct superior. I would have thought you might have more than a passing interest in him. But for the moment, I think we'd better do something about friend Jarrot here."

"What would you suggest?"

"A little more of this Napoleon down him for a start. A pity to waste good cognac, but there it is." He pulled the unconscious Jarrot's head back by the hair and forced the neck of the bottle between his teeth. He glanced over his shoulder. "I do hope you can manage to get me a ticket for Friday's performance. I'd hate to miss it."

At five-thirty the following morning it was still raining heavily when the night patrolman for the area stopped by the slipway that ran into the Seine opposite Rue de Gagny.

His cape was soaked, and he was thoroughly miserable as he paused under a chestnut tree to light a cigarette. As the mist lifted a little from the river, he saw something in the water at the end of the slipway.

As he approached, he discerned it to be the back of a Citroën truck, the front end of which was under the surface. He waded down into the freezing water, took a deep breath, reached for the door handle, and pulled it open. He surfaced with Claud Jarrot in his arms.

At the inquest, which took place a week later, the medical evidence submitted indicated a level of alcohol in the blood many times in excess of the maximum permitted for vehicle drivers. The coroner's verdict was simple. Death by accident.

The concert on Friday was everything the audience could have hoped for. At the reception afterward, hosted by the Greek Ambassador, France's Minister for the Interior himself was present. While he and the Ambassador conferred in one corner, Mikali held court in another.

It was only as the press of well-wishers slackened around Mikali that Deville approached.

"Glad you could come," Mikali said as they shook hands.

"My dear chap, I wouldn't have missed it. You were brilliant—quite brilliant."

Mikali looked around the room, crowded with some of the most fashionable and important people in Paris.

"Strange how much apart I suddenly feel from all this."

"Alone in the crowd?"

"I suppose so."

"I've felt like that for something like twenty-five years. Walking the knife edge of danger. Waiting for the final day. The knock on the door." Deville smiled. "It has its own excitement."

"Like being on a constant high?" Mikali said. "You think it will come, this final day of yours?"

"Probably when I least expect it and for the most stupid and trivial of reasons."

Mikali said, "Don't go away. I must have a word with the Minister of the Interior. I'll see you later."

"Of course."

The Minister was saying to the Greek Ambassador, "Naturally, we are doing everything in our power to wipe out this—this blot on French honor, but to be frank with you, Ambassador, this assassin of yours seems to have vanished off the face of the earth. But only for the moment. We'll get him, sooner or later, I promise you."

Mikali heard all of this as he approached. He smiled. "Your Excellencies, I'm honored you could both attend tonight."

"A privilege, Monsieur Mikali." The Minister snapped his fingers, and a waiter hurried forward with champagne on a tray. They all took a glass. "An astonishing performance."

The Greek Ambassador raised his glass. "To you, my dear Mikali, and to your genius. Greece is proud of you."

As Mikali raised his own glass in return, Jean Paul Deville toasted him in the mirror.

General George Stephanakis arrived at the Hilton Hotel in West Berlin on the afternoon of the 2nd of November. The management gave him a suite on the fourth floor, with adjoining rooms for his aides. They also made sure, as a courtesy, that the room service waiter was a Greek—and also the chambermaid.

Her name was Zia Boudakis, age nineteen, a small girl with dark hair and olive skin. In a few years, she would have a weight problem, but not yet, and that evening, as she let herself into the suite with her passkey, she looked undeniably attractive in the dark stockings and short, black, uniform dress.

The General would be back at eight, they'd told her that, so she busied herself quickly in turning down the beds and generally tidying the suite. She folded the coverlets, then turned to put them away in the wardrobe, pulling across the sliding door.

The man standing inside was dressed in black pants and sweater, his head covered with a ski mask through which only his eyes and nose and lips showed. There was a nylon line around his waist—she noticed that and that the hand that grabbed her throat, choking off her scream, was gloved. And then she was inside in the dark with him, the door closed, leaving only a chink through which the room could be seen.

He released his grip, and in her terror, she spoke instinctively in Greek. "Don't kill me!"

"Heh, a Greek girl," he said, to her total astonishment in her own language. She recognized the accent at once.

"Oh, my god, you're the one who killed Colonel Vassilikos in Paris."

"That's right, my love." He swung her around, a hand lightly circling her throat. "I won't harm you, if you're a good girl. But if you're not—if you try to warn him in any way—I'll kill you."

"Yes," she moaned.

"Good. What time does he get in?"

"Eight o'clock."

He glanced at his wrist. "We've got twenty minutes to wait. We'll just have to make ourselves comfortable, won't we?"

He leaned against the wall, holding her against

him. She was no longer afraid, at least not as she had
been at first, but excited in a strange way, aware of
him hard against her, one hand around her waist.
She started to move against him, only a little at first
and then more as he laughed and kissed her on the
neck.

Before long she was more excited than she had
ever been at the hands of the crude young fellows in
the olive groves at the side of the village back home.
There, in the darkness, she turned to meet him as he
pushed her against the wall, easing the dark dress up
above her thighs.

Afterward, he tied her wrists very gently behind her
and breathed in her ear, "There, you've had what you
wanted, so be a good girl and keep quiet."

He tied a handkerchief around her mouth to gag
her, again with surprising gentleness, and waited.
There was the sound of the key in the lock, the door
opened and General Stephanakis was ushered in by
two of his aides.

They were all in uniform. He turned and said,
"I'm going to have a shower and change. Come back
in forty-five minutes. We'll eat here."

They saluted and left, and he closed the door.
Stephanakis dropped his cap on the bed and started
to unbutton his tunic. Behind him, the door of the
wardrobe rolled back and Mikali stepped out. He
held a pistol with a silencer in his right hand.
Stephanakis gazed at him in stupefaction, and Mikali
pulled up the ski mask.

"Oh, my god," the General said. "You—you are the
Cretan."

"Welcome to Berlin," Mikali said, pulling the trig-
ger.

Mikali turned off all the lights, pulled on his ski mask again, then opened the window and uncoiled the nylon line wound about his waist. A few moments later, he was rappelling down to the flat roof of the garage in the darkness four floors below. It was no great trick. In training at Gasfa on the Moroccan coast in the old days, a Legion paratrooper had been expected to rappel down a 300-foot cliff or fail his course.

Safely on the roof, he pulled down the nylon line, coiled it quickly about his waist, then dropped over the edge of the garage to the ground.

He paused by some garbage cans in the alley and took off his ski mask, which he folded neatly and slipped into one pocket. Then he pulled an ordinary paper shopping bag from behind the garbage cans and took out a cheap, dark raincoat, which he pulled on.

A few moments later, he was walking away briskly through the crowded evening streets, back to his hotel. At nine-thirty he was at the University of Berlin, giving a recital of the works of Bach and Beethoven to a packed hall.

The following morning, Jean Paul Deville received a cable from Berlin. It said, "Your mitzvah much appreciated. Perhaps I can do the same for you some time."

There was no signature.

TWO

The British Secret Intelligence Service, known more correctly as DI5, does not officially exist, is not even established by law although it does in fact occupy a large white and red brick building in the West End of London not far from the Hilton Hotel.

Those whom it employs are faceless, anonymous men who spend their time in a ceaseless battle of wits aimed at controlling the activities of the agents of foreign powers in Great Britain and increasingly what has become an even more serious problem: the forces of European terrorism.

But DI5 can only carry out an investigation. It has no powers of arrest. Any effectiveness it has at all depends in the final analysis on the cooperation of the Special Branch of the Metropolitan Police at Scotland Yard. It is they who make the arrests so that those anonymous men of DI5 never have to appear in court.

Which explained why, on the night of the shooting of Maxwell Cohen, it was Detective Chief Superintendent Harry Baker who got out of the police Jaguar outside the mortuary in Cromwell Road just after nine o'clock and hurried up the steps.

Baker was by birth a Yorkshireman from Halifax in the West Riding. He'd been a policeman for twenty-

four years. A long time to be disliked by the general
public and work a three-shift system that only gave
you one weekend in seven at home with the family.
A fact his wife no longer commented on for the simple reason that she'd packed her bags and moved out
six years previously.

Baker had gray hair and a badly broken nose, a
relic of his rugby-playing days, giving him the air of
an amiable prizefighter, an air which was deceptive
for it concealed one of the sharpest minds in Special
Branch.

His assistant, Detective Inspector George Stewart,
waited in the foyer smoking a cigarette. He dropped
it to the floor, put a foot on it, and came forward.

Baker said, "All right—tell me."

"Girl of fourteen—Megan Helen Morgan." He had
his notebook open now. "Mother, Mrs. Helen Wood.
Married to the Reverend Francis Wood, rector of
Steeple Durham in Essex. I spoke to him on the phone
half an hour ago. They're on their way now."

"Now wait a minute," Baker said. "I'm beginning
to get a bit confused."

"The girl's landlady is in here, sir. A Mrs. Carter."

He opened a door marked "Waiting Room," and
Baker moved in. The woman who sat by the window
was stout and middle-aged and wore a brown raincoat. Her face was blotched, swollen by weeping.

"This is Chief Superintendent Baker. He's in charge
of the case, Mrs. Carter," Stewart said. "Would you
tell him what you told me now?"

She said in a low voice, "Megan lodges with me.
Her mother lives in Essex, you see."

"Yes, we know that."

"She was at the Italia Conte school. You know?

Singing, dancing, acting, things like that. She wanted to go on the stage. That's why she was here, lodging with me," she explained again, patiently.

"And tonight?"

"They were rehearsing all afternoon for a musical they're doing. I told her to be careful." She turned to gaze vacantly out of the window. "I never did like her being out after dark on that bike."

There was a silence. Baker put a hand on her shoulder, then nodded to Stewart, and they went out.

"Is Doctor Evans here yet?"

"On his way, sir. Would you like to see the body?"

"No, I'll keep that unpleasantness for later. I've got two girls of my own, remember. In any case, Evans can't start cutting until the mother's made formal identification."

"Any news on Mr. Cohen, sir?"

"Still alive, that's all you can say, with a bullet in his brain. They're operating now."

"Are you going to wait here for Mrs. Wood?"

"Yes, I think so. The office knows where I am. See if you can find us some tea."

Stewart went off, and Baker lit a cigarette and looked out through the glass doors. He was uneasy in a way he hadn't been for years. Among its other duties, the Special Branch was always given the task of acting as bodyguard to visiting heads of state and other ranking VIPs. The department was justly proud of the fact that they'd never failed yet in that particular task.

But this business tonight with Max Cohen—this was something else again. International terrorism of the most vicious kind, here in London.

Stewart appeared with tea in two paper cups. "Cheer up, sir. We'll get the bastard."

"Not if it's who I think it is," Harry Baker told him.

At that moment, John Mikali walked back on stage to take another standing ovation. He exited down the gangway known to the artists as the Bullrun. The stage manager was waiting there and handed him a towel.

Mikali wiped sweat from his face. "That's it," he said. "If they want any more, they'll have to buy tickets for Tuesday."

"Most of them already have, Mr. Mikali." The manager's voice was attractive—full of its own character, what some people would call good Boston American— and matched the lazy charm he could switch on instantly when required. He smiled. "The champagne's waiting in your dressing room. Any visitors?"

"Nothing under twenty-one, George." Mikali smiled. "I've had a very young week."

In the Greek Room he stripped off his tailcoat and shirt and pulled on a terrycloth robe. Then he switched on the portable radio on the dressing table and reached for the champagne bottle, Krug, non-vintage. He put a little crushed ice in the bottom of the glass and filled it.

As he savored the first, delicious, ice-cold mouthful, the music on the radio was interrupted for a news-flash. Mr. Maxwell Cohen, victim of an unknown assassin earlier that evening, had been operated on successfully. He was now in intensive care under heavy police guard. There was every prospect that he would make a full recovery.

Foreign news sources reported that responsibility for the attack had been claimed by Black September, Al Fatah's vengeance group, formed during 1971 to eliminate all enemies of the Palestine revolution. They gave as their excuse Maxwell Cohen's considerable support for Zionism.

Mikali closed his eyes momentarily, was aware of the burning truck, the four *fellagha* walking around, drifting toward him, the smile on the face of the leader, the one with the knife in his hand. And then the image changed to the tunnel darkness, the white, terrified face of the girl, briefly glimpsed.

He opened his eyes, switched off the radio, and toasted himself in the glass. "Less than perfection, old buddy. Less than perfection and that won't do at all."

There was a knock at the door. When he opened it the corridor seemed crowded with young women, mainly students to judge by their university scarves.

"Can we come in, Mr. Mikali?"

"Why not." John Mikali smiled, the insolent charm firmly back in place. "All life is here with the great Mikali. Enter and beware."

Baker stood in the foyer of the mortuary with Francis Wood. There was nothing particularly clerical looking about him. Baker judged him to be about sixty, a tall, kindly man with graying beard that badly needed trimming. He wore a dark car coat and a blue, polo-neck sweater.

"Your wife, sir?" Baker nodded to where Helen Wood stood at the door talking to Mrs. Carter. "She's taking all this remarkably well."

"A lady of considerable character, Superintendent. She paints, you know. Water colors mostly. She had quite a reputation, under her previous name."

"Morgan, sir? Yes, I was wondering about that. Mrs. Wood was widowed, I presume?"

"No, Superintendent—divorced." Francis Wood smiled faintly. "That would surprise you, the Church of England holding the views it does. The explanation is simple enough. To use an old-fashioned term, I happen to have private means. I can afford to steer my own boat. There was a gap of a year or two when we first got married when I was out of a job, and then my present bishop wrote to me about Steeple Durham. Hardly the hub of the universe, but the people there had been without a rector for six years and were willing to have me. And my bishop, I might add, is a man of notoriously liberal views."

"And the child's father? Where could we contact him? He'll need to be notified."

Before Wood could answer, Mrs. Carter left, and his wife turned and came toward them. She was thirty-seven, Baker knew that from the information supplied by Stewart. She had ash blond hair tied at the nape of her neck, pulled back from a face of extraordinary beauty and the calmest eyes he had ever seen in his life. She wore an old military trenchcoat that had once carried a captain's three pips in the epaulettes; his policeman's sharp eyes noticed the holes.

"I'm sorry to have to ask you this, but it's time for formal identification, Mrs. Wood."

"If you'd be good enough to lead the way, Superintendent," she said in a low, sweet voice.

* * *

Doctor Evans, the pathologist, waited in the postmortem room, flanked by two male technicians, already wearing white overalls and boots and long, palegreen, rubber gloves.

The room was illuminated by fluorescent lighting so bright that it hurt the eyes, and there was a row of half a dozen stainless steel operating tables.

The child lay on her back on the one nearest the door, covered by a white sheet, her head raised on a wooden block. Helen Wood and her husband approached, followed by Baker and Stewart.

Baker said, "This isn't going to be nice, Mrs. Wood, but it has to be done."

"Please," she said.

He nodded to Evans, who raised the sheet, exposing the head only. The girl's eyes were closed, the face unmarked, but the rest of the head was bound in a white rubber hood.

"Yes," Helen Wood whispered. "That's Megan."

Evans covered the face again and Baker said, "Right, we can go."

"What happens now?" she said. "To her?"

It was Francis Wood who said, "There has to be an autopsy, my dear. That's the law. To establish legal cause of death for the coroner's inquest."

"I want to stay," she said.

It was Baker who by some instinct got it exactly right. "Hang around here if you want to," he said, "but within five minutes, you'll think you're in a butcher's shop. I don't think you'd want to remember her like that."

It was brutal, it was direct, and it worked so that

she broke at once, falling against Wood, half-fainting. Stewart ran to help him. Together, they got her from the room.

Baker turned to Evans and saw only pity on his face. "Yes, I know, Doc. A hell of a way to make a living."

He walked out. Evans turned and nodded. One of the technicians switched on a tape recorder, the other removed the sheet from the dead girl's body.

Evans started to speak in a dry unemotional voice. "Time, 11:15 P.M. July 21, 1972. Pathologist in charge, Mervyn Evans, senior lecturer in forensic pathology, University of London Medical School. Subject, female, age fourteen years one month. Megan Helen Morgan. Died approximately 7:15 P.M. this date, as a result of a hit-and-run driving accident."

One of the technicians pulled back the rubber skull cap, revealing immediate evidence of massive cranial fracture.

Continuing to speak in that same precise voice, detailing every move he made, Evans reached for a scalpel and drew it around the skull.

Francis Wood came in through the swing doors and found Baker and Stewart waiting in the foyer.

"She'll be all right now. She's in the car."

"What will you do, sir? Go to a hotel?"

"No, she wants to go home."

"A tricky drive at this time of night on those Essex country roads."

"I was a padre with the Royal Artillery in Korea in the winter of 1950, when a million Chinese came out of Manchuria and chased us south again. I drove a

Bedford truck through heavy snow for four hundred miles, and they were never very far behind. We were short on drivers, you see."

"A hell of a way to take your advanced driver's course," Baker commented.

"One interesting aspect of life, Superintendent, is that some experiences are so terrible, anything that comes after seems like a bonus."

They were talking for the sake of talking now, and they both knew it. Baker said, "Just one thing, sir. I've had a phone call from my superiors. It would seem that for security reasons, no direct link will be made publicly between your daughter's death and the Cohen affair. I hope you and your wife can accept that."

"Frankly, Superintendent, I think you'll find that my wife would infinitely prefer this terrible business to be handled as quietly as possible."

He turned toward the door, then paused. "But we were forgetting. You asked me about Megan's father."

"That's right, sir. Where can we contact him?" Baker nodded and Stewart got out his notebook.

"Rather difficult, I'm afraid. He's out of the country."

"Abroad, sir?"

"It depends entirely on your point of view. Belfast, Superintendent, that's where he is at the moment. Colonel Asa Morgan, the Parachute Regiment. The right department of the Ministry of Defence would be able to help you contact him, I suppose, but you'd know far more about that than me."

"Yes, sir, leave it to us."

"I'll say good night then."

The door swung behind him. Stewart said, "Colonel

Asa Morgan, Parachute Regiment. You know something, sir, I shouldn't think he'll be too pleased when
he hears about this, a man like that."

"And that's the understatement of the bloody age,"
Baker said violently.

"You know him, sir?"

"Yes, Inspector. You could say that."

Baker made straight for the porter's office, phoned
Scotland Yard, and asked to be put through to Assistant Commissioner Joe Harvey, Head of the Special
Branch, who, he knew, had already installed himself
there for the night with a camp bed in his office.

"Harry Baker here, sir," he said when Harvey
answered. "I'm at the mortuary. The girl who our
friend ran down in the Paddington tunnel while
making his escape—her mother's just left after making a formal identification. A Mrs. Helen Wood.

"I thought the kid's name was Morgan?"

"Her mother's divorced, sir. Remarried to a vicar
of all things." Baker hesitated. "Look, sir, you're not
going to like this one little bit. Her father. . . ."

He hesitated again. Harvey said, "Spit it out, Harry,
for Christ's sake."

"Is Asa Morgan."

There was a moment of silence, then Harvey said,
"Dear god in heaven, that's all we needed."

"Last I heard he was in Trucial Oman with the
Special Air Service. Know what they are, George?"

Baker was standing at the window of his office. It
was a little after midnight, and rain drummed against
the glass.

Stewart passed him a cup of tea. "Can't say I do,
sir."

"What the military refer to as an elite unit. The army likes to keep as quiet about this one as they possibly can. Any serving soldier can volunteer. A three-year tour is the rule, I believe."

"And what exactly do they do?"

"Anything too rough for anyone else to handle. The nearest thing to the SS we've got in the British Army. At the moment, they're in Oman on loan to the Sultan, knocking merry hell out of his Marxist rebels in the mountains. They also served in Malaya during the Emergency. That's where I first came across them."

"I didn't know you were out there, sir."

"On temporary assignment. They weren't doing too well with the Chinese communist underground, so they decided to see if some real coppers could help. That's where I met Morgan."

"What about him, sir?" Stewart asked. "What's so special?"

"The right word you've chosen, that's for sure." Baker filled his pipe slowly. "He must be damn near fifty now, Asa. A Welsh miner's son from the Rhondda. I don't know what happened to him earlier in the war, but I know he was one of the poor sods they dropped in at Arnhem. He was a sergeant then. Got a field commission as a second lieutenant afterward."

"Then what?"

"Palestine. His first taste of urban guerrillas, he used to say. Then he was seconded to the Ulster Rifles when they went to Korea. Captured by the Chinese. They had him for a year, those bastards. I know some people thought all that brainwashing stuff they used on our lads out there had really gone to his head."

"What do you mean, sir?"

"When he came back, he wrote this treatise about what he called a new concept of revolutionary warfare. Kept quoting Mao Tse-tung as if he was the Bible. I suppose the General Staff decided he'd either turned communist or knew what he was talking about, so they sent him to Malaya, which is where I met him. We worked together for quite a time."

"Did you do any good?"

"We won, didn't we? The only communist insurrection since the second world war to be successfully crushed was Malaya."

"And Morgan?"

"I saw him again for a while in Nicosia during the Cyprus thing when I was seconded out there on the same sort of deal. Come to think of it, he'd just got married before leaving the UK, I remember that now, so the kid's age would fit. I remember hearing he was in Aden in 1967 because he got a DSO for saving the necks of a bunch of Argyle and Sutherland Highlanders who got ambushed in the Crater district."

"He sounds quite a man."

"Oh, yes, you could say that. The original soldier monk. The army's everything to him. Family and home rolled into one. I'm not surprised his wife left him."

"I wonder what he'll do, sir, when he hears about his daughter."

"God knows, George, but I can imagine."

The wind rattled the window and outside, rain drifted across the rooftops from the Thames.

THREE

In Belfast that day, extraordinary things had been happening also. A day that was to go down in the history of the war in Ulster as Bloody Friday.

The first bomb exploded at 2:10 P.M. at Smithfield Bus Station, the last at 3:15 at the Cavehill Road Shopping Centre.

Twenty-two bombs in all, in locations scattered all over the city, usually where people might be expected to be present in large numbers. Protestant or Catholic, it made no difference. By the end of the day nine people were dead and 130 injured.

At midnight, the army was still out in force. No less than twelve of the bombs which had exploded that day were in the New Lodge Road area, which was the responsibility of 40 Commando, Royal Marines.

In a side street littered with glass and rubble, off the New Lodge Road itself, a dozen marines crouched against a wall opposite what had once been Cohan's Select Bar, which was burning fiercely. Two officers stood casually in the middle of the street surveying the scene. One was a marine lieutenant. The other wore a paratrooper's red beret and a camouflage uni-

form, open at the neck, no badges of rank in evidence
and no flak jacket.

He had the dark, ravaged face of a man who had got
to know the world he inhabited too well and now had
only contempt for it. A small, dark man with good
shoulders, full of restless vitality that was somehow
accentuated by the bamboo swagger stick he tapped
against his right knee.

"Who's the para?" one marine whispered to another.

"Suns Special Section at Staff—Colonel Morgan. A
right bastard, so I've heard," the man next to him replied.

On the flat roof of a block of flats seventy-five yards
away, two men crouched by the parapet. One of
them was Liam O'Hagan, at that time chief intelligence officer for the Provisional IRA in Ulster. He
was examining the scene outside Cohan's Bar with the
aid of a pair of Zeiss night glasses.

The young man at his side carried a conventional
.303 Lee Enfield rifle of the type much favored by both
British Army and IRA snipers. It had an infrared
image intensifier fitted to it so that he could search
out a target in the dark.

He squinted through it now as he leaned the barrel
on the parapet. "I'll take the bloody paratrooper,
first."

"No you won't," O'Hagan told him softly.

"And why not?"

"Because I say so."

A Land-Rover swept around the corner below, followed by another very close behind. They had been
stripped to the bare essentials so that the driver and

three soldiers who crouched in the rear of each vehicle behind him were completely exposed. They were paratroopers, efficient, tough-looking young men in red berets and flak jackets, their Sterling submachine guns ready for instant action.

"Would you look at that now. Just asking to be chopped down, the dumb bastards. You'll not be telling me I can't have a crack at one of them?"

"It would be your last," O'Hagan told him. "They know exactly what they're doing. They perfected that open display technique in Aden. The crew of each vehicle looks after the other. Without armor plating to get in the way they can return fire instantly."

"Bloody SS," the boy said.

O'Hagan chuckled. "A hell of a thing to say to a man who once held the King's commission."

Down below, Asa Morgan climbed in beside the driver of the first Land-Rover, and the two vehicles moved away.

The marine lieutenant gave an order, and the section stood up and moved out. The street was silent now, only the flames still burning fiercely in Cohan's Bar, the occasional explosion of a bottle inside as the heat got to it.

"Mother of god, what a waste of good whiskey," Liam O'Hagan said. "Ah, well, the day will come, or so my Socialist Democratic comrades tell me, when not only will Ireland be free and united again, but with whiskey on tap like water in every decent man's house."

He grinned and slapped the boy on the shoulder. "And now, Seumas, my boy, I think we should get the hell out of here."

* * *

Morgan stood by the desk in the O.C.'s office at the Grand Central Hotel in Royal Avenue, the base for the city center regiment and billet for five hundred soldiers.

He stared down at the message in his hand blankly, and the young staff officer who had brought it from H.Q. shuffled uncomfortably.

"The G.O.C. has asked me to offer his sincere condolences. A terrible business. He's authorized your onward transportation to London by first available flight."

Morgan frowned. "That's very kind of him. But what about Operation Motorman?"

"Your duties will be assigned to someone else, Colonel. Orders from the Minister of Defence."

"Then I'd better start packing."

Somewhere in the distance there was the dull crump of an explosion and the rattle of machine gun fire. The young officer started in alarm.

"Nothing to worry about," Asa Morgan told him. "Belfast night sounds, that's all," and he walked out.

Steeple Durham was in Essex, not far from the Blackwater River. Marsh country, creeks, long grass stirring to change color constantly as if brushed by an invisible presence, the gurgle of water everywhere. An alien world inhabited mainly by birds. Curlew and redshank and brent geese coming south from Siberia to winter on the flats.

The village was a tiny, scattered community, Saxon in origin. The crypt of the church was that early at least, although the rest was Norman.

Francis Wood was working in the cemetery, cutting the grass verges with an old hand mower, when the silver sports car drew up at the gate and Asa Morgan got out. He wore slacks, a dark-blue polo-neck sweater and a brown leather bomber jacket.

"Hello, Francis," he said.

Francis Wood looked across at the Carrera Targa. "Still got the Porsche, I see."

"Nothing else to spend my money on. I keep on the flat in Gresham Place. There's a basement garage there. It's very convenient."

Rooks lifted out of the beech trees above their heads, calling angrily. Wood said, "I'm sorry, Asa. More than I could ever say."

"When's the funeral?"

"Tomorrow afternoon. Two-thirty."

"Are you officiating?"

"Unless you have any objection."

"Don't be stupid, Francis. How's Helen taking it?"

"She hasn't broken down yet, if that's what you mean. If you'd like to see her, you'll find her on the dike, painting. I'd tread very softly, if I were you."

"Why?"

"Surely they explained the peculiar circumstances of Megan's death."

"She was killed by a hit-and-run driver."

"There was rather more to it than that, Asa."

Morgan looked at him. "Then you'd better tell me about it, hadn't you?"

Morgan followed the path through the lych gate, around the gray stone rectory with its pantile roof, and took the track along the dike toward the estuary. He could see her from a long way off, seated at her easel, wearing the old military trenchcoat he'd bought the year they got married.

She glanced over her shoulder at the sound of his approach, then carried on painting. He stood behind her for a while without saying anything. It was a water color, of course, her favorite medium. A view of the marsh and the sea and a gray sky full of rain beyond, that was very fine indeed.

"You get better."

"Hello, Asa."

He sat on a grass bank to one side of her, smoking. She kept on painting, not looking at him once.

"How was Belfast?"

"Not too good."

"I'm glad," she said. "You deserve each other."

He said calmly, "I used to think that phrase had a particular application where we were concerned."

"No, Asa, whatever else I may have deserved in this life I never earned you."

"I never pretended to be anything other than I was."

"We went to bed together on our wedding night, and I woke up in the morning with a stranger. Every rotten little war they came up with, you were the first to volunteer. Cyprus, Borneo, Aden, the Oman, and now that butcher's shop across the Irish Sea."

"That's what they pay me for. You knew what you were taking on."

She was angry now. "Like hell I did. Certainly not Cyprus and the things you did there for Ferguson."

"Another kind of soldiering, hunting urban guerrillas," he said. "The rules are different."

"What rules? Torture, brainwashing? Lean a man against a wall on his fingertips with a bucket on his head for twenty-four hours? Isn't that what the newspapers accused you of in Nicosia? Are you still using that one in Belfast, or have you come up with some more acceptable refinement?"

He got up, his face bleak. "This isn't getting us anywhere."

"Do you know why I left?" she said. "Do you know what finally decided me? When you were in Aden. When I read in the papers how after they'd ambushed one of your patrols, you went into the Crater on foot, totally unarmed except for that damned swagger stick, and walked in front of the armored car to draw the fire, daring the rebels to come to the window and take a shot at you. When I read that, saw the photo on every front page, I packed my bags because I knew then, Asa, that I'd been married to a walking dead man for ten years."

Morgan said, "I didn't kill her, Helen."

"No, but someone very much like you did."

It was perhaps the cruelest thing she could have said. All color drained from his face. For a moment, she wanted to reach out, hold him in her arms again. To bind him to her as if she could contain the incredible vitality of the man, that elemental core to his being that had always eluded her. But that was foolishness of the worst order, doomed to failure as it had always failed before.

She stifled any pity she might have felt and carried on coldly, "Has Francis told you about the funeral arrangements?"

"Yes."

"We're hoping for a very quiet affair. There's to be no public connection with the Cohen business for security reasons, which is one good thing. If you'd like to see her, she's at an undertakers in Grantham. Pool and Son—George Street. And now I'd like you to go, Asa."

He stood there for a long moment, looking at her, then walked away.

Mr. Henry Pool opened an inner door and led the way through into a chapel of rest. The atmosphere was heavy with the scent of flowers, and taped music provided a suitable devotional background. There were half a dozen cubicles on either side, and Mr. Pool ushered Morgan into one of them. There were flowers everywhere, and an oak coffin stood on a draped trolley, the lid partially back.

The assistant who had first greeted Morgan in the shop on his arrival, a tall, thin, young man called Garvey, dressed in a dark suit and black tie, stood on the other side of the coffin.

The girl's eyes were closed, lips slightly parted, touched with color, the face heavily made up.

Harvey said, "The best I could do, Mr. Pool." He turned to Morgan. "Massive cranial damage, sir. Very difficult."

But Morgan didn't hear him for, as he looked down on his daughter's face for the last time, bile rose into his mouth.

He turned. "Thank you," he said to the mortician and went out, managing to hold himself together until he reached his car.

When he was ushered into Harry Baker's office by Stewart later that afternoon, Baker was standing at the window looking out. He turned.

"Hello, Asa. It's been a long time."

"Harry."

"The good Reverend's been talking has he?"

"That's right."

Morgan sat down, and Baker said, "George Stewart, my inspector."

He sat himself, behind the desk. Morgan said, "All right, Harry. What can you tell me?"

"Nothing," Baker replied. "Security rating, priority one. Special Branch is only supplying the muscle. DI5 is in charge. Group Four has new powers, directly from the Prime Minister himself, to coordinate the handling of all cases of terrorism, subversion, and the like."

"Who's in charge?"

"Ferguson."

"He would be. God in heaven, it's like coming round full circle, isn't it? When can I see him?"

Baker glanced at his watch. "In about thirty-five minutes at his flat in Cavendish Square. He prefers to see you there." He got to his feet. "Come on—I'll take you myself."

Morgan stood up. "No need for that."

"Orders, old son." Baker smiled. "And you know how Ferguson feels about people who don't carry them out."

Brigadier Charles Ferguson was a large, kindly-looking man whose crumpled blue suit seemed a size too big. The only military aspect to his appearance was the Guards tie. The untidy gray hair, the double chin, the half-moon spectacles with which he was reading the *Financial Times* by the fire when Morgan and Baker were ushered in, all conspired to give him the look of some minor professor.

"Asa, my dear boy, how nice to see you."

The voice was slightly plummy, a little overdone, rather like the aging actor in a second-rate touring company who wants to make sure they can hear him at the back of the house.

"All right, Kim. Tea for three," he said to the manservant, an ex-Ghurka *naik*, who waited patiently by the door.

The Ghurka retired, and Morgan looked around the room. The Adam fireplace was real, and so was the fire which burned there. The rest was Georgian also. Everything matched to perfection, even the heavy curtains.

"Nice, isn't it?" Ferguson said. "My second girl, Ellie, she did it for me. In interior decorating now."

Morgan moved to the window and looked into the square. "You always did do rather well for yourself."

"Oh dear, are you going to be tiresome, Asa? That *is* a pity. Very well, let's get it over with. You wanted to see me?"

Morgan glanced across at Baker who was seated in a leather armchair on the other side of the room, filling his pipe. "According to Harry, it was the other way round."

"Was it?" Ferguson said cheerfully.

The Ghurka came in with a tray, which he placed by the fire, and then retired. Ferguson picked up the teapot.

"For Christ's sake," Morgan exploded violently.

"All right, Asa. You are by now aware that the man who shot Maxwell Cohen is the same one who knocked down your daughter in the Paddington Tunnel. Am I correct?"

"Yes."

"And you'd very naturally like to get your hands on him. And so would we. So would the intelligence organizations of most of the major nations. You see, the one thing we do know for certain about the gentleman involved is that he's performed the same sort of exercise with rather spectacular success in various parts of the world for something like three years now."

"And what's being done about it?"

"You can safely leave that to us. I've been in touch with the Ministry of Defence. They inform me that in these special circumstances, you're to be granted a month's leave." Ferguson was serious now. "I'd bury your dead and then go as far away as possible for a while, if I were you, Asa."

"Would you indeed?" The Welsh accent was much more noticeable now as it always was in times of stress. Morgan turned to Baker. "And you, Harry? Is that what you'd do?"

Baker looked troubled. Ferguson said, "They're considering promoting you on the autumn list, or had you heard a whisper already? Brigadier, Asa, at your present age, means you should make major general at least before you retire. Something to be proud of."

"Who for?"

"Don't spoil it, Asa. You've come a long way."

"For a little Welsh pit boy who walked into the recruiting office with the arse out of his trousers, isn't that what you mean?"

Morgan went out, slamming the door.

Baker said, "You were a big rough on him, sir."

"Exactly what I intended, Chief Superintendent. He'll be back when he's reached boiling point."

* * *

The interior of the church of St. Martin at Steeple Durham was sparse and beautiful in its simplicity. Norman pillars rising to a roof that was richly carved with figures, both human and animal. Perhaps because at the period it was built it had been used as a place of refuge, there were no windows at ground level. The only light was from round, clerestory windows high up under the roof, so that the church itself was a place of shadows.

Harry Baker and Stewart arrived just after two and found Francis Wood waiting in the porch in his vestments.

"Chief Superintendent—Inspector. It's good of you both to come."

"No news, I'm afraid, sir."

"No arrest, you mean?" Wood smiled gently. "What possible difference could it make to us now if there were?"

"I saw Colonel Morgan yesterday. His sentiments were rather different."

"Knowing Asa, I would imagine so."

People started to arrive, mainly on foot, obviously villagers. Wood greeted them, and then the gate in the wall on the other side of the churchyard, which gave access to the rectory garden, opened and his wife appeared.

She was not dressed for mourning, but wore a simple gray suit with a pleated skirt, tan shoes, and stockings. Her hair was tied back with a velvet bow as on the first occasion Baker had met her. She was unnaturally calm considering the circumstances.

She nodded to Baker. "Superintendent."

Baker, for once, couldn't think of a thing to say.

Francis Wood kissed her briefly on the cheek, and she moved on inside. The hearse pulled up at the lych gate, and a few moments later the coffin was brought forward on the shoulders of Harry Pool, his son, and four assistants, all suitably garbed in black coats.

Wood went forward to greet them. Baker said, "You know what I hate about this sort of thing, George? The fact that they've probably done two already today. Same hearse, same black overcoats, same appropriate expressions."

"No sign of Morgan, sir."

"So I'd observed," Baker said and added as the procession moved toward them, "Let's get inside now we're here."

They sat in a pew halfway down the church, and the cortege moved past them, Francis Wood reciting the Order for the Burial of the Dead.

> I am the resurrection and the life, saith the Lord: he that believeth in me, though he were dead, yet shall he live: and whosoever liveth and believeth in me shall never die.

The coffin was placed before the altar rail, the bearers retired. There was a pause, and Wood carried on.

> Lord, thou hast been our refuge: from one generation to another. . . .

The door opened, then shut again so loudly that he paused and looked up from the prayer book. Heads turned. Asa Morgan stood there in full uniform, razor-

sharp, polished Sam Brown belt gleaming, medals
hanging in a neat row beneath the SAS wings above
the tunic pocket. He removed the red beret, sat down
in the rear pew.

The one person who had not turned was Helen
Wood. She sat alone in the front pew, shoulders
straight, staring ahead. There was the briefest of
pauses, and then her husband carried on in a loud,
clear voice.

As they moved out to the churchyard, thunder
rumbled in the distance, and the first heavy spots of
rain dotted the flagstones of the path.

"One of life's greatest clichés," Baker observed.
"Eight times out of ten it rains at funerals. That's
why I brought this thing."

He opened his umbrella, and he and Stewart followed at the tail end of the villagers as they made
their way between the headstones toward the freshly
dug grave.

Most of them stayed at a respectful distance while
Helen Wood stood at the edge of the grave facing
her husband. Asa Morgan was behind the rector, his
red beret tilted forward at the exact regulation angle.

Francis Wood continued with the committal, rais-
ing his voice a little as the rain increased in force.
His wife, at the correct moment, dropped to one
knee to pick up a handful of soil to cast into the
open grave. She remained there for a moment, then
glanced up and found that Morgan had moved forward to stand beside her husband.

Francis Wood carried on without faltering:

Earth to earth, ashes to ashes, dust to dust; in sure and certain hope of the Resurrection.

Morgan took the red beret from his head and dropped it into the open grave on top of the coffin. His ex-wife stood up slowly, her eyes never leaving his face. He turned, marched away through the tombstones, and went into the church.

"Which should give them something to talk about in the village for quite some time," Baker observed.

When Francis Wood went into the church a few minutes later, he found Morgan sitting in the front pew, arms folded, staring up at the altar.

Wood said, "Well Asa, you didn't come to pray, so what exactly do you want?"

"Not if that's the best you can do, the claptrap you handed us out there," Morgan told him. *"Forasmuch as it hath pleased Almighty God of his great mercy to take unto himself the soul of our dear sister here departed.* What in the hell is that supposed to mean, Francis?"

"I don't know, Asa. You see, for me, it's a matter of faith. Faith in God's purpose for all of us."

"That's really very comforting." Morgan stood up and climbed the steps to the pulpit.

"All right, Asa, say what you have to say."

At the back of the church Baker and Stewart stood in the shadows by the door, listening.

Morgan said, "I'm trying to reconcile the fact of God's mercy with a little girl on a bicycle getting in the way of a rabid fanatic, fleeing from an attempted murder. You'll be interested to know, by the way, that an Arab terrorist group named Black September has claimed credit. A nice word, you must admit. All in the terminology."

There was an unnatural calm to him now, and he gripped the edge of the pulpit so tightly that his knuckles turned white.

Wood said, "Asa, God punishes, men only take revenge. I think I know the road you wish to take, and I tell you this now. You will find nothing at the end of it. No answer—no satisfaction—nothing."

Morgan looked around him. "I never realized before what a good view you had up here." He came down the steps, walked briskly up the aisle and went out.

Baker and Stewart followed him. It was raining harder than ever now, and they watched him march bare-headed to the lych gate and cross to the Porsche.

Baker said to Stewart, "You take the car and get after him. I'll take the train back to London. Stick to him like glue. I want to know where he goes and what he does. Lose him and I'll have you."

Stewart had little difficulty keeping the silver Porsche in plain view. Even after skirting London and joining the M1 motorway north, Morgan seldom did more than seventy, moving into the fast lane only when it was necessary to pass a heavy truck or some other particularly slow-moving vehicle.

Just outside Doncaster, he pulled into a service area for petrol. Stewart did the same, keeping well back. The Porsche moved across to the car park, and Morgan got out, reached inside, and pulled out a military trenchcoat which he put on over his uniform. Then he walked across to the self-service cafe.

Stewart parked a few cars away, then went to the toilet. When he came out, he checked that the Porsche was still in view, then crossed to the cafe and peered inside. There was no sign of Morgan.

He turned quickly, but he had not been mistaken. The Porsche was still there, and then he saw the Colonel crouched beside his own car.

As Stewart hurried toward him, Morgan stood up and Stewart saw that his right front tire was flat.

"Here, what the hell do you think you're doing?" he demanded angrily.

Morgan kicked the wheel. "Looks like you're in trouble, Inspector. I'd get hold of a policeman if I were you."

Morgan walked to the Porsche, climbed in, and drove rapidly away.

Mikali rose late that morning, and it was eleven o'clock before he went for his usual run in Hyde Park in spite of the heavy rain. Not that it bothered him. He liked the rain. It gave him a safe, enclosed feeling, rather like being in a little world of your own.

He finally got back to the apartment in Upper Grosvenor Street and opened the door to the aroma of freshly ground coffee. At first he assumed the girl from the previous night hadn't gone home, and then Jean Paul Deville appeared in the kitchen doorway.

"Ah, there you are. Let myself in with the contingency key. I hope you don't mind."

Mikali got a towel from the bathroom and mopped the sweat from his face. "When did you get in?"

"The breakfast plane. I thought we should chat."

He returned to his coffee making. Mikali said, "It didn't go too smoothly."

"You shot him in the head at pointblank range.

Who could ask for more? And we've achieved what we set out to do. A major assassination attempt in the heart of London. Headlines in every newspaper in the world and wonderful publicity for the Palestinian cause. Black September is delighted. Their man in Paris came to see me last night. It got a little rough this one, I understand. Were you worried?"

"When I was in Algiers, the Arabs had a saying. 'It comes as God wills.' However carefully you plan, one of these days, someone turns up where they shouldn't be. The gun that's never been known to jam, does. That's what will kill me in the end, and you, when you least expect it."

"Very possibly," Deville said. "Like the girl on the bicycle in the tunnel?"

"That was regrettable. I tried to avoid her, but there was nothing to be done. There was the briefest of mentions in both London evening papers, but what I can't understand is why they've made no connection with the Cohen affair."

"Yes, I wondered about that. I had my friends in London investigate. It seems the girl's parents were divorced some time ago. The father is a paratroop colonel named Morgan—Asa Morgan. Serving in Ireland at the moment. My friends most obligingly ran him through the computer for me, and he has quite a record. Expert in subversion, urban guerrilla techniques, advanced interrogation methods. Was even a Chinese prisoner in Korea. It makes sense that the British Army would prefer to keep a very low profile on a man like that, which would explain the official handling of the matter."

"They're also keeping a very low profile on the Cretan." Mikali spooned tea into the pot.

"What's that supposed to mean? That you're afraid someone else will get the credit?"

Mikali laughed. "Go to hell."

"Soon enough, my friend." Deville took his office and sat by the window. "To revolutionaries the world over from the Red Brigade to the IRA, the Cretan is a living legend. But make no mistake. The files of every Western intelligence agency record in minute detail each of your operations. By disclosing as little as possible to the public, they hope to improve their chances of catching you. Besides, everybody loves a winner. You might even become popular, and that would never do."

"It's a thought."

Deville took a folded sheet of notepaper from his pocket and pushed it across. "For your own safety, naturally," he smiled, "I've changed your emergency postbox number again, not only in London but also in Manchester and Edinburgh. Learn and burn."

"Okay." Mikali poured a cup of tea.

"Your performance the other night—were you satisfied?"

"Tolerably. I'm never happy with the Albert Hall acoustics, but the ambience is great."

"And now a holiday. What do you intend to do? Go to Hydra?"

"A few days in Cambridge first."

"Dr. Katherine Riley?" Deville said. "That's fast becoming a habit. Are you serious?"

"She's company," Mikali said. "No more than that, but then good company's damned hard to find in this lousy world, don't you agree?"

He unzipped the right-hand pocket of his track suit and took out a small rather ugly automatic, perhaps six inches long with a curious-looking barrel, which he placed on the table.

Deville picked it up. "What is it?"

"A Czech Ceska. This particular model was manufactured by the Germans when they took over the factory during the war. It incorporates a very effective silencer."

"Any good?"

"SS intelligence used them."

Deville put it down carefully. "You always go armed, even when running in the park?"

"My dear Deville, when I go onto the stage of the Albert Hall to give a concert, I carry this little item. Paris, Berlin—it's all the same."

"But why?"

Mikali poured himself a cup of tea, added sugar and milk, English style. "Tell me," he said. "Do you still carry a cyanide capsule?"

"Of course."

"Why have you never offered me one?"

Deville shrugged. "Because I could never conceive of a situation in which you would use it."

"Exactly." Mikali smiled and picked up the Ceska. "When that totally unexpected moment arrives, when they come to take me, I'll have this in my hand. Even in the Green Room at the Albert Hall."

"I see," Deville said. "You go down firing. The soldier's end, face toward the enemy." He sighed, and there was genuine affection in his voice now. "My dear John, you really are the most romantic fool at heart. Is that how you see yourself? The last Samurai."

Mikali opened the window and stepped onto the balcony. The sun was shining as he looked out across the park. It was going to be a warm day.

He turned. "Oscar Wilde once said that life is a bad quarter of an hour made up of exquisite moments."

"Which brings us back to Cambridge and Dr. Riley," Deville said.

Mikali smiled. "Exactly. Very definitely one of the more exquisite moments he was referring to."

FOUR

By evening Morgan had reached Leeds. He left the city by the A65 making for the Yorkshire Dales through Otley, Ilkley, and Skipton, moving up into a high dark landscape of desolate moors surmounted by an occasional low mountain peak.

The village of Malham is set in the midst of the most rugged limestone scenery in Yorkshire. He reached it as darkness was falling, drove on for another mile before finally turning through a five-barred gate to a small, graystone cottage set among trees in half an acre of garden.

Strictly speaking, it was now Helen's part of the settlement, but when he checked, the key was under the stone where it had always been kept. He opened the door, then went and got his things from the car.

There was that faintly damp smell that came from lack of use, but there was a fire laid ready on the hearth. He put a match to it and went exploring upstairs, where there were two bedrooms and a bath.

He found what he wanted in one of the wardrobes. His old climbing gear. Boots, corduroy pants, and heavy woollen sweaters. He took them downstairs along with a sleeping bag and spread them in front of the fire. Then he got a bottle of Scotch from his carryall, climbed into the sleeping bag, and lay in front of the fire.

He piled on the logs and drank whiskey—a great deal of whiskey—because he didn't want to think of his daughter. Not then. That would come later. After a while, he slept.

A couple of miles beyond Malham, a footpath leads to the cliffs of Gordale Scar. Asa Morgan had last visited this place with his daughter on her twelfth birthday. Walking steadily across the boggy ground that morning through heavy rain, he could hear again her excited voice as they rounded the rocky corner and Gordale Scar came into view, the waterfall pouring down the center, heavier than usual because of the rain.

The only way forward had been by a rockclimb up the steep buttress on the left, and he had pushed her on ahead, staying close behind—just in case. Afterward, there was the long struggle up the scree past the upper waterfall and then the path following the edge of the ravine.

He plowed on through thick mist and rain for mile after mile, totally trapped in the past. It was as if she was still there, hurrying on ahead into the mist, then suddenly reappearing, with a rush, to tell him of some discovery.

And for a while he was a fourteen-year-old boy again, in that first week out of school. Up at five and off over the mountain with a packet of his mother's cheese sandwiches and a flask of cold tea.

Six miles hard walking every morning to reach the pit that had killed his father.

He never forgot that first day. The sickening jolt as the cage dropped, two thousand feet down, into a nightmare world of darkness and despair and back-breaking labor.

And the six-mile tramp back at the end of his first shift, so tired that he'd thought he would never make it. Later, sitting in the old zinc tub in front of the fire while she scrubbed the coal dust from his body, he knew only one thing with certainty. There had to be something better, for there was something in him, he felt it, aching to break out.

And there was, for as some were born to act, others gifted to be great surgeons or musicians. Asa Morgan was a soldier by nature. A born leader. For him, the military life was as much a calling as the ministry was for others. So, greatest irony of all, it was the war that saved him; that took him out of the slagheaps and coal mines of the Rhondda for good—and into the Army.

The walk circled back toward Malham, and it was on the inward leg of the journey as he descended what was known as Dry Valley that it happened. He came to an overhang, a large boulder beside it, where they had sheltered from the rain to eat their sandwiches.

The pent-up agony erupted inside him. "No!" he cried. "No!" and turned, as if running from the Devil himself, slipping and sliding on the treacherous surface as he stumbled down the valley.

Suddenly he found himself on the limestone pavement that he knew led to the brink of the great 240-

foot clig of Malham Cove. The wind snatched the mist away, and the whole of the Dale stretched below him.

It rose up inside him like white-hot lava now, a rage such as he had never known.

"I'm coming you bastard!" he screamed. "I'm coming!"

He ran across the limestone slabs and started down the path as fast as he could go.

By noon of the following day he was knocking at the door of the flat in Cavendish Square. It was opened by the Ghurka, Kim, in his neat white jacket, brass buttons polished. Morgan moved straight past him without a word and found Ferguson seated at his desk in the living room, half-moon spectacles on the end of his nose, working his way through a pile of papers.

He glanced up and removed them. "You *have* been a naughty boy. Poor old Stewart wasn't exactly received with open arms on his return. You've probably set the poor devil's promotion back a couple of years."

"I want him, Charles," Morgan said. "I'll do anything you say. Play it any way you like, but you must give me my chance."

Ferguson got up and moved to the window. "Revenge, Bacon said, is a kind of wild justice and that won't do. Won't do at all. Too emotional. Bound to impair your judgment. And you're not exactly twenty-five anymore, now are you?" He shook his head firmly. "No, you finish your leave, then it's back to Belfast."

"Then I'll resign my commission."

"You can't, not in your case. It's your security classi-
fication, you see, Asa. Makes you rather special. You're
with us for the duration. Just like the good old war
days."

"All right." Morgan put up his hands defensively.
"A month, that's what you said I had, and a month it
is then."

He turned and walked out before Ferguson could
make any reply.

He was calmer now, completely in control again.
That primordial outburst at Malham, the mad drive
south, had drained the excess emotion out of him.
He was one more a professional—cold, calculating,
and capable of total objectivity.

But where to start, that was the problem. He was
sitting in the living room of the Gresham Place flat
just after four, working his way through several different newspapers with accounts of the shooting,
when the door bell rang. When he opened it, Harry
Baker was standing there, holding a leather briefcase.

He walked straight in. "Bit rough on young Stewart,
weren't you? I mean, the lad's got to learn."

Morgan followed him into the living room and
stood waiting, hands in pockets. "All right, Harry,
what do you want?"

"Ferguson phoned me. Said you'd been on his back
again."

"Did he also tell you he'd warned me off?"

"Yes."

"So?"

Baker took out his pipe and started to fill it. "You
saved my life in Nicosia, Asa. If it hadn't been for
you, I'd have taken a bullet in the head from that

EOKA gunman. You shoved me down and took it in the back instead."

"We all make mistakes."

"If Ferguson finds out about this, I'm finished, but to hell with it." Baker opened the briefcase, produced a manila folder, and tossed it on the table. "There you are, Asa. Everything there is to know, and that isn't a great deal, on the man who shot Maxwell Cohen and killed Megan. The man we call the Cretan Lover."

FIVE

Baker stood in front of the fire, warming himself as Morgan started to work his way through the file.

"As you can see, the first time he appeared on the scene was in 1969. The Vassilikos killing. That's when the newspapers first referred to him as the Cretan."

"Because the chauffeur was so sure he'd spoken with a Cretan accent?"

"Which, according to the file, was confirmed by the maid at the Hilton in West Berlin a month later in November when he got General Stephanakis."

Morgan read on. "This business with the girl in the wardrobe while they were waiting for Stephanakis to appear? It's genuine?"

"Oh, yes."

"Which explains the Cretan Lover tag?"

"That and a similar case you'll find mentioned in there. And that Boudakis girl—it wasn't rape. A psychiatrist had a session with her. His impression was that she'd fallen for the man."

"From the details listed in here, I'd say a great many Greeks might be cheering for him," Morgan said. "Both Vassilikos and General Stephanakis seem to have been a couple of butchers."

"All right," Baker said. "So our friend is just a

simple Cretan peasant, a hero of the Resistance who
doesn't like the present regime in Greece, a regime
he sees as fascist. He decides to do something about it.
Fine—except for one rather important point. Since
then, he's been responsible for one assassination after
another the world over. Oh, the credit's usually been
claimed by some appropriate terrorist group, but we
know, as do most of the world's leading intelligence
organizations, when the Cretan has been responsible.
His touch is distinctive and unmistakable. Read on.
You'll see what I mean."

He sat by the fire and relit his pipe, and Morgan
continued to go through the file.

In June, 1970, the Cretan had killed, in his hotel
room, Colonel Rafael Gallegos, Chief of Police for
the Basque country that straddles the Pyrenees between Spain and France. The killing was a carbon
copy of the murder of General Stephanakis in Paris.
Responsibility had been claimed by the Basque Na-
tionalist movement, the ETA, which had been fighting for years for separation from Spain.

In September of the same year, General Severo
Falção, head of the Brazilian secret police, had been
assassinated in Rio de Janeiro by a traffic policeman
who had stopped his car on a quiet country road
leading out of the city to the General's home. As in
the Vassilikos killing, only the General and his bodyguards died. The chauffeur had been allowed to go.

In November, 1970, he had murdered George Henry
Daly, an insurance executive in Boston. What the
newspapers had not been told was that Daly was
actually Major Sergei Kulakov, who had defected
to the Americans five years before from the Red
Army's Berlin intelligence station. The CIA had

squeezed him dry and then provided him with what they had fondly imagined to be a brand new identity. His wife had described the Cretan perfectly. He could have killed her and didn't.

In 1971, in Toronto, there was Henry Jackson, an economist, another case of a defecting Russian agent under an assumed name.

Later that year, the Israeli Consul General in Istanbul. The Turkish People's Liberation Army had claimed credit for that.

Then came one of the most spectacular affairs of all. His killing of the Italian film director, Mario Forlani, at the Cannes Film Festival. The Black Brigade in Rome, the fascist answer to the Red Brigade, claimed credit. They'd threatened Forlani on a number of occasions because of a film he had made ridiculing Mussolini.

"So, he isn't some Marxist fanatic," Morgan commented.

"You mean the Cannes business? That was a hell of an affair. The French had the hotel Forlani was staying at guarded like Fort Knox. Garde Mobile all over the place. Plain clothes security men inside. Everybody was staying there. Half the uncrowned heads of Europe, most of what counts for stars these days in Hollywood. John Mikali, the pianist, Sophia Loren, David Niven, Paul Newman, and god knows who else."

"And he pulled it off in the middle of that lot?"

"What happened was simple. Forlani appeared from his apartment on the fifteenth floor with three girl friends to go down to dinner. There were two policemen on his door, another on the lift."

"And?"

"The Cretan simply materialized at the end of the corridor, shot him in the heart with a handgun, at that range, mind you. Was away through the fire door like a flash."

"And no trace?"

"Vanished off the face of the earth. The French police turned the place inside out, but they didn't get a thing. Most of the celebrities left that night. Couldn't get away fast enough. It caused one hell of a stink."

"Then?"

"It's in the file. Killed Helmut Klein, the East German Minister of Finance, who was visiting Frankfurt University last November. The campus was under heavy security. He holed up with a girl called Lieselott Hoffman who, it later transpired, was a Baader-Meinhoff sympathizer. She took in a rifle under orders of the Red Army Faction. Was told to hold it for pick-up."

"And the Cretan turned up?"

"After dark and wearing that damned mask of his."

Morgan examined the file again. "According to this, Klein emerged from a reception at the director's home just after ten. The Cretan got him from three hundred yards using an image intensifier. One hell of a shot."

"Then cleared off. The girl was caught trying to dispose of the gun. Most of the details emerged during her interrogation. Seems he'd given her what he gave the maid at the Hilton in Berlin, and she was another who didn't seem to mind. She was sprung from a prison van en route to jail by a combat squad of the Red Army Faction."

"And totally disappeared?"

"Until she was arrested in London in February of

this year working in a boutique. Claimed she'd married a gentleman called Harry Fowler, a waiter from Camden Town, only he can't be found. It would, of course, have made her a British citizen. The Germans want her back, both East and West variety. Naturally, the civil liberty groups here want her kept. She's at a special remand center at Tangmere, near Cambridge. A source of considerable embarrassment to the government."

"I can imagine." Morgan read on in silence for a moment. "This psychologist's report on the girl is really quite excellent. Who did it?"

"A woman called Riley. Dr. Katherine Riley. An American. She's a fellow at one of the Cambridge colleges. She's been allowed to visit the Hoffmann girl regularly."

"Why?"

"It's her field, terrorism. She's interviewed nearly every well-known European terrorist in prison, when they've allowed her to. Wrote a book about it eighteen months ago called *The Terrorist Phenomenon*."

"I remember now," Morgan said. "I read it." He reached for a cigarette. "By my reckoning, our friend has knocked off around a dozen very important people in just under three years. That's quite a score."

"And he doesn't take sides." Baker said. "The Cretan peasant who seemed so antifascist ends up shooting an East German cabinet minister and a communist film director."

"But also still finds time for the odd fascist."

"And two very important Russian defectors whom both American and Canadian intelligence thought they'd taken care of more than adequately."

Morgan said, "Just what is the latest on the international terrorist front? I'm slightly out of touch since the Ulster business."

"There are definite links now between groups around the world," Baker said. "For example, the Japanese who were responsible for the massacre at Tel Aviv airport were trained at Lebanese terrorist training camps. Their arms, mainly grenades and Kalashnikovs, were provided by the Baader-Meinhoff gang. The Palestine Liberation Front were also involved."

"Quite a combination."

"Our information is that earlier this year, a secret conference of guerrilla organizations held in Dublin was attended by Maoist and anarchist representatives from all over the world."

"With the IRA as hosts?"

"That would depend on which branch of the IRA you're speaking of."

"Maoists—anarchists—to hell with all of them. It's the Cretan I want." Morgan picked up a pencil and pulled a pad forward. "What do we really know about him?"

"Physically small," Baker said.

"But extremely powerful."

"Highly intelligent, resourceful. Obviously able to move around the world with no difficulty whatsoever."

"A soldier."

"What makes you think that?"

"The way he operates, the precision, the organization. When he has a target, that's what he goes for. There's nothing indiscriminate about him. On several occasions he's spared people's lives. The chauffeurs', for example, in Paris and Rio."

"But not Megan."

"No." Morgan nodded calmly. "He ran her down like a dog. His one mistake."

He studied the notes he'd made on the pad, and Baker said, "Don't forget the most important thing. He's a Cretan."

"Who speaks German, French, Spanish, and English? A trained soldier? A world traveler?" Morgan shook his head. "I'd amend that one, if I were you. What we're after is a man who for some reason can pass as a Cretan if he wants to."

"And where would you start looking for a man like that?"

Morgan shrugged. "I don't know—not at the moment. The Hoffmann girl. There could be something there. Maybe she's not telling everything she knows. This Dr. Riley of yours might be worth a visit. Have you met her?"

"I have had that pleasure. She doesn't like policemen. One thing that isn't in that file, by the way. The bullet they took out of Cohen's brain indicates a Mauser, but a very unusual one; 7.63mm, Model 1932, and with a bulbous silencer. They were used by certain German security units during the war."

"Yes, I know the gun you mean," Morgan said. "They only manufactured a few."

"That's right. And they're in very short supply these days, virtually unobtainable. The computer shows only one as having been used to kill in the United Kingdom ever. That was an army intelligence sergeant last year in Londonderry."

"The Cretan? In Ulster?" Morgan was astonished.

"No—a Provisional hit man named Terence Murphy. He was shot dead by a Commando patrol as he

made a run for it along with a man called Pat Phelan.
As a matter of interest, he had one, too. We tried to
trace the dealer the guns had come from, but no
luck."

"An interesting possibility," Morgan said softly.
"That the gun used to shoot Cohen might have come
from the same source."

"I've got people working on that now," Baker said.
"But frankly, we didn't get very far last time, so. . . ."
He picked up the file and replaced it in his brief-
case. "Now you know as much as I do about the
Cretan. What do you intend to do?"

"I'll think of something."

"I bet you will," Baker said grimly and opened the
door. "We're all square now, Asa, just remember
that."

Morgan gave him a few moments only, then grabbed
his coat and went after him. He arrived in the main
entrance to see Baker walking toward the end of the
street. The Superintendent stood on the corner, at-
tempting to hail a taxi. Morgan went back inside,
hurried down to the garage, got into the Porsche,
and started the engine.

He was waiting under the trees outside Ferguson's
apartment in Cavendish Square when the taxi drew
up and Baker got out. He paid the driver and went
inside. Morgan gave him a few minutes and followed.

When Kim opened the door, he walked straight
past him and through into the living room. Ferguson
was at his desk, the file in front of him; Baker stood
at his side.

"Christ Almighty!" Baker said bitterly.

Ferguson sighed. "Oh dear, you are being awkward, aren't you, Asa?"

"All right," Morgan said. "Let's stop playing silly bastards. You want this Cretan character, and so do I, so why not say so officially and be done with it."

"But that's just it, dear boy. Nothing official. That's the whole point."

"Oh, I see." Morgan glanced at Baker. "I was supposed to be grateful for favors received from my old mate here and go roaring off like a wild man to see what I could find out on my own. And all my own fault if I cocked it up, eh?"

Ferguson leaned back. "And could you, Asa? Go roaring off and find anything, I mean? Anything of value?"

"The Mauser," Morgan said. "If I could trace the arms dealer who supplied it, that would do for a start."

"And where in the hell would you find that information?" Baker demanded.

"Belfast."

"Belfast!" Baker said in amazement. "You must be crazy."

"Let's put it this way. There are people there on entirely the wrong side, who might be willing to help me for old times sake."

"Like Liam O'Hagan? Because you once served together? All you'll get there is a bullet in the head."

"And what else, Asa?" Ferguson interrupted. "What else would you need?"

"I'd like to interview Lieselott Hoffmann before I leave for Belfast. Tomorrow morning would be fine."

Ferguson said, "Arrange that with Dr. Riley, Superintendent."

"I'd also like a list of all the hits mentioned in that file. Dates, places, the works."

Morgan walked to the door. Ferguson said, "Asa, as far as I'm concerned, you're on leave for a month."

"Of course."

"On the other hand, if there's anything we can do. . . ."

"I know," Morgan said. "Don't hesitate to call."

In 1947, as the first rumblings of the Cold War were heard on the horizon, J. Parnell Thomas and his House Committee on Un-American Activities had decided to examine the Hollywood film industry for signs of communist subversion.

Nineteen writers, producers, and directors formed a resistance group, declaring that it was none of the committee's business what their political opinions were. Eleven were called to Washington to answer for themselves in public. One, Bertholt Brecht, departed for East Germany in a hurry. The remaining ten all refused to answer, using the freedom of speech guarantee contained in the first amendment of the U.S. Constitution.

The affair sent shock waves all the way down through the industry, involving far more than the famous ten. In the period that followed, many actors, writers, and directors had their reputations so damaged by Senate investigations that they could not work under their own names again for many years.

Sean Riley, an Irish—American writer with a reputation for plain speaking, was one of the casualties. In spite of his two best-screenplay Oscars, he suddenly found himself unable to get work of any kind. His

wife, who had suffered from heart trouble for years,
was unable to take the strain and worry of that terrible period. She died in 1950, the year her husband
refused to appear before a Senate subcommittee
headed by Joseph McCarthy.

Riley didn't surrender. He simply withdrew into the
country, a rambling old Spanish–American farmhouse
in the San Fernando Valley, taking his eight-year-
old daughter with him.

For years, he made a living as what is known in the
industry as a script doctor. Anyone in trouble with a
screenplay took it to Riley and he rewrote it for a
fee. Naturally, his name never appeared in the credits.

It was not, in the end, such a bad life. He wrote
two or three novels, planted a vineyard, and raised
his daughter with love and understanding and grace
to respect the land and what was best in people and
never to be afraid.

She was an angular, olive-skinned, awkward girl
with gray-green eyes and black hair inherited from
her mother, a Jewess from Warsaw. At UCLA, she
took her degree in psychology in 1962, then did research in experimental psychiatry at the Tavistock
Clinic in London, and took her doctorate at Cambridge University by 1965.

She went to Vienna to the Holzer Institute for the
Criminally Insane to follow her particular interest,
the psychopathology of violence. It was here that she
first came into contact with that startling phenomenon
of our times, the urban guerrilla. The terrorist from
the middle-class home.

During the years that followed, she pursued this
study, interviewing her subjects in most of the major
cities of Europe, working, where she had to, for the

state authorities involved, although this was not a situation she was happy with.

She kept the closest of contacts with her father, returning home at least twice a year. He visited her in Europe, mainly when the developing Italian film scene took him to Rome and new opportunities. Once again, his name appeared on the credits. He won screenplay awards in Berlin, in Paris, in London. And then, in 1970, he collapsed with a massive heart attack at the San Fernando Valley farmhouse.

She was in Paris at the time, at the Sorbonne, and flew home at once. He hung on, waited for her, so that when she entered his room at the Cedars of Lebanon Hospital, the blue eyes in the strong tanned face that was suddenly so old opened instantly. She took his hand, and he died.

They all came to the funeral. Directors, actors, producers, front-office men who hadn't spoken to him during the bad years. Who'd turned and walked the other way when they saw him coming. Now that he was dead there was even talk that the Academy was considering a special award.

As a Catholic of the old-fashioned variety, she had him buried instead of cremated and stood at the cemetery, shaking one hand after the other as they all filed past, hating every coward, every hypocrite there.

Afterward, she fled back to the farmhouse in the Valley, but that was no good—no good at all with memories of him everywhere.

There was no one to turn to, for in one respect—in her relations with the opposite sex—he had never been able to help her. Her dealings with men had always been brief and unsatisfactory emotionally and therefore unsatisfactory physically. The blunt truth was that she had never found anyone who matched up to her father.

When she was close to the final edge of things, salvation appeared in the shape of an airmail letter with an English stamp postmarked Cambridge, which dropped into her mailbox one morning. It contained the offer of a fellowship at her old college, New Hall, and she grabbed with both hands, fleeing to the only other refuge she had ever known in her life.

And things had gone well for her. It was like coming home. There was the work, there was her book, and there was Cambridge in all its glory, particularly on that beautiful April morning in 1972, when she first met John Mikali.

She worked all night on the proofs of the fifth edition of her book, the publishers wanting them back by Friday. Instead of going to bed, she followed her set routine. Put on a track suit, got out her bicycle, and rode down toward the center of the city, clean and calm and beautiful in the morning.

Fifteen minutes later, she was running on the footpath along the Backs, the lawns that slope down to the River Cam. She was thoroughly enjoying herself, pleased with the night's work, relishing the keen morning smell, and then she became aware of the sound of someone overtaking her and Mikali appeared at her side.

He wore a very simple navy blue track suit and running shoes. A white towel was wrapped around his neck.

"Nice morning for it," he said.

She recognized him at once, could hardly fail to
for posters featuring his usual photo had been plastered all over Cambridge for a fortnight.

"Yes, it usually is."

He smiled instantly. "Hey, a fellow American. This
must be my day. Are you an exchange student or something?"

The Irish side of her rose quickly to the surface,
and she laughed out loud. "Those days are long gone.
I'm what they call a don here. I teach at the University. My name's Katherine Riley. I'm from California."

"Good god, so am I. My name's Mikali—John
Mikali."

She took his hand with a slight reluctance, aware of
a tingling excitement, a coldness in her belly that
was new to her.

"Yes, I know. You're playing Rachmaninov's
Fourth tonight with the London Symphony."

"I trust you'll be there."

"Are you joking? Some students queued overnight
to catch the box office the first day it opened. There
hasn't been a ticket available for that concert since
then."

"Nonsense," he said. "Where do you live?"

"New Hall."

"I'll have a ticket delivered there by noon." He
smiled with incredible charm.

There was no way she could say no, or even wanted
to. "That would be marvelous."

"Afterward, they're throwing a reception for me at
Trinity College. Can I send you a card for that as
well? It could be a bore, but not if you come." Before she could reply, he glanced at his watch. "I

hadn't realized the time. I've got a four-hour re-hearsal this morning, and Previn is a hard task-master—see you tonight."

He turned and ran away across the Backs, very fast indeed. She stood there, watching him go, aware of the power in him, more excited than she had ever been in her life.

At the reception, she stood watching him on the other side of the room, in the velvet suit, the open black silk shirt, the golden crucifix around his neck, all of which had become his trademark. He was restless as they crowded around, his eyes searching the room constantly. When he found her, the smile was instant, and he reached for two glasses of cham-pagne from a tray carried by a passing waiter and made straight for her alone.

"I phoned your college," he said. "Why didn't you tell me? Dr. Riley—Fellow of New Hall. All that stuff."

"It didn't seem important."

"Was I good tonight?"

"You know you were," she said simply and took the champagne from him.

There was a sudden, strange look in his eyes. It was as if, in some way, he had made a discovery he had not looked for.

He smiled and raised his glass. "To Katherine Riley, a nice Catholic girl, with wit, perception, and ex-quisite musical taste who is going to take me the hell out of here within the next three minutes and show me Cambridge."

"Jewish," she said. "My mother was, you see, and that's what counts."

"Okay, I'll amend it. Katherine Riley, a nice Jewish girl. Does that mean you can cook as well?"

"Oh, yes."

"Excellent! Now, let's get out of here. You can take me on a punt in the moonlight, show me the romance of all those gleaming spires of yours."

It rained after the first half an hour so that they were both soaked to the skin by the time they managed to abandon the punt at the side of the river.

Later, when the taxi dropped them at New Hall, it was raining even harder, and they arrived at the door to her rooms as wet as two human beings could possibly be.

When she got the door open and made to enter, he took her arm gently, "No," he said. "The first time I carry you across the threshold. It's an old Greek custom. We're very ethnic, you know."

Afterward, somewhere close to three o'clock when they finally stopped, she turned to him in bed as he reached for a cigarette.

"That was nice. I never knew it could be like that."

"Go to sleep," he said gently, putting an arm around her.

It had stopped raining now, and moonlight filtered into the room. He lay there for quite a while, smoking and staring up at the ceiling, his face grave. When she moaned in her sleep, his arm tightened around her instinctively.

"Do you realize Milton was responsible for this tree?" she demanded.

They were sitting under the Mulberry tree in the

Fellows' garden of Christ's College, the tree the great poet was reputed to have planted himself.

"I'm totally indifferent." Mikali kissed her on the neck. "Nothing matters on a day like this. Spring in Cambridge, and you have to work."

"For the rest of the week, then I'm due a vacation."

"I don't know, Katherine. This work you do. Violence, killing, terrorism. That's a hell of a field for a woman. No—let me amend that. A hell of a field for anyone."

"Oh, come on," she said. "What about your time in the Legion in Algeria. I've read those magazine articles. I mean, what scene were you playing then?"

He shrugged. "I was just a kid. I joined up on impulse. It was an emotional thing. But ycu—you really seek them out. Someone told me last night that you're working on this German girl, the one with the Baader-Meinhoff connections. I didn't know she was over here."

"Yes, she's at Tangmere. It's a special institution not far from here. Government sponsored."

"Oh, I see. You're handling her case officially?"

She hesitated. "Yes, that's the only way I could get in to see her, but I hope I've won her trust as well."

"Didn't she hide this guy the newspapers call the Cretan in her room at Frankfurt the night he shot that East German Minister?"

"That's right."

"I was there myself," he said. "Giving a concert in the university." They stood up and started to walk. "I don't understand. Surely the police could have got some sort of description of him out of her. Enough to trace him. I've always understood the Germans were pretty thorough that way."

"He wore a ski mask. You know the kind of thing? Holes for the eyes, nose, and mouth. She couldn't describe him, even if she wanted to."

"What do you mean?"

Katherine Riley smiled. "Apparently, he filled in the time making love to her."

"Wearing the ski mask? Say, that's heavy stuff."

"I wouldn't know. I haven't tried it."

Later, in a punt on the river, he said, "Katherine, I have a villa in Hydra. Do you know where that is?"

"Yes."

"The house itself is way down the coast. You can only reach it by boat or over the mountains on foot or on mule. Actually, there is a telephone line all the way across the mountains. In fact, if you ever get lost, look for the telephone poles and follow them."

"Lost?"

"You said you were due a vacation this weekend. It occurred to me that you might like to come to Hydra. I've got three weeks going spare, then I'm due in Vienna. Would you consider it?"

"I already have."

Later, on the telephone to Deville, he said, "I've established contact as you suggested, and I can assure you that there's no problem as concerns the little German package. None at all."

"Good, so that's taken care of. What do you do now?"

"I'm leaving for Hydra for three weeks on Saturday. I'm taking Dr. Riley with me."

Deville for once was astonished. "Good heavens, why, John?"

"Because I want to," Mikali answered and replaced the receiver.

SIX

Katherine Riley was having lunch in her study at the desk by the window; salad sandwiches, cold milk, and the over-written thesis of one of her weaker students.

There was a knock at the door, and Morgan entered. He wore a dark, polo-neck sweater and gray jacket in Donegal tweed. The only thing military about him was the trenchcoat which hung loosely from his shoulders.

"Yes?" she said although she knew already who this must be.

"Morgan," he said. "Asa Morgan. I believe Chief Superintendent Baker of Special Branch has been in touch with you."

She sat there, looking up at him, a sandwich in one hand, a pen in the other. "Colonel Morgan, isn't it? Asa Morgan? Parachute Regiment?"

"You say that as if it has some importance."

"I read that pamphlet you wrote for the Ministry of Defence after Korea. It does happen to be my field."

"Something in common."

"Oh, no," she said. "Not as far as I'm concerned. That little unpleasantness you got yourself into in Cyprus during the EOKA struggle. I looked you up,

Colonel. At the time, the newspapers suggested you'd have fitted into the SS rather well."

"The purpose of terrorism is to terrorize," Morgan told her. "Lenin said that. Back in 1921, Michael Collins lived by that creed. He said it was the only way a small country could defeat a nation. If urban guerrillas are your specialty, Doctor, you know as well as I do how they work. Indiscriminate bombing campaigns, motiveless terror, the deliberate slaughter of the innocent. Women, kids. My brief in Cyprus was to stop it, and I did."

"By the use of interrogation methods that were reminiscent of the Gestapo more than anything else."

"No," he said. "Quite wrong. Anything worthwhile I had to offer came by courtesy of the Chinese. They gave me personal instruction at a camp called Ti-pai in Manchuria."

She sat there, staring up at him, aware that she should be angry and wasn't, which was strange because this man represented everything she despised most. Uniformed authority, the military machine that was once more chewing up the youth of her own country and spitting them out in Vietnam.

"Harry Baker told me it was coppers you didn't like," he said. "He was wrong. Obviously it's uniforms."

"Perhaps."

He lit a cigarette. "That's better. You almost smiled, and the corners of your mouth started turning up instead of down."

"Damn you," she said.

He sat on the edge of the desk. "Do I get to see the Hoffmann girl?"

"From what Baker tells me, this is to do with the

Maxwell Cohen shooting. Special Branch think it was the Cretan again."

"That's right."

"And you think you might get a lead on him from Lieselott?" She shook her head. "She wouldn't tell you, even if she could."

"Because he made love to her?"

She shook her head. "I don't think you understand. To someone like her, he's almost a god. A symbol of what they believe in."

"Don't tell me, let me guess. The purity of violence."

She opened a drawer and took out a yellow pamphlet. "Someone sent me this from the Sorbonne the other day. This was printed by one of the student bodies. They're supposed to be at university getting an education—and what an education." She opened the pamphlet. "Listen to this advice for demonstrators. When punching policemen, leather gloves should be worn. Newspapers wrapped around the body reduce the effectiveness of rifle butts. One antiflu pill taken half an hour before the riot begins, another when the grenades start coming over, reduces the sickness you're supposed to get from inhaling the gas."

"I hadn't come across that one before," Morgan commented. "I must remember. When do I get to see her?"

"All right, waste your time if you want to. Have you got a car?"

"Yes."

"I've made an appointment for three. It will take twenty minutes to get there. You can pick me up at two-thirty. Now, if you wouldn't mind."

He picked up his briefcase and raincoat. "Do you always wear your hair held back like that?"

"What in the hell has it got to do with you?"

"Let it hang loose if I were you, girl," he said. "On a good day, it might even make you look like a real woman."

The door closed softly behind him. She sat there, her mouth open in astonishment.

The interview room at Tangmere Special Remand Centre was surprisingly pleasant. Patterned wallpaper, fitted carpet, a table, modern chairs. The barred windows seemed almost incongruous.

"Rather pleasant, really," Morgan said with some irony, peering into the garden.

"This is not a normal prison nor is it supposed to be," Katherine Riley told him. "It is a psychiatric institution. . . ."

"Aimed at rehabilitation, recovery, and let us all rejoice for god is good."

Before she could reply, the door was unlocked, and Lieselott Hoffmann was ushered in. The woman prison officer withdrew, locking the door again.

She was a small, plain-faced girl with short blonde hair. She wore jeans and a denim shirt. She ignored Morgan and said in excellent English, "Who's your friend?"

"Colonel Morgan. He'd like to ask you a few questions." Katherine Riley produced cigarettes, gave her one, and a light.

"About the Cretan," Morgan said.

The girl turned sharply, her face blank, and then she turned back to Katherine Riley. "What's happened?"

"There's been a shooting in London. A prominent Zionist. Black September claims credit, but the police think it was the Cretan."

Lieselott Hoffmann turned on Morgan and raised a clenched fist. "Power to the people."

"Which people, you silly little bitch?"

She lowered her hand, a strange uncertainty on her face, and he opened his briefcase and took out a sheaf of photos.

"I thought you might care to be put in touch with reality for a change. See what your Cretan's been up to over the years."

She approached the table, and Katherine Riley followed.

"That's a Colonel Vassilikos in the back of his car in Paris. As you can see, his skull has fragmented. The man kneeling beside him is one of his bodyguards. Those are his brains showing through."

The expression on her face didn't alter in the slightest as he threw down one photo after another of the Cretan's victims. The last was of Megan, taken in the Paddington tunnel, lying in the gutter where she had been found.

"Who was she?"

"My daughter," Morgan said. "She was fourteen. He ran her down in a car he stole to make his escape after shooting Cohen."

She turned to Katherine Riley, an expression of total indifference on her face. "Can I go now?"

And Katherine Riley, in a gesture totally alien to her nature, struck her across the face, overwhelmed by the horror of it.

Morgan was between them, his hands on her arms, his voice soft, insistent. "Easy, girl. Let it go."

Behind them, Lieselott Hoffmann walked to the door and pressed the bell. After a while it opened, and she passed through without a word.

Beyond his shoulder, Katherine Riley could see the photo of Megan clearly, the bloody mask of the face, and felt physically sick.

"I'm sorry," she whispered. "So sorry."

"Ah, Kate," he said. "Rule number one. Never apologize, never explain. Now, let's get out of here and find ourselves a drink."

"Asa?" she said. "That's a strange name."

"From the Bible," he told her and, for a moment he became very Welsh indeed. "A religious woman, my mam. Chapel twice every Sunday when I was a boy."

"And where was that?"

"A village in the Rhondda Valley in Wales. Coal miners, slagheaps. A place to get out of. My father was killed in a roof fall when I was eight. The company gave my mother ten shillings a week pension. I went down the pit myself at fourteen, came up for the last time four years later to join the army."

"And never looked back?"

"I loved it," he said. "Soldiering. I'd never felt so right. And the army was good to me. I was a sergeant at Arnhem, then I got a commission in the field as second lieutenant. After the war, they kept me on. Sent me to Sandhurst."

"And your background? Didn't that ever give you problems in a place like that?"

"Oh, any fool can learn how to handle a knife and fork and being Welsh, you see, I always knew I was better than any bloody Englishman who walked the earth, even if he'd been to Eton." He smiled, mocking her now. "Very intellectual people, we are. I surprised them there. I didn't only read Clausewitz on war. I knew my Wu Ch'i as well. Heavy stuff, you see."

"I bet you were the original bastard."

"I had to be, girl. I had to be better, see? Languages, for instance. Not that they were any problem. Learn to speak Welsh fluently, anything else seems easy."

They were sitting at a small table, one of a number outside a pub on the banks of the River Cam. It was very pleasant in the early evening sun.

"What about your wife? How has she taken all this?"

"With her usual firmness, as far as I could judge." He shrugged. "That finished quite some time ago. She never took kindly to military life, or my version of it. She's a painter by profession and a very good one. We met in the National Gallery one Sunday morning. One of those monumental errors people make in life so frequently. I think it was the uniform that did it, and the red beret."

"She liked that?"

"Not for long."

"What went wrong?"

"She visited me in Cyprus during the EOKA campaign. We were driving through Nicosia one day behind a doctor from one of the cavalry regiments who'd been spending his spare time giving free medical aid to peasants in the villages of the Troodos mountains. He stopped at some traffic lights, and a couple of EOKA terrorists ran forward and blew his brains out through the window."

"And you took them on?"

"I was armed, naturally."

"And you killed them both?"

"Yes. Unfortunately, one of them turned out to be only fifteen."

"And she found that hard to take?"

"All those Westerns. People expect you to shoot them in the arm or the shoulder or something neat like that. When it's real, you've only time to do one thing. Shoot to kill. And always twice, to make sure, otherwise he gets one off at you as he goes down."

"And she was different after that?"

"Not so much the boy. I think it was seeing me do it. Told me she couldn't forget the look on my face. As it happened, she was pregnant anyway, but she never slept with me again after that."

"I'm sorry."

"Why should you be. She believes in life you see. She saw me as some kind of public executioner. She's married to a country parson now. The sort of man who believes in anything and everything, so they do rather well together."

She said, "I'm sorry about your daughter."

"I should have known better," he said. "A stupid idea to think I could shock that girl into some kind of response."

"For the ones like her, it's like a religion," she said. "They believe all that cant dished out by people like Sartre. The mystical view of violence as ennobling. Terrorists are fond of the romantic viewpoint. They claim to be heroes of the revolution, yet disdain the rules of war. They claim to speak for the people and usually speak only for themselves."

"And the Cretan," he said. "What kind of man is he?"

"What do you think?"

He told her of the discussion he and Baker had had on the subject and their eventual conclusion.

She nodded. "Yes—I can go along with that. The business of a military background is the one point I'd disagree with you on."

"Why?"

"The Cubans have been offering excellent military training to terrorists from all over the world for many years now, and then there are the Russians. These days, they take students from most foreign countries into Patrice Lumumba university in Moscow. The KGB is always on the lookout for promising material."

"I know," he said, "but I think there's more to the Cretan than that. A soldier's instinct for another soldier if you like. What makes a man like him tick, that's what I'd like to know. Not ideology—there's no pattern to his killings that would indicate that."

"You want the psychologist's viewpoint?"

"Why not?"

"Okay—here goes. Some time ago I got involved in a study of Grand Prix drivers. What came out was that the greater the stress, the better they function. Most of them are only truly alive, truly operating to their full potential, in conditions of maximum danger. The most successful Grand Prix driver is the one who's prepared to simply push any car which gets in his way off the track. His image is one of ultimate masculinity, but he loves engines, cars, the machinery of his trade more than he could love any woman. The race is the perfect challenge, with death as the only alternative. It's a game which always excites, never ceases to satisfy."

"The constant challenge. One man against. . . ."
Morgan frowned. "Against what?"

"Himself, perhaps. A psychopathic personality, certainly, otherwise he could never take the guilt associated with his killings."

"And seeking death, is that what you're saying?
That he has a death wish?"

"I shouldn't imagine it would bother him in the slightest. We have tapes of tests pilots on the point of death in crashing airplanes who, instead of screaming in fear, are still trying to work out aloud what it is that went wrong. He's that kind of man." She hesitated. "A man, I should imagine, very like you."

"Good," Morgan said. "That gives me a chance at him then." He glanced at his watch. "I must get going. I've an appointment in London this evening."

As they walked back to the Porsche, she said, "What will you do now. Isn't this about as far as you can go?"

"No," he said. "The gun that was used to shoot Cohen. If I could trace where it came from."

"Do you think you can?"

"There's a man I know in Belfast who might be able to help. I'll have to see." She got into the Porsche. He closed the door, went around, and got behind the wheel. "Can I see you again when I get back?"

She hesitated. Did she really want to see this man who had appeared so unexpectedly in her life and made her question everything she believed in? And yet, he was there, and nothing would be quite the same again.

The simple truth was some part of her wanted to see him again. She said, "I'll see you, if you'd like to."

"Wouldn't have asked if I didn't, would I?"

* * *

Security Factors Ltd. was in a small cul-de-sac off Great Portland Street. It was just after seven when Morgan went up the stairs and tried the door marked OFFICE. It was locked, but there was a light on inside. He pressed the bell and waited. There was a shadow behind the glass; the door opened.

Jock Kelso was fifty-five and looked forty, in spite of his close-cropped gray hair. He was over six feet tall, tanned and fit-looking, a man to avoid in one situation or to lean on in another. He had served in the Scots Guards and then the Parachute Regiment for twenty-five years, five of them as Regimental Sergeant-Major to Morgan.

"Hello, Jock." Morgan moved inside. "How's the security business?"

Kelso led the way through into another office, small and uncluttered, a neat desk, green filing cabinets, carpets on the wall. It was here that the real business of the firm was contracted. From this office, mercenaries had gone out to fight in the Congo, the Sudan, the Oman, and a dozen other dirty little wars, for Jock Kelso was in the death business. He knew, and so did Morgan.

He poured whiskey into two paper cups and said, "I heard about Megan. I'm sorry."

"I want the man responsible," Morgan said.

"Anything I can do, Colonel, you know that."

"Fair enough, Jock. I've got a lead. It could mean something or nothing, but it means going back to Belfast to find out."

"Out of uniform?" Kelso looked grave. "They get their hands on you, Colonel, they'll have your eyes."

"Get word to O'Hagan," Morgan said. "Tell him I'll be at the Europa in Belfast from tomorrow afternoon. That I must see him. Can you do that?"

"Yes," Kelso said. "If that's what you want."

"It is, Jock, it is. How have you been managing since your wife died?"

"Fine. My daughter, Amy, she's still at home. Looks after me just fine."

"She must be about twenty now? She engaged to be married or anything?"

"Not her." Kelso laughed. "Got her head screwed on right, that one. She's in business for herself as a florist. Doing very well, especially on the delivery side. Amazing how they grow. One minute, they're just kids, the next. . . ."

He paused awkwardly. Morgan emptied his paper cup and shivered. "Cold tonight. I must be getting old."

"But not as cold as Korea, Colonel."

"No," Morgan said softly. "Nothing could ever quite match up to that. I'll let you know when I get back."

Kelso listened to him descending the stairs, then picked up the telephone, and called for a taxi.

It deposited him twenty minutes later outside the Harp of Erin, a public house in the Portobello Road, which as its name implied, was much frequented by London Irish.

The bar was crowded, an old man in the corner playing a concertina and singing a famous Irish street ballad, "Bold Robert Emmet." As Kelso entered, the entire room was joining in the chorus of—"tried as a traitor, a rebel, a spy; but no one can call me a knave or a coward, a hero I lived and a hero I'll die."

There was more than one unfriendly look as he shouldered his way through to the frosted glass door marked SNUG. When he went in, he found three men sitting at a small table playing whist.

The big man facing him was named Patrick Murphy, and he was organizer for north London of Sinn Fein, the political wing of the Provisional IRA.

"Jock?" he said.

"It's important," Kelso told him.

Murphy nodded, the other two got up and went out. "Well?"

"I've got a message for O'Hagan."

"And which O'Hagan would that be?"

"Don't play games with me, Patsy, we soldiered together too long. Tell O'Hagan that Asa Morgan will be at the Europa from tomorrow, and he wants to see him as soon as possible on personal business."

"What kind of personal business?"

"That's for them to discuss."

Kelso opened the door, pushed his way back through the crowd, and returned to the taxi he'd left waiting. As it drove away, he was sweating slightly.

In the snug, Murphy sat thinking for a while, then he leaned over the bar and called the landlady. He offered her a couple of pound notes.

"Change these for tenpence pieces, Norah, love. I want to call Belfast."

"Sure and you can use my phone, can't you?"

"Not for this one, I can't. You never know who might be listening."

She shrugged, gave him the silver from the till, and

he went out of the side door and walked down the street to the public telephone box on the corner.

The following morning, just after nine, there was a knock at Katherine Riley's study door. As she glanced up, Mikali appeared.

"When did you get in?" she demanded.

"Flew up this morning in my new second-hand Cessna. Got a couple of days to spare, then concerts in Paris, Berlin, Rome. Afterward, I thought of going to Hydra again for a while. How about you? You seemed to enjoy it last time."

"Yes," she said, remembering. She was in his arms now, aware of that surging physical excitement that never failed. "I've got one hell of a work load this term," she said.

"All right, let's discuss it over lunch."

"Just give me ten minutes to change."

"Five," he said and sat on the desk and lit a cigarette as she went into her bedroom. "So, you've been busy this week? Doing what?"

"The same old routine," she called. "Except for the Hoffmann girl. I saw her yesterday in rather strange circumstances."

"Is that so?" He leaned against the door. "Tell me about it."

Later, as they walked out to the car, he made an excuse, went back inside the college, stopped at the first public phone and dialed Paris.

When Deville answered, he said quickly, "The man Morgan, I want the complete file. Everything there is to know. The works, including photo. Can your people in London supply this?"

"Of course. You can pick it up at the London post box there any time after seven this evening. Do I take it you are experiencing trouble?"

"He's been to see the German package, not that it got him anywhere. My information is he's now gone to Ulster looking for a lead that might help him trace the tool employed."

Deville chuckled. "He's running in the wrong direction. A blind alley."

"Of course," Mikali said. "But it's as well to be prepared. I'll keep in touch."

He replaced the receiver and went out to the car. "And now," he said to Katherine Riley as he got behind the wheel. "Let's have some fun."

SEVEN

The Europa Hotel in Belfast stands in Great Victoria Street, rising twelve stories above the railway station next to it. Since it had opened in 1971, more than twenty-five separate bombing attacks had been made on it by the IRA.

Morgan remembered that statistic as he stood at the window of his room on the fourth floor and looked down to the bus station and the Protestant stronghold of Sandy Row.

A cold east wind blew in from Belfast Lough, driving rain across the mean street of the devastated city. He was restless and frustrated. This was his second day here, and nothing had happened.

He had stayed in the hotel, only left his room to go down to the dining room or the bar, had spent most of the previous night sitting in the darkness by the window, a night punctuated by the sounds of bombs exploding or the occasional rattle of small-arms fire.

He was worried because this was Friday and in less than forty-eight hours, at 4:00 A.M. on Monday, the 31st of July, Motorman was to go into action— the biggest operation mounted by the British Army since Suez. A planned invasion of all the so-called no-go areas dominated by the IRA in Belfast and Londonderry. Once that went into operation, O'Hagan would be certain to drop completely out of sight for a while, might even run south to the Republic if he wasn't arrested.

In the end, he could stand it no more, pulled on his jacket, and took the lift down to the foyer. He told the desk clerk that he'd be in the bar, sat himself on a high stool, and ordered Irish whiskey—Bushmills.

Perhaps he'd expected too much from O'Hagan. Perhaps the gulf was too wide now.

He sipped a little of his whiskey, and a uniformed porter tapped him on the shoulder. "Colonel Morgan? Your taxi's here, sir."

The driver was an old man badly in need of a shave. Seated in the rear, Morgan was aware of the eyes watching him in the driving mirror. Not a word was said as they drove through gathering darkness and rain. At most main street corners there were soldiers of one kind or another, but there was a considerable amount of traffic on the road and a surprising number of people about.

They were somewhere on the Falls Road, with the Catholic Turf Lodge area on the left. Morgan knew that, and then the old man turned into one of the mean little side streets.

There was a builder's yard at the end. As they approached, the high gate swung open. They drove inside, the gate closed behind them.

Above a door, there was a lamp that illuminated the yard. The old Ford van standing next to it had "Kilroy's Bakery" painted on the side.

There was silence, only the rain. The old man spoke for the first time. "I think you'd better get out, mister."

This was the most dangerous moment, Morgan knew that. The moment that would tell him whether his calculated risk had paid off or not. He lit a cigarette calmly, then opened the door and got out.

A heavily-built man in a dark anorak, the hood up, came around from behind the van holding a Kalashnikov assault rifle. Morgan waited. There were footsteps, and a second figure emerged from the darkness, a tall man in an old belted raincoat and tweed cap. He was very young, little more than a boy. As he came close, Morgan saw the face beneath the peaked cap, the dark, tormented eyes that hinted at a soul in hell.

"If you'd be good enough to assume the position, Colonel."

He was Belfast, his accent said as much, and he knew his job, running his hands expertly over Morgan as the Colonel leaned against the side of the van, arms braced.

Finally satisfied, he opened the rear doors. "All right, Colonel. Inside."

He climbed in after Morgan, the other man handed him the rifle and closed the doors. Morgan heard him walk around to the cab. A moment later, they drove away.

The journey took no more than ten minutes. The van stopped, the driver came around and opened the doors. The boy jumped out and Morgan followed him. The street was a scene of desolation, littered with glass. Most of the lamps were smashed, and a warehouse on the other side had been reduced to a heap of rubble.

The small terrace houses showed little sign of life except for the odd chink of light where a curtain was badly drawn. The boy lit a cigarette and tossed the match away.

"A grand place to raise your kids, wouldn't you say, Colonel?" he said without looking at Morgan, then started across the road, hands in the pockets of his old raincoat.

Morgan followed him. There was a small cafe on the corner. The boy pushed the door open and entered. It wasn't much of a place. There was a row of brown-painted booths down one side, a marble-topped bar on the other with a large old-fashioned tea urn operated by a gas burner.

There didn't seem to be any customers. The only sign of life was the old, gray-haired woman in the soiled white apron who sat by the urn reading a paper. She glanced at Morgan briefly, then nodded to the boy.

A quiet voice called softly from the end booth, "Bring the Colonel down here, Seumas."

Liam O'Hagan was eating eggs and chips, a mug of tea at his elbow. He was in his early forties with dark curly hair and the face of a genial prizefighter. He wore a denim shirt open at the neck and a donkey jacket and looked like a shipyard worker who'd stopped off for a bite to eat on his way home.

"Hello, Asa," he said. "You're looking well."

The boy went to the counter and asked for two teas. Morgan sat down. "A bit young for it, isn't he?"

"Who, Seumas?" O'Hagan laughed. "They didn't think so in the Falls Road, back in August '69 when the Orange mobs swept in to burn the place to the ground, chase out every Catholic family who lived there. It was a handful of IRA men who took to the streets that night to hold them off, and Seumas was one of them."

"He must have been all of sixteen at the time."

"Eighteen, Asa," O'Hagan said. "He turned up with a .45 Webley revolver his grandfather had brought home from the First World War. Fought at my side that night. Has looked after my interests ever since."

"Looked after you?"

"With a handgun, he's the best I've ever seen."

Seumas returned with a mug of tea, which he put down at Morgan's elbow. He went back to the counter and sat on a stool at the far end, watching the door as he drank his tea.

"I'm impressed."

O'Hagan said, "What is it you want, Asa?"

"The winter of 1950, Liam, in Korea when you were the worst national service second lieutenant in the Ulster Rifles."

"Those were the days," O'Hagan said. "God, but we were impressed when a big man like you turned up on attachment. A real soldier, medals, everything."

"When the Chinese encircled us on the Imjin, when the regiment had to carve its way out, I went back for you, Liam, when you took that bullet in the foot. I brought you out. You owe me for that."

O'Hagan wiped his mouth, took half a bottle of whiskey from his pocket and sweetened his tea. He did the same for Morgan.

"Paid in full," he said. "Bloody Friday, Asa, you were standing in Lewis Street at midnight, outside Cohan's Bar, which was burning rather well at the time. The boy and I were on the roof opposite. He wanted to blow your head off. I wouldn't let him. So if you're come looking for any special favors, Asa, maybe you've wasted your time?"

"A good day for you, that," Morgan said bitterly. "Around one hundred and forty dead and injured."

"Be your age. The fire storm those RAF bombs raised in Hamburg in July, '43, killed more people in three days than the atom bomb did at Hiroshima. The only difference between the bomb dropped from twenty thousand feet and the one left under a cafe table in a parcel is that the airman can't see what he's doing."

"And where does it all end, Liam, all the violence, the killing?"

"A united Ireland."

"And then what? What do you do when it's all over?"

O'Hagan frowned. "What in the hell are you talking about?"

"You're going to win, aren't you? You must believe that, or there wouldn't be any point to it, or don't you ever want it to stop? Do you want it to go on for ever, like stage six at MGM? Up the Republic! Thompson guns and trenchcoats. My life for Ireland."

"To hell with you, Asa," O'Hagan said. "What do you want?"

"Remember my daughter, Megan?"

O'Hagan nodded. "How old is she now? Fourteen or fifteen, I suppose."

"You read about the Maxwell Cohen shooting last week?"

"That was the Black September, not us."

"The man responsible had to hijack a car to get away with the police hard after him. Megan was cycling home from school through the Paddington Tunnel. He ran her down. Left her lying in the gutter, like a dog."

"Mother of god!" O'Hagan said.

"I wouldn't let it upset you. It happened on Bloody Friday, so what's one extra more or less."

O'Hagan's face was grim. "All right, Asa. What do you want?"

"Full details haven't been released to the press for security reasons, but it looks as if the man responsible is the one known as the Cretan."

"I've heard of him."

"He shot Cohen using a very unusual handgun. A silenced Mauser, one of a batch made for SS security men during the war. They don't often turn up now."

"I see," O'Hagan said. "If you could trace the dealer who supplied it?"

"Exactly. According to Special Branch, the only recorded killing in the UK using such a gun was of an Army Intelligence sergeant in Londonderry by a Provisional gunman named Terence Murphy. He was shot dead by Commandos while making a run for it along with a man called Pat Phelan who also had one."

"And you'd like to know where they got them from?" O'Hagan shrugged. "There's only one problem."

"And what would that be?"

"Terry Murphy and Phelan weren't Provos. They

were to start with, but then last September, they joined a splinter group called the Sons of Erin led by Brendan Tully."

"I've heard of him," Morgan said. "Another of your purity of violence types?"

"That's our Brendan. Mad as a hatter. Lights a candle to the Virgin every night of his life, yet he'd shoot the Pope if he thought it would advance the cause."

"Would he tell you where they got those Mausers?"

"Maybe."

"Liam, I need to know. It's the only lead I've got."

O'Hagan nodded slowly. "You want this man badly. What for—justice?"

"To hell with justice, I want to see him dead."

"That's honest, anyway. I'll see what I can do. You go back to the Europa and wait."

"How long?"

"A couple of days—perhaps three."

"That's no good."

"Why not?"

Morgan was in too deep to draw back now. "By Monday night, they'll have Belfast sewn up so tight that even a mouse couldn't slip through the net."

"Interesting," O'Hagan said, and the door burst open.

Seumas was already on his feet, and O'Hagan produced a Browning Hi Power from his pocket with some speed and held it in his lap under the table.

A great brute of a man stood swaying drunkenly just inside the door. He wore a soiled reefer coat and denim overalls and his eyes were bloodshot. He didn't appear to notice O'Hagan and Morgan and ignored Seumas, lurching across to the counter and holding on to it with both hands as if to prop himself up.

"I'm collecting," he said to the old woman. "Funds for the Organization. Ten quid, ma, and we'll call it quits. Otherwise we close you down."

She wasn't in the least afraid. Simply poured tea into a mug, spooned sugar into it, and pushed it across the counter.

"Drink that, lad, then sober up and go home. You've come to the wrong shop."

He sent the mug flying with a sweep of his hand. "Ten quid, you old bitch, or I smash the place up."

There was a Luger in Seumas's right hand, the barrel up under the man's chin. The boy didn't say a word. It was O'Hagan who spoke.

"The IRA, is it? Which brigade?" The big man glared at him stupidly, and O'Hagan said, "Outside with him, Seumas."

The boy swung the man around and sent him staggering through the door. O'Hagan got to his feet and went after them and Morgan followed.

The big man stood under one of the few street lamps still working, rain soaking his head, Seumas to one side covering him with the Luger. O'Hagan walked forward, paused, then kicked him viciously in the crotch so that he cried out and went down on his knees.

"All right," O'Hagan said. "You know what to do."

Seumas moved in close, the barrel of the Luger poking into the back of the man's right kneecap and then he simply blew it off with a single shot.

The man screamed in agony and rolled over. O'Hagan stood looking down at him.

"There's good men dead and in their graves fighting the bloody British Army, and bastards like you spit on them."

At the same moment, a couple of stripped-down Land-Rovers turned the corner at the end of the street and braked to a halt. Morgan was aware of the uniforms, and a spotlight was turned on.

"Stay exactly where you are," a voice echoed over a loudhailer in crisp, public-school English, but O'Hagan and Seumas had already ducked into the alley at the side of the cafe. Morgan went after them, running like hell.

There was a six-foot brick wall at the end of the street, and they were scrambling over it as the first soldiers turned into the alley. They found themselves in a builder's yard and blundered across in darkness to a double wooden door. Seumas got the judas gate open, and they were out and into the street as the first soldier arrived on the other side of the wall.

The boy and O'Hagan seemed to know exactly where they were going. Morgan followed at their heels, twisting and turning through a dark rabbit warren of mean streets, and the sounds of pursuit grew fainter. Finally, they came out on the banks of a small canal, and Seumas paused beside some bushes. He took a small flashlight from his pocket and, as he switched it on, there was a tremendous explosion from the direction of the city's center, followed by three more in rapid succession.

O'Hagan looked at his watch. "Right on time for once." He grinned at Morgan. "Just think, you could have been shot by one of your own people. There's irony for you."

"Now what?" Morgan asked.

"We get the hell out of here. Get it open, Seumas."

In the light of the boy's flashlight, Morgan saw that he had pulled back the bushes revealing a manhole cover, which he removed. He descended a steel ladder. Morgan hesitated, then went after him, and O'Hagan followed, pulling the manhole cover back into place.

Morgan found himself in a tunnel so small that he had to crouch. The boy took a large spot lamp form a ledge and switched it on. He started forward and Morgan went after him, aware of the sound of rushing water in the distance.

They came out on the concrete bank of a large tunnel, and in the light of the spot he saw that a brown foaming stream coursed down the center. The smell was very unpleasant.

"The main sewer," Seumas said. "All that Protestant shit from the Shankhill. Don't worry, Colonel. We'll pass right underneath and come up amongst friends in the Ardoyne."

"Then what?" Morgan asked.

"I think, under the circumstances, we'd do better out of town tonight," O'Hagan said. "You, too, Asa."

"You'll never make it," Morgan told him, "not after those bombs. They'll plug every road out of the city up tight."

"Ah, there are ways," O'Hagan said. "You'd be surprised. Now, let's get moving."

They emerged some twenty minutes later in what appeared to be a factory yard behind a high brick wall. When the boy turned the light on the building itself, Morgan saw considerable evidence of bomb damage and that all the windows had been blocked with corrugated iron.

They paused at large double doors locked with a padlock and chain, and O'Hagan produced a key. "This was a wholesale booze warehouse, owned by a London firm. After the third bomb, they decided they'd had enough."

He got the doors open, and Morgan and Seumas moved in. O'Hagan closed the doors, and the boy fumbled in the dark. There was the click of a switch, and a single bulb turned on.

"Nice of them not to cut off the electricity," O'Hagan said.

Morgan found himself standing in a garage. In the center there was some sort of vehicle covered with a dust sheet. O'Hagan moved across and pulled the sheet away, revealing an army Land-Rover. The painted board mounted at the front said: EMERGENCY —BOMB DISPOSAL.

"Neat, eh?" O'Hagan said. "And we've never been stopped yet. Come to think of it, you should feel right at home in this situation, Asa." He went around to the back of the Land-Rover, opened it, and took out a camouflage jacket, which he threw across. "Everything we need in here. You'll have to drop a couple of ranks though. Best I can manage are a captain's pips. I'll be sergeant, and Seumas our driver."

"To what end?" Morgan demanded. "Where are we going?"

"You wanted to know where those Mausers came from. All right—we'll go and ask Brendan Tully."

* * *

It worked like a charm, all the way out of the city on the Antrim Road. They were waved through three separate roadblocks by military police without hesitation. At a fourth, where there was a queue of vehicles being checked, Seumas simply sounded his horn and passed on the wrong side of the road.

Outside Ballymena, O'Hagan told the boy to pull up at the public telephone box. He was inside for no more than three minutes. When he returned, he was smiling.

"He's expecting us. The Glenariff road through the Antrim mountains."

Morgan said, "How do you explain me?"

O'Hagan grinned. "You still speak Welsh, don't you? He loves to try out his Irish, Brendan. Learned it when he and McStiophan were in prison together. Welsh and Irish—they must have something in common surely."

Twenty miles along the road through the mountains, they came to a sign indicating Coley to the left. Seumas turned, following a narrow, twisting road between dry stone walls, climbing higher and higher into the mountains.

In the first gray light of dawn they came over a rise onto a small plateau backed by beech trees. There was a barn, doors standing open, and an old Jeep. Two men stood beside it. They were both dressed like farm laborers, one in a patched corduroy jacket and cloth cap, the younger one in denim overalls and Wellington boots.

"The one in the cap is Tim Pat Keogh, Tully's

right-hand man. The other's Jackie Rafferty. A bit touched in the head, that one. He usually does what Tully tells him to and likes it," O'Hagan said.

Seumas braked to a halt, and the two men came forward. "Good day to you, Mr. O'Hagan," Keogh said. "If you'd leave the Land-Rover in the barn, we'll take you up to the farm in the Jeep."

O'Hagan nodded to Seumas who drove the vehicle under cover. They all got out, and, as they emerged. Keogh and Rafferty closed the barn door. O'Hagan had slung a Sterling submachine gun over one shoulder, and Morgan carried a Smith & Wesson .38 service revolver in a standard issue webbing holster.

Keogh said, "A friendly visit, is it, Mr. O'Hagan."

O'Hagan said, "Don't be bloody stupid, Tim Pat. Now let's get up to the farm. I could do with some breakfast. It's been a hard night."

The farm was a poor sort of place, in a small hollow backed up against the side of the mountains for protection against the wind. The outbuildings were badly in need of repairs, and the yard was thick with mud.

Brendan Tully was a tall, handsome, lean-faced man with one side of his mouth hooked into a slight perpetual half-smile as if permanently amused by the world and its inhabitants. He greeted them at the door. He'd obviously just got out of bed and wore an old robe over pajamas.

"Liam!" he cried. "You're a sight for sore eyes, in spite of that bloody uniform. Come away in."

They followed him into the kitchen where a wood fire burned on an open hearth. An old woman, a black shawl about her shoulders against the morning chill, was at the stove preparing breakfast.

"Don't worry about her. She's deaf as a post. Seumas, lad." He clapped the boy on the shoulder. "I've still got a place for you, if you fancy some real action."

"I'm content where I am, Mr. Tully."

Tully eyed Morgan curiously. "And who might this be?"

"An old friend. Dai Lewis of the Free Wales Army. They helped us out with guns in autumn of '69, remember, when things were bad."

"Does he speak Welsh then?"

"A bloody poor sort of Welshman I'd be if I didn't," Morgan answered in his native tongue.

Tully was delighted. "Marvelous," he said. "Only I didn't understand a word of it. Now, let's start the day right, while the old bag there gets the food ready."

He produced a whiskey jug and glasses. O'Hagan said, "A bit early even for you."

"A short life, eh?" Tully was obviously in high spirits. "Anyway what brings you out this way?"

"Oh, things were a little bit warm in town last night, and then Dai came over to see me from Cardiff. Let him tell you himself."

He accepted the glass Tully passed him, and Morgan said, sounding very Welsh indeed, "We've decided to go active properly this time, Mr. Tully. Talking to the bloody English about an independent Wales is wasted breath."

"Seven hundred years of talking to the buggers we've had, and where's it got us?" Tully asked him.

O'Hagan said, "What Dai and his people are after are some silenced pistols. He thought I might be able to help, and then I remembered those two lads of yours who died last year. Terry Murphy and young Phelan. Wasn't it silenced Mausers they were carrying?"

"That's right," Tully said. "And damned difficult to come by they were."

"Can we ask where you got them?"

"The Jago brothers—two of the biggest villains in London." Tully turned to Morgan. "I don't know if they'll still have what you want, but watch them. They'd dig up their grandmother and sell the corpse if they thought there was money in it."

There was a strange, nervous unease to him, and his eyes were very bright. He swallowed some of his whiskey and said to O'Hagan, "I'm glad you've come. I'd like to talk. Something of considerable importance to the whole movement."

"Is that so?" O'Hagan was interested and wary at the same time.

"Come in the living room. I'll show you. We've time before breakfast." Tully could hardly contain himself. "It'll only take a few minutes. They can wait for us."

He went through into the living room. O'Hagan glanced at Morgan and Seumas, then followed reluctantly.

"Close the door, man," Tully said impatiently, then opened a drawer in the old mahogany table and took out a map which he unrolled.

O'Hagan joined him and saw that the map was of the west coast of Scotland including the islands of the Outer Hebrides.

"What's all this?"

"This island here, Skerryvore," Tully pointed. "It's a missile training base. One of my boys, Michael Bell, was a corporal technician there. Knows the place backwards."

"So?"

"It seems that on Thursdays once a fortnight, an officer and nine men drive up by road from Glasgow Airport to Mallaig. From there, they go to Skerryvore by boat. Let's say their truck is stopped on the way to Mallaig one Thursday, and I'm waiting with nine of my men to take their place, including Michael Bell, of course."

"But why?" O'Hagan said. "What's the name of the game?"

"The thing they're testing on that island is called Hunter, a medium range missile. Not atomic, but a new kind of explosive that would cause a very big bang indeed. One of those things on target could take out a square mile of London."

"You must be crazy," O'Hagan told him angrily. "Rockets on London? What are you trying to do? Lose everything we've fought for?"

"But it's the only way, don't you see? Take the struggle to the enemy's own doorstep."

"Kill thousands at one blow—totally alienate world opinion?" O'Hagan shook his head. "Brendan, at the moment in the eyes of many people abroad, we're a gallant little handful taking on an army. That's how we'll win in the end. Not by defeating the British Army, but by making the whole thing so unpleasant that they'll withdraw of their own accord, just like they did in Aden and Cyprus and all those other places. But this . . ." He shook his head. "This is madness. The Army Council would never approve such a scheme. It would be like shooting the Queen— counterproductive."

"You mean you'll tell the Army Council about this?"

"Of course I will. What else do you expect me to do? I'm Chief Intelligence Officer for Ulster, aren't I?"

"All right," Tully said defensively. "So I was wrong. If the Council won't back me, then there's no way we can do it, that's obvious. I'll see if breakfast is ready."

He went into the kitchen where Morgan, Seumas, and Keogh sat at the table. He moved to the front door and found Rafferty leaning inside the Jeep, oil- ing the brake pedal shaft. Rafferty straightened and turned.

Tully's face was distorted with fury. "Dump them, Jackie. Three with one blow. No messing. You under- stand?"

"Yes, Mr. Tully," Rafferty said without the slight- est flicker of emotion. "One of those Russians pencil timers should do it, and the plastique."

"Get to it then." Tully went back into the kitchen. O'Hagan was just coming out of the living room. He had the map under one arm and the Sterling sub- machine gun ready for action in his right hand.

"I've suddenly lost my appetite." Outside there was the sound of the Jeep starting up and driving away. "Where in the hell has he gone?"

"For milk," Tully said. "We don't have a cow here. Liam, let's be reasonable."

"Just keep your distance." O'Hagan nodded to Mor- gan and the boy. "All right, you two. Seumas, watch my back."

They moved into the yard. As they reached the gate, Tully shouted from the door, "Liam, listen to me."

But O'Hagan simply increased his walking speed. Morgan said, "What in the hell was all that about?"

"Nothing to do with you," O'Hagan said. "A matter for the Army Council." He shook his head. "That lunatic. How could he even have imagined I'd go for such a scheme."

They went over the rise and down to the barn. The doors were still closed and there was no sign of the Jeep.

He said to Morgan and Seumas, "You cover me while I get the Land-Rover out, just in case they try anything funny," and he tossed the Sterling to Morgan.

He got the barn door open. Morgan turned away, aware of him moving inside. The Land-Rover door slammed as O'Hagan got in. There was a colossal explosion, a blast of hot air, and Morgan was flung forward onto his face.

He got to his knees, turned and found Seumas trying to get up, clutching his arm where a piece of metal was embedded like shrapnel.

The barn was an inferno, the wreck of the Land-Rover blazing fiercely.

Morgan was aware of the sound of an engine, dragged Seumas to his feet and shoved him into the trees, crouching down beside him. The Jeep approached. It braked to a halt and Rafferty got out.

He walked forward, a hand shielding his face from the heat, going as close as he dared. Morgan stood up and emerged from the bushes.

"Rafferty?"

As Rafferty swung to face him, Morgan emptied
the Sterling in three bursts, driving him back into
the furnace of the barn. He threw the Sterling after
him, picked up Seumas and got him to the Jeep.

As he climbed behind the wheel he said, "Do you
know where we can find you a doctor? A safe doctor."

"The Hibernian Nursing Home for the Aged. It's
two miles this side of Ballymena," Seumas told him
and fainted.

Morgan removed the camouflage uniform in the
washroom and stuffed it into a laundry basket. Underneath, he still wore his ordinary clothes. He checked
his wallet, then washed his face and hands and returned to the small surgery.

The old doctor, Kelly, who appeared to run the
place, and a young nun were bending over Seumas
whose arm and shoulder were bandaged. His eyes
closed.

Doctor Kelly turned to Morgan. "He'll sleep now.
I've given him an injection. Good as new in a week."

Seumas opened his eyes. "You going, Colonel?"

"Back to London. I've things to do. You know, you
never did tell me your second name."

The boy smiled weakly. "Keegan."

Morgan wrote his London telephone number on
the doctor's prescription pad and tore it off. "If you
think I can help anytime, give me a ring."

He moved to the door. "Why, Colonel? Why did
they do it?"

"From what I could gather, Tully had come up
with some scheme or other that Liam didn't approve.

He was going to inform the Army Council. I suppose this was Tully's way of stopping that."

"I'll see him in hell first," Seumas said and closed his eyes.

At the first public telephone box he came to, Morgan phoned Army Intelligence Headquarters at Lisburn and in as convincing an Ulster accent as he could muster indicated where Brendan Tully and the Sons of Erin might be found, although he suspected they would already be long gone.

Then he caught a train in Ballymena for Belfast and went straight to the Europa, where he checked out. By three o'clock he was at Aldergrove Airport waiting for the London flight.

John Mikali, twenty-eight thousand feet over Sweden, en route for Helsinki, was working his way through the file on Asa Morgan. Deville's friends in London had really been most thorough. Not only every aspect of Morgan's career in finest detail, but also details of his known associates, with photographs. Ferguson figured prominently as head of the antiterrorist squad, Group Four, and so did Baker, although Mikali was already familiar with the Yorkshireman. Deville had a file on Special Branch personnel and Mikali had spent many hours in the past scanning their faces. Had done the same with their counterparts in Paris, Berlin, and most other major cities he was in the habit of visiting.

He studied Asa Morgan's photograph again for quite a while then leaned back, thinking about it.

Not that he was worried. There was no way Morgan could get to him. Not a single clue, not a single hint of a lead. The tracks were too well covered.

A blonde stewardess, an attractive girl with an excellent figure that was definitely enhanced by the navy blue uniform of British Airways, leaned over him.

"Are you giving a concert in Helsinki, Mr. Mikali?"

"Yes. The Brahms Concerto tomorrow night with the national state orchestra."

"I'd love to come if I can get a ticket," she said. "We're on stopover for two days."

She really was rather pretty. He smiled lazily. "Let me know where you're staying, and I'll have one sent around to you. And there's a party afterward, if you've nothing better to do."

Her face was flushed now, and the breasts seemed to strain against the light, white, nylon blouse.

"That would be marvelous. Is there anything I can get you?"

"Half a bottle of champagne, I think."

He sat there staring out of the window, feeling rather tired, but the truth was that he wasn't really in the mood for this concert. What he needed was a holiday. No need to return to London. He would fly to Athens from Helsinki after the concert. Even if there wasn't a direct flight and he had to go via Paris or Munich, he could be in Athens sometime during the afternoon. And then Hydra.

The thought was extremely pleasant, and his spirits lifted as she brought the champagne. As he sipped it slowly, savoring the coldness, he found himself opening Morgan's file and starting to work his way through it again.

EIGHT

Harvey Jago inspected himself carefully in the bathroom mirror. In the red velvet jacket with the white silk scarf at the throat, the blond hair carefully combed, he made an imposing figure. He still looked like a useful light-heavyweight—good for fifteen rounds any day of the week—which was what he had been in early life, and the signs were there in the broken nose, the scar tissue around the eyes. He could have had the nose straightened, but women liked it. It gave him a kind of rugged geniality, but it was the eyes that indicated the real man. Hard and cruel and pitiless.

This morning he was far from happy, for the previous evening one of his many business ventures, a house in Belgravia where young ladies in his employ catered to the whims of clients of the highest prestige, had been raided by the police.

It was not the embarrassment caused to the two peers of the realm and three members of parliament who had temporarily found themselves in the hands of the police that worried Jago—that was their lookout. He wasn't even worried about the fines that would have to be paid on behalf of the girls or the loss of the night's takings.

There was certainly no possibility of his personal involvement. The property was in someone else's name. That was what he kept front men for. No, what really annoyed him was the lack of warning from those police officers on the Vice Squad who received handsome weekly stipends to see that Jago's establishments were left alone. Somebody's head was going to have to roll.

He walked into the living room and stood at the window of his penthouse apartment. It gave him a continuing pleasure to look out across Green Park to Buckingham Palace, which was why he'd bought the place. A long way from the back street in Stepney in which he'd been raised.

Maria, the little Filipino maid, brought coffee on a tray. He waited while she filled his cup and handed it to him.

"Thanks, love," he said.

As she walked away, neat and trim in black dress and stockings, his brother, Arnold, entered. He was ten years younger than Jago. With thinning hair and hollow cheeks, he managed to look undernourished and anxious at the same time. Underneath that surface appearance he had a brain that operated like a computer in matters of finance.

"Lovely arse on her, that girl," Jago said. "I'd give her a going over, Arnold, I really would, only you know what I've always said about messing about with the staff."

Arnold, who already had an arrangement with Maria, which he was terrified his brother would find out about, said, "Quite right, Harvey."

"What's last night going to cost me?"

"Between thirteen and fifteen grand. I can't be more

certain because of the legal end. Some of those girls are three-time losers, Harvey. It could mean the nick. They'll need a top brief and that comes expensive."

"Anything it takes, Arnold. Another thing. The Vice Squad. I want to know who let us down, and I want to know today."

"It's being taken care of," Arnold said. "There's a bloke to see you. Name of Morgan."

"What's he want?"

"Wouldn't say, but he told me to give you this." Arnold handed him a wad of twenty-pound notes with a Midland Bank wrapper still around them. "Five hundred."

Jago held them to his nose. "God, how I love the smell of this stuff. Okay, Arnold, wheel him in. Let's see what his game is."

Morgan wore a polo-neck sweater and hadn't bothered to unbutton his military trenchcoat. Jago poured himself a Scotch and looked him over.

"Mr. Morgan," Arnold said and stood by the door.

"Colonel, actually."

Jago made a face. "So what am I supposed to do, curtsey?" He picked up the five hundred pounds. "I'm a busy man, and all this buys you is limited conversation. Speak your piece, or move on."

"It's quite simple," Morgan said. "The Cohen shooting last week. The gun used was a Mauser 7.63mm, series 1932, with the SS bulbous silencer, a weapon of some rarity these days. Your organization supplied two of them to the IRA last year."

"Who says so?" Arnold put in.

Morgan kept his eyes on Jago. "A man called Brendan Tully. I was with him in Ulster yesterday."

"Now look here," Arnold began, but his brother stilled him with a hand.

"You're not the law, so what's your angle?"

"The man who shot Cohen ran my daughter down while making his escape. Killed her. I'd like to find him."

"I get it now," Jago said. "You think the Mauser he used might have come from the same source as the others?"

"It would seem reasonable." Morgan took a second packet of banknotes from his pocket and tossed it on the table. "Another five hundred there, Mr. Jago, so you see, I'm prepared to pay for the information."

"It'll cost you," Jago said.

"How much?"

"Another grand."

"All right—when?"

"I don't deal with that end of things myself. I'll need to talk to the guy who does. I should know by tonight, if there is anything to know. I own a club in Chelsea, the Flamingo on Cheyne Walk. I'll see you there around nine."

"All right."

Morgan turned to the door, and Jago said, "And Colonel Morgan. Don't forget the other thousand."

"Of course not, Mr. Jago. I keep my word."

"Delighted to hear it."

"See that *you* do."

Jago said softly, "Is that a threat, Colonel?"

"Yes, come to think of it, I suppose it is," Morgan told him and went out.

There was silence. Jago said, "You know something, Arnold? That's the first time anyone's given me the hard word in years, and we can't have that, now can we? Bad for business. I'm going to take a personal interest in Colonel Morgan. Very personal. Make sure there's a couple of good lads laid on for tonight. Dustbin men."

"Yes, Harvey."

Arnold turned to go out, and Jago added, "Another thing, from now on we stop selling hardware to those Micks across there. They're all puddled, I've told you before. Stick to the Arabs in future."

Back at the flat, Morgan put the coffee percolator on and then telephoned Security Factors Limited. Jock Kelso sounded relieved to hear his voice.

"You're back then. Thank god for that. Did you see O'Hagan?"

"Briefly," Morgan said. "I'm afraid he's dead, Jock. Car bomb. I was lucky not to go with him."

There was a heavy silence, then Kelso said, "Did you find out what you wanted to know?"

"Oh, yes, that's why I'm ringing. What can you tell me about the Jago brothers?"

"Probably the most important gangsters in London," Kelso said. "Even the Mafia walk cautiously around those two. Arnold, the skinny one, is the brains. His elder brother, Harvey, is no fool either. Used to be a prizefighter."

"A nasty piece of work. I've met him."

"And that's an understatement. Last year an Italian gambler called Pacelli tried to palm loaded dice at one of Jago's gaming clubs. You know what Jago did? Cut off the top joint of each finger on Pacelli's right hand with garden shears. Are you trying to tell me he's the source of the Mausers?"

"That's the way it looks. I'm seeing him tonight. A place called the Flamingo in Cheyne Walk. Is it respectable?"

"Strictly top people."

"Which means he'll behave himself. Tell me, Jock, how does he make his money?"

"Gaming clubs, protection, high-class whorehouses."

"And that's it?"

"He does have one other profitable sideline an associate of mine was involved in. It's not far from Cheyne Walk, near Chelsea Creek. A paint factory called Wetherby and Sons."

"And?"

"It's what's known in the trade as a cut-liquor still. What they usually do is hijack a tanker carrying Scotch whiskey, or something similar, on the motorway. It's then heavily diluted with water. They have their own bottling plant and all the best labels. Supply labels. Supply clubs all over the country."

"And the police—don't they know any of this?"

"They can never get close, and when they do, there's always some front man in between to take the drop. I'd stay clear if I were you, unless you're prepared to go all the way."

"Oh, but I am, Jock. I am."

Morgan was sitting at his desk cleaning a Smith & Wesson Magnum when the phone rang. It was Kate Riley. "You're back," she said.

"Yes, last night."

"Did you get anywhere?"

"I'll know that for sure later on tonight. Where are you calling from—Cambridge?"

"No, I'm in town for a few days, working at the

Tavistock Clinic. I've borrowed the apartment of a colleague who's in New York for a month. It's in Kensington. Douro Place."

"I'll tell you what," Morgan said. "I've got an appointment with the worst villain in London tonight. I would have thought that was exactly the sort of subject you were looking for, Doctor, with your special interest in matters violent. I'm meeting him at the Flamingo in Cheyne Walk."

"But that's one of the most exclusive nightclubs in town."

"So they tell me. You find yourself a pretty frock, comb your hair, and I might be persuaded to take you."

"You're on," she said.

The place was everything they'd said it would be. Soft lights, sweet music, attentive waiters, the ultimate in luxury. Morgan and Kate Riley were obviously expected, were led to a corner table that was one of the best in the house.

The headwaiter snapped a finger, and a champagne bucket appeared. "Mr. Jago's compliments, sir. Tonight you are his guests."

From his office high above the main restaurant, Harvey Jago, resplendent in a black velvet evening suit, watched them through an ornamental grill.

"I like the look of his bird, Arnold. Real class, there. You can always tell."

"What about him, Harvey. He's a colonel and all that, isn't he?"

"Rubbish," Jago said. "I don't know what his story is, but he's off the same length of street as you and me."

"Shall I have him up?"

"Not just yet. Let them enjoy their meal. I mean, it's the dessert that counts, isn't it, Arnold?"

"What about men?" Morgan asked her.

"None of your business."

"What do you do for a bit of action and passion, then?"

The headwaiter interrupted, whispering discreetly in Morgan's ear. He left Kate to finish the champagne and followed the man out and through a door marked PRIVATE. There was a flight of carpeted stair. Arnold waited at the top.

"This way, Colonel."

Morgan went up the stairs and entered the office, which was Jago's pride and joy and had been put together for him by one of the best interior designers in London. Everything was Chinese, and some of the art objects had cost him a great deal of money.

Jago sat behind the desk, smoking a cigar. "There you are. They looking after you all right down there?"

"Fine," Morgan said. "But my time is as limited as yours, Mr. Jago. The information you promised me?"

"Didn't we say something about another grand, Arnold?" Jago said.

Morgan produced an envelope from his inside pocket. "We'll hear what you have to say first. Then you get this."

Jago sighed. "Well, now, that's going to prove rather difficult. You see, I'm afraid we haven't been able to come up with the information you require."

"Can't or won't?" Morgan asked.

"You can amuse yourself long winter evenings thinking about that one."

"And the thousand pounds I paid you earlier today?"

"My time, old sport, is valuable." Jago looked at his watch. "Show the Colonel out, Arnold. I've got things to do."

Morgan walked to the door, paused, and picked up a large Chinese vase from a lacquer table. "Early nineteenth century," he said. "Not particularly rare, but nice."

He dropped it on the floor, where it shattered into a hundred pieces. "And that, my friend, is just the beginning," he said and walked out.

Jago came around the desk on the run. He stood looking down at the broken pieces of the vase, his face working, then turned to his brother.

"You know what to do, and tell them to make it good. If he ever does come out of hospital, I want it to be on sticks."

Morgan had parked the Porsche some distance away. Kate Riley had her arm in his as they walked.

She said, "So he wouldn't come through?"

"That's about the size of it."

"What are you going to do now?"

"Persuade him to think again."

They turned into the side street where he had left the Porsche.

Arnold Jago paused on the corner with two men. One of them was small and badly in need of a shave. The other was at least six feet tall with a hard, rawboned face and big hands.

"Right, Bailey," Arnold said. "Make it good."

"Leave it to us, Mr. Jago."

The two men started along the pavement beside the parked cars and Bailey paused, pulling the smaller man to a halt. Morgan and Kate Riley seemed to have completely disappeared.

He took an anxious step forward. Morgan moved up the steps from the basement area of one of the tall Victorian houses, swung the small man around and kneed him in the groin.

He went down with a groan and Bailey turned to find Morgan standing on the other side of the writhing body, face clear in the lamplight as Kate Riley came up from the area behind him.

"Looking for me, are you?"

Bailey moved in fast. Afterward, he could never be certain of what had happened. His feet were kicked expertly from beneath him, and he landed hard on the wet pavement. As he got up, Morgan seized his right wrist twisting it around and up, locking the shoulder as in a vise. Bailey gave a cry of agony as the muscle started to tear. Still keeping that terrible hold in position, Morgan ran him head first into the railings.

He took Kate Riley by the arm and walked her along the sidewalk to the Porsche. As he handed her in she said, "You really believe in going all the way, don't you?"

"Interesting," he said as he got in beside her, "that you're not tearing out your hair over my brutal fascist ways, a nice, virginal, liberal academic like yourself."

"They asked for it, those two. They got it," she said. "You must have displeased Mr. Jago considerably."

"I think you could say that," he said and drove away.

He stopped outside the house in Douro Place and walked her to the door.

"Aren't you coming in?" she asked.

"I've got things to do."

"Such as?"

"Teach Harvey Jago his manners."

"Do you need me?"

"Not really. What I intend is by any definition a criminal act. I'd rather you weren't involved in case something goes wrong. I'll be in touch."

He went down the steps to the Porsche before she could argue. She opened the door and went inside. Arnold Jago got out of his car from where he had parked it further along the street. He checked the number of the house, then returned to his car and drove away.

Ferguson was working alone at his desk in the Cavendish Square apartment, the only sound the Glenn Miller orchestra playing softly on the record player on the table behind him.

It was his secret vice, listening to the big band sounds of his youth. Not only Miller but great British bands like Lew Stone, Joe Loss with Al Bowlly singing. It took Ferguson right back to the war with warm nostalgia. To 1940, when things had been really bad. But at least you knew where you were—knew just how far you had to go. Whereas now? The real enemy might actually be sitting on a parliamentary bench. Probably was.

The telephone, the red one at his left hand, buzzed

softly. He checked his watch. It was almost ten o'clock as he lifted the receiver.

"Say who you are."

"Baker, sir."

"Working late tonight, Superintendent."

"Desk work—you know how it is, sir. I thought you'd like to know Asa Morgan got back from Belfast in one piece. Security noted him passing through Heathrow last night."

"But we don't know what he got up to while he was there?"

"No, sir."

"Have you checked with Army Intelligence at Lisburn on O'Hagan?"

"Yes, but he's dropped out of sight. Hardly surprising with Operation Motorman in full swing."

"And what's Morgan up to tonight?"

"Seems to have something going for him with Doctor Riley, the psychologist from Cambridge. She's staying at a flat in Douro Street. Morgan picked her up at eight-thirty. They were both dressed for what looked like a big night out."

"And where did they go?"

"I don't know, sir. My man lost them."

"How amazing," Ferguson said. "Is that what we pay him for, to play the incompetent idiot?"

"Look, sir, this kind of thing is Morgan's business. He's been at it for years now, you know that. Malaya, Cyprus, Aden, now Ulster. He can smell a tail the moment he steps out of the door. He has an instinct for it. It's the only way he kept alive all those years."

"All right, Superintendent, cut the eulogy. What you're really saying is that there's no way he can be followed if he doesn't want to be."

"Not unless I put a six-car team on him, sir, with full radio control from Central."

"No," Ferguson said. "Don't do that. In fact, do nothing. Pull your man off completely. Let's give Asa his head for a day or two. Then we'll see where we're at."

He put down the receiver. At the other end, Harry Baker buzzed through on the intercom to the sergeant in the outer office.

"George, you can pull Mackenzie out of Gresham Place."

"Right, sir. Any further orders on that one?"

"I'll let you know."

Baker put down the receiger, sighed heavily, then started to work his way through the pile of paper that littered his desk.

NINE

Not that any of it mattered for at the very moment Mackenzie received word on his radio to go home, Morgan was hailing a cab at the corner of Pont Street after leaving the apartment by scaling the wall of the rear courtyard.

He had carefully reconnoitered the situation in daylight earlier that afternoon and knew exactly what he was doing. He told the driver to drop him at St. Mark's College on the Kings Road. From there, Chelsea Creek was only a brisk five-minute walk.

The paint factory of Wetherby and Sons stood on a pier jutting out into the creek on the other side from the power station. Morgan paused in the shadows, tightening the soft, black leather gloves he wore, took a ski mask from the pocket of his jacket and pulled it over his head.

The front gates were barred and flooded with the glare of security lights. There was also a sign warning of dog patrols, although that could mean something or nothing.

He'd already established the way in during his afternoon visit. There was a concrete weir, water pouring over it, stretching toward the maze of steelwork propping up the pier on which the factory stood.

He went down the bank and started across, taking his time at first, gauging the force of the water. But it wasn't anything he couldn't cope with, rising half-way up his calves, and the apron of the weir was broad enough although green with slime and treach-erous underfoot.

It took him no more than a couple of minutes to reach the far end. He paused for a moment, then climbed the maintenance ladder to the pier above, reaching the yard at the rear of the factory.

There was a fire escape to the first floor. The door at the top was held fast with an iron bar, a padlock on the end. Morgan produced a two-foot steel jimmy from inside his left boot, inserted it into the clasp of the padlock and twisted. It snapped instantly, and he was inside.

From now on he was into uncharted territory. Didn't even know what he intended next, for he was not sure what he would find.

He used his torch with care, noting that this floor held the bottling plant. There was a heavy smell of liquor to everything. He unscrewed the cap of one of several drums he found at one end of the room and sniffed. Industrial alcohol. So, Jago was cutting good Scotch with more than water. With the kind of poison that was known to make people go blind.

From a window he could look down into the main courtyard. There was a hut by the gate, and he could see a uniformed security guard reading in a chair, feet up on a desk. A large Alsatian slept on the floor beside him.

Morgan moved cautiously down wooden stairs and found himself in a large garage. There were two vans and a three-ton truck, which contained dozens of cases of a very prestigious brand of Scotch whiskey, or so it seemed.

There were big double doors held together by a locking bar. He peered through a window beside the doors and saw that a small ramp led down to the yard below. From that point, he couldn't even see the security guard, only the lighted window of the hut.

He thought about it for a while, then went back upstairs to the bottling rooms, unscrewed the cap on one of the drums of industrial alcohol, and put it on its side so the contents spilled across the floor.

He returned downstairs, leaned in the cab of the truck, put the gear stick into neutral, and released the handbrake. Then he removed the locking bar and very carefully pulled back the double doors.

There was no sign of life from the hut at all. He went around to the rear of the truck, put his back to it, and pushed. It started to roll, slowly at first, and then the front wheels were on the ramp. Its speed increased so suddenly that he lost his balance and fell.

As Morgan got to his feet and ran for the stairs, the truck lumbered across the yard and crashed into the double gates, tearing them from their hinges, and grinding to a halt in the street outside.

By that time, he was already halfway across the bottling room. He paused to strike a match and tossed it into the pool of industrial alcohol, which flared immediately, like gas exploding, driving him back out through the fire escape door.

Halfway across the weir he glanced back to see flames blossom at the first-floor windows. He turned and waded on, climbing up to the road and hurrying away quickly through the maze of side streets leading to the Kings Road.

Jago was still at the club when he received the news, and he wasn't pleased. "What in the hell goes on?" he demanded. "Is someone trying to move in or what?"

"I don't know, Harvey," Arnold told him.

"And the Scotch in the truck they found in the street? Where was that from?"

"Export stuff on the way to Harwich Docks. The boys lifted it the other night outside a truckers cafe in Croydon."

"Jesus," Harvey said. "That's all I need. Coppers nosing into everything, and maybe some burk left his fingerprints in the wrong place."

"They can't get within a mile of you, Harvey," Arnold assured him eagerly. "The lease on that place is in the name of an Irish geezer called Murphy."

"Then you get him on the first plane back to the Republic, and I mean like yesterday."

"No sweat, Harvey, he's already there. Some Dublin drunk who hadn't been over in years. That's why I picked him."

The phone rang. Jago lifted it and said, "Yes, what is it?"

"Ready to talk now, Mr. Jago, or would you care for a further demonstration?" Morgan said.

"You bastard."

"It's been said before, but let's get back to business. The source of the Mausers. Any information you can give me, and I'm off your back for good."

Arnold was listening on the desk speaker. He

opened his mouth, and Jago motioned him to silence.

"Okay, friend, you win. The character who handles that end of my business interests is called Goldman. Hymie Goldman. I'll get in touch with him and ring you back."

"Is that a promise?" There was a certain irony in Morgan's voice.

Jago glanced at his watch. "No later than one o'clock."

He put down the receiver and poured himself a Scotch. He drank it slowly, reflectively, without saying a word. Arnold groaned inside for he had seen the expression before, knew what it meant.

"All right, Arnold, this is what you do. Get Andy—Andy Ford. Then you go round to Douro Street and pick up Morgan's bird. We'll all meet up together at Wapping." He glanced at his watch. "I'll give you an hour."

"Harvey, this could be real trouble. Why not tell him what he wants to know. Get him off our backs."

"I could say because I've had it out with Hymie Goldman and there's nothing to tell."

"Oh, god," Arnold said.

"But that isn't enough. I mean, what he did to the booze plant was bad, but it's more than that, Arnold. He threatened me—me! Now we can't have that, can we?" He patted his brother on the cheek. "Get moving, sweetheart, we haven't got all night."

It was perhaps forty minutes later that Morgan's phone rang. "All right, Colonel, you win. Farmer's Wharfe, Wapping. You'll find a warehouse on the dock called Century Export Company. I'll be there

in half an hour with the guy who handled the trans-
action you're interested in."

"That's nice," Morgan said. "What will it cost me?"

"The original extra grand we agreed on. I don't
see why I shouldn't have that." Jago tried to sound
injured. "Afterward, just stay off my back. I don't
want police trouble. It costs time and money, and
I'm a capitalist all the way through."

Morgan put down the phone, opened the right-
hand drawer of the desk, and took out first a Walther
PPK, then a Carswell silencer, which he fitted over
the muzzle of the Walther, whistling tunelessly. Then
he removed the magazine from the butt, emptied it,
and started to reload carefully, taking his time.

The warehouse was old with heavy stone walls and
dated from the great days of Victorian sailing ships
when Britain's merchant navy had reigned supreme.

The place was full of packing cases, and Jago sat in
the rear of his Rolls-Royce Silver Shadow beside Kate
Riley, drinking brandy from the portable bar.

"You sure you won't have one, sweetheart?"

"You go to hell," she said.

"Now that isn't nice."

Arnold was by the door, and Ford, a little, dark,
dangerous-looking Scot in a green parka of the kind
issued to American forces for winter use, was sitting
on a packing case. He was nursing a sawed-off shotgun.

"Get that bloody thing out of sight," Harvey said,
tossing him a car rug, and checked his watch. "He
should be here any minute."

High above them on the fire-escape catwalk, Morgan peered down, carefully noting every detail of the situation. Ford and the shotgun, Arnold by the door, Jago in the rear of the Rolls with Kate.

Very quietly, he went back down the fire escape, then hurried along to the end of the street where he'd left the Porsche. He'd expected trouble, of course. Was prepared for it. Now, because of Kate, he was angry. As he got behind the wheel, his hands were shaking slightly.

Arnold said, "He's coming, I can hear him."

There was the roaring of the Porsche's V6 engine outside, then silence as it was switched off. The judas gate opened and Morgan stepped through. His military trenchcoat hung open, his hands pushed deep into the pockets.

Kate, never so frightened in her life, yet desperately concerned for Morgan, grabbed for the door handle, got it open, and was out and stumbling toward him.

"It's a trap, Asa!" she cried. "They've been waiting for you."

Morgan got an arm around her. Harvey Jago laughed and got out of the Rolls holding the brandy flask in one hand, a silver cup in the other.

"No need for that," he said delightedly. "I mean we're all friends here, isn't that so, Colonel?"

Morgan smiled down at her, the coldest smile she'd ever seen, and she noticed for the first time that there were strange gold flecks in his eyes.

"Did they hurt you?"

"No."

"That's all right then."

He pushed her behind him and turned to Jago. "I

don't think your friend remembered to cock that shotgun when he put it under the rug."

"Andy!" Jago cried.

Ford was already tossing the car rug aside, his
thumbs reaching for the hammer. Morgan's hand appeared through the front of the trenchcoat, holding
the Walther. It coughed twice, both bullets striking
Ford, killing him instantly. The shotgun flew into the
air as the little Scot went back over the packing case.

Kate gave a sudden moan, and Morgan was aware
of her fingers digging into his shoulder. "Outside,
girl," he said. "Wait for me in the car."

"Asa this has gone far enough."

"In the car, girl."

She went. The judas closed softly behind her. Jago
and his brother waited together by the Rolls.

"Tell him, Harvey. For Christ's sake tell him the
truth."

"All right," Jago said. "So I made a mistake. You
can't blame a man for trying, Morgan. I mean you
and me, we're off the same length of street. It takes
one to know one."

"Exactly." Morgan took careful aim and shot off
part of Jago's left ear.

Jago screamed and fell back against the Rolls,
clutching the side of his head, blood pouring between
his fingers.

Arnold ran forward and grabbed him by the lapels.
"Tell him, Harvey, for god's sake. He's a madman,
this one. He'll have us all."

"All right! All right!" Jago said, and the essential
toughness of the man was still there in spite of the
pain. "Okay, you bastard, here's how it was. Hymie

Goldman supplied those Micks in Ulster with the
two Mausers amongst other things. Then a couple
of weeks ago he was sitting in here checking stock on
his own. What we call special stock. He always does
that on Wednesday night. Next thing he knows, this
geezer in a ski mask appears from the shadows. Drops
him a grand in old notes in an envelope and asks for
a silenced handgun. Says a friend recommended him."

"And?"

"Hymie still had one of those silenced Mausers left.
He gave it to him with a box of ammo, and he was
away."

"I see." Morgan raised the Walther. "I think I'll
have the right ear this time."

"I'm telling you the truth, I swear it," Jago cried,
and for the first time there was real panic in his
voice.

Morgan lowered the Walther. "Yes, I'm afraid you
are from the sound of it." He looked across at Ford,
lying back, mouth gaping, one leg propped up on the
packing case. "I don't know what you'll do with him,
but I imagine you have your ways."

He walked to the door. As he opened the judas, Jago
screamed, "I'll have you, Morgan. I'll have you for
this."

Morgan turned. "No," he said softly. "I don't think
you will. I think you'll find on sober reflection, Mr.
Jago, that the best thing to do is put it all down to
experience and forget it."

The door closed behind him. They heard the engine start, and the Porsche moved away.

The side of Jago's head, his hand and shoulder,
were saturated in blood, but he was still in control.

"Harvey?" Arnold said, trembling with fright.

"It's all right. Get Doc Jordan on the phone. Tell him I've had an accident. We'll meet him at that private nursing home in Bailey Street."

Arnold glanced across at Andy Ford. "And him?"

"Just another drunken little Jock gone missing. Ring Sam at the club. Tell him I want the recovery team round here fast. I want this place clean by morning. They can dump him in the new Hendon bypass. There's five hundred tons of wet concrete a night pumping into those foundations. Thank god for progress. Now, help me into the car. You'll have to drive."

Arnold did as he was told. "I'm sorry, Harvey." He was almost in tears.

"Never mind, Arnold. He was right, that bastard. Put it all down to experience, and forget it."

He patted his brother on the cheek and fainted.

When they reached Douro Street, Morgan switched off the engine and turned to face her.

"I'm sorry about that."

"No, you're not," she said. "You're a driven man, Asa, I see that now. You'll do anything to reach this mystical goal of yours. Pull anyone down with you as you nearly pulled me down tonight. And to what end? Are you any further forward?"

"No."

"Asa, you're too rich for my blood. I'm going straight in to pack, and then I'm driving back to Cambridge now—tonight. I've had it."

"If you're worried about what happened back there, don't be. The last thing Jago wants is police nosing around."

"You mean he'll have no trouble in disposing of

the body? For god's sake, Asa, does that make it all right?"

She got out of the car and slammed the door. He stayed behind the wheel and pressed the button so that the electrically operated window slid down silently.

"I'm sorry girl," he said. "But I've no choice, see?"

He started the engine and drove away. She stood there for quite a while, listening to the sound of the Porsche fade, then slowly, wearily, she went up the steps, fumbled for her key, and got the door open.

TEN

It was raining heavily in the first gray light of dawn as Seumas Keegan went up the path to the back door of the cottage two miles outside Ballymena on the Antrim road. He was tired clean through to the bone, and his right arm hurt like hell in spite of the white sling the doctor had given him.

Tim Pat Keogh had watched him approach from behind the kitchen curtain. Tully sat at the table by the fire eating bacon and eggs.

Tim Pat was holding a Sterling submachine gun. He said, "It's Keegan, and he doesn't look too good. Shall I take him out?"

"Not yet," Tully said. "Let's see what he wants."

Tim Pat opened the door. Seumas Keegan stood there, his face under the tweed cap pale and drawn, the old belted trenchcoat saturated by the heavy rain.

"Christ Jesus, but you look like a corpse walking," Tim Pat said.

"Could I see Mr. Tully?" Seumas asked.

Tim Pat pulled him into the kitchen and ran his hands over him expertly. He found a Colt automatic in the left-hand pocket of the trenchcoat and placed it on the table.

Tully kept on eating, looking the boy over at the same time. "What do you want?"

"You said you could always use a good man, Mr. Tully."

Tully poured himself another cup of tea. "What's wrong with your arm?"

Seumas glanced down at the sling. "Broken, Mr. Tully."

"Now there's a thing," Tully said. "I mean, with a gun in your right hand, you were the best there was, O'Hagan always swore to that. But with your left, he said you couldn't hit a barn door."

"A month or two, I'll be as good as new, Mr. Tully, if you'd give me the chance."

There was desperation on the boy's ravaged face now. Tully picked his teeth with a match. "I don't think so, Seumas. To be honest with you, I'd say you could do with a long rest. Wouldn't you agree, Tim Pat?"

"I would indeed, Mr. Tully." Tim Pat smiled and cocked the Sterling.

Seumas stood there, shoulders hunched, head down for a moment, but when he looked up he was actually smiling.

"Somehow, that's what I thought you'd say, Mr. Tully."

He fired the Luger he was holding inside the sling twice, killing Tim Pat instantly.

As the big man's body was hurled back against the dresser, crockery cascading to the floor, Tully pulled at the drawer in the table frantically, reaching for the gun inside. Keegan's third shot took him in the left shoulder, spinning him around, knocking him off the chair.

He crouched there for a moment, crying aloud in agony as he tried to get up. Keegan fired again, the bullet smashing into the base of Tully's skull, driving him headfirst into the open hearth to sprawl across the burning logs.

There was a sudden spurt of flame as his jacket caught fire. Seumas stood there looking down at him for a moment, then turned and let himself out.

Morgan had tried going to bed but had slept only fitfully. Just after six, he gave up and went into the kitchen. He was making the coffee when the phone rang. He could tell it was a public call box by the tone. There was the rattle of coins and then the unmistakable Ulster accent.

"Is that you, Colonel? This is Keegan—Seumas Keegan."

"Where are you?"

"Not far from Ballymena. I thought you'd like to know I've just taken care of Tully and Tim Pat Keogh."

"Permanently?"

"As the coffin lid closing."

There was a silence. Morgan said, "Now what?"

"I'll go down South for a rest."

"And then?"

"What do you think, Colonel. Once in, never out. That's what we say in the IRA, you know that. You're a good man, but you're on the wrong side entirely."

"I'll try to remember that next time we meet."

"I hope for both our sakes that never happens."

The phone went dead. Morgan stood there for a moment, then replaced the receiver.

"Up the Republic, Seumas Keegan," he said softly, and went back into the kitchen.

He sat by the window, drinking his coffee, over-
tired and depressed and not because he'd killed a man.
There had been too many over the years for that. And
he had no regrets. Ford had been, after all, a mur-
derer by profession.

"And so are you, old son," Morgan said softly to
himself in Welsh. "Or, at least, that's what some people might argue."

He thought of Kate Riley then and of what she
had said. She'd been right. He was no further forward.
He'd had two possible leads only. Lieselott Hoffmann
and the Mausers. Both had led him only into blind
alleys.

So, what was left? The newspaper, the magazines
on the table, each with a different account of the
Cohen shooting. How many times had he pored over
them? He pulled the *Telegraph* forward and once
again worked his way through the relevant article.

When he finished, he poured another coffee and sat
back. Of course, the one thing was missing was the
death of Megan in the tunnel because the press had
not been allowed to link the two events.

There was a mention, entirely separate, treating it
as an ordinary hit-and-run accident in which the
driver of a stolen car had run down a young school-
girl and later abandoned the vehicle in Craven Hill
Gardens, Bayswater.

It was with no particular emotion he realized that
for some reason, he hadn't actually visited the place
where the Cretan had dumped the car. Not that there
could be anything worth seeing. On the other hand,

what else was there to do when you were at the final
end of things at six o'clock on a wet, gray London
morning.

He parked the Porsche in Craven Hill Gardens and
sat there with the Geographia map book of London
on his knees, open at the relevant page, tracing the
course of the Cretan's wild progress that night, imagining the panic as things had started to go wrong. And
when he'd dumped the car, what then?

Morgan got out and started along the sidewalk, doing what seemed natural. He turned into Leinster
Terrace and there, only a few yards away, was the
busy Bayswater Road, Kensington Gardens opposite.

"And that's where I'd have gone in your situation,
boyo," Morgan said. "Straight across the road, head
down in the darkness, and run like hell to the other
side."

When he crossed the road, he made automatically
for the nearest entrance and followed the path, passing the Round Pond on his right. In spite of the
hour, there were people about, the occasional jogger
in track suit or early-morning-riser exercising a dog.

He emerged at Queens Gate, opposite the Albert
Hall. From here, anything was possible. The subway
would have been the obvious place to make for. Once
on a tube train, the possibilities were endless.

He went back across Kensington Gardens to the
place where Leinster Terrace joined the Bayswater
Road and paused, full of anger and frustration, unable to let go.

"You must have gone somewhere, you bastard," he
said softly. "But where?"

He crossed the road and started to walk along the

sidewalk toward Queensway. It was hopeless, of course, he knew that as he paused warily at the Italian restaurant on the corner and lit a cigarette.

There were a number of posters on the wall beside the main window of the restaurant. It was the pale, handsome face that caught his attention first, the dark eyes and the name Mikali in bold black type.

He started to turn away, but the coincidence made him turn again to read the poster, remembering that according to the file Baker had shown him, Mikali had been one of the celebrities present in the hotel at the Cannes Film Festival when the Cretan had shot the Italian film director for the Black Brigade.

And then he saw the date on the poster and the time. Friday, July 21, 1972, at 8:00 P.M.

It wasn't possible, it was absolutely crazy and yet he found himself turning and hurrying back along the sidewalk to Leinster Terrace. He stood there for a moment, imagining the Cretan dumping the car and emerging here.

In the far distance, he could see the dome of the Albert Hall above the trees. He crossed the road quickly and plunged into the park.

He went down the steps from the Albert Memorial, crossed Kensington Gore, dodging the early morning traffic, and paused outside the front entrance of the Albert Hall. There was a selection of posters on the boards, advertising various concerts and their programs. Daniel Barenboim, Previn, Moura Lympany, and John Mikali.

The Vienna Philharmonic and John Mikali playing Rachmaninov's *Second Piano Concerto*, Friday, July 21, 1972, at 8:00 P.M.

"Oh, my god," Morgan said aloud. "This was where he was making for. It had to be. That's why he came through the Paddington Tunnel. That's why he dumped the car in Bayswater."

He turned and walked away quickly.

It was nonsense and yet, when he got back to the flat, he started to go through those newspapers again. The facts of the Cohen shooting and Megan's death were both mentioned on different pages of the *Daily Telegraph* for Saturday, the twenty-second.

He found the music page, and there it was. A lengthy piece by the paper's critic reviewing the concert of the previous evening and a picture of the pianist alongside.

Morgan studied it for quite some time. The handsome, serious face, the dark hair, the eyes. It was stupid, of course, but he went and got *Who's Who* from the bookshelf anyway and looked Mikali up. And then a couple of sentences seemed to leap right out at him. The reference to Mikali's service in the French Foreign Legion paratroopers in Algiers—and he didn't feel stupid anymore.

It was just after nine when Betty, Bruno Fischer's secretary, unlocked the door of his office in Golden Square and walked in. She's hardly had time to get her coat off when the phone rang.

"Good morning," she said. "Fischer Agency."

"Is Mr. Fischer in yet?" It was a man's voice, rather deep with a touch of Welsh about it.

She sat on the edge of the desk. "We never see Mr. Fischer much before eleven."

"I am right, he does represent John Mikali?"

"Yes."

"My name's Lewis," Asa Morgan told her. "I'm a postgraduate student at the Royal College of Music doing a thesis on contemporary concert pianists. I was wondering whether Mr. Mikali might be available for an interview?"

"I'm afraid not," she said. "He's just had a concert in Helsinki, then flown straight to Greece on holiday. He has a villa there on Hydra."

"And when might you be expecting him back?"

"He has a concert in Vienna in ten days time, but he'd probably fly there direct from Athens. I really couldn't say when he'll be back in London, and there wouldn't be any kind of guarantee that he could see you."

"That's a pity," Morgan said. "I'd hoped to be able to question him about particular cities he likes to play in. Any personal favorites and why."

"Paris," she said. "I should say he plays Paris and London more than anywhere else."

"And Frankfurt?" Morgan enquired. "Has he ever played there?"

"I should say so."

"Why do you say that?"

"He was giving a concert at the university there last year when that East German minister was assassinated."

"Thank you," Morgan said. "You've been more than helpful."

He sat by the phone, thinking about it. There had to be something wrong. It was too simple. And then the phone rang.

Kate Riley said, "Asa, I'm sorry. I was so shattered by what happened. . . ."

"Where are you?"

"Back in Cambridge at New Hall."

"Hell of a thing happened to me this morning," he said. "I visited the street where the Cretan dumped the car that night, moved on foot from there, as he might have done."

"All supposition, of course."

"But it took me across Kensington Gardens to the Albert Hall. Where I noticed a poster. One of many, but more interesting than the others, advertising a concert at eight o'clock on the night Megan died."

"A concert?" She was aware of a coldness in her, a quickening of breath.

"John Mikali playing Rachmaninov's *Second Piano Concerto*, and that name struck a chord. An Italian film director called Forlani was shot dead in his hotel at the Cannes Film Festival in 1971 by the Cretan, who vanished completely in spite of the French security guards. Mikali was one of a number of famous celebrities staying in the hotel at the same time."

"Well?"

"Last year, when that East German minister was killed at Frankfurt, guess who was giving a concert at the university?"

She took a deep breath. "Asa, this is nonsense. John Mikali is one of the greatest pianists in the world. An international celebrity."

"Who spent two years in the Foreign Legion as a kid," Morgan said. "All right, so it doesn't sound very probable, but at least it's worth following up."

"Have you spoken to Chief Superintendent Baker about your suspicions?"

"Have I hell? This is mine—nobody else's. I'm going to do some more checking. I'll keep you posted."

After he had put the phone down, she got her address book and quickly found Bruno Fischer's number. When he answered, he sounded as if he was still in bed.

"Bruno—Katherine Riley."

"And what can I do for you so early in the morning?"

"When's John due back from Helsinki?"

"He isn't. He decided he needed a break. Flew straight to Athens and carried on to Hydra. He'll be there now if you want him. You've got the number, haven't you? The one good thing about that barbaric place is that he has a phone."

She rang off then turned to another page. One thing about Hydra. It was possible to get through direct by automatic trunk dialing. She punched out the lengthy series of numbers. It took her three separate attempts before she got through.

"John, is that you?"

"Katherine. Where are you?" He sounded pleased.

"Cambridge. I think I can get away for a few days. Can I come over?"

"You certainly can. When do I expect you?"

She glanced at her watch. "I've a few things to clear up here, but I might just catch the afternoon flight. If not, this evening at the latest. That would mean I couldn't get across to the island till tomorrow morning."

"I'll have Constantine waiting at the dock for you."

After he had gone, she sat there for a long time without moving. She could not accept any of that. It had to be nonsense. It had to be. At that moment, she actually found herself hating Asa Morgan with all her heart.

* * *

Morgan waited at the counter of the *Telegraph* information department in Fleet Street. The pleasant young lady he'd stated his requirements to five minutes earlier returned with a bulky file.

"Mikali—John," she said, "and there's a lot of him."

Which there was. Morgan took it to one of the tables, sat down, and started to work his way through. There were gaps, of course. The clippings were mainly English and American, but there were also some French. A review of a concert to fit with the Vassilikos assassination, another that matched the Russian in Toronto.

Finally, there was an article in *Paris Match*, which Morgan read slowly. His French was only fair, but he managed to get the gist of it. It was an account of Mikali's time in the Legion, and there was a particularly graphic description of the affair at Kasfa.

Then he turned to the next page and saw the pictures. One of Mikali in paratrooper's beret and camouflage uniform, holding a machine carbine with negligent ease. The other, a close-up of him wearing the regulation white kepi of the fully trained legionnaire.

Morgan looked at that hard young face, the cropped hair, the blank eyes, the mouth. He closed the file. It was enough. He had found the Cretan.

It was just after one when Baker was admitted to Ferguson's flat by Kim. The Brigadier was enjoying a sandwich lunch by the fire. He was also reading the *Times*.

"You look agitated, Superintendent!"

"Asa's left for Athens on the eleven o'clock plane. Special Branch at Heathrow had no authority to stop him, but the news did finally percolate through to us."

"By which time he'd gone, naturally. British Airways, I presume?"

"Olympic."

"How very unpatriotic of him."

"I checked with them. It seems he booked the flight by phone and arrived with ten minutes to spare to pick up his ticket. He only had hand luggage with him."

"Greece," Ferguson said. "And Cretan. Somehow they really do seem to fit together, don't they? I don't like it."

"Do you want me to notify Greek Special Branch in Athens to pick him up?"

"Certainly not."

"All right, sir, do we have a DI5 man at our embassy there?"

"Actually we do. A Captain Rourke, assistant in the military attaché's office."

"Maybe he could follow Morgan when he gets in?"

"It's certainly a thought, Superintendent, except for the unfortunate fact that as you yourself pointed out, Asa Morgan can't be followed unless he wants to be. Still, if you'd like to give Rourke a ring, please do so. The red phone generally achieves the quickest results."

He returned to the *Times*, Baker went to the desk, picked up the red telephone, and asked to be put through on the scrambler to the British Embassy in Athens.

* * *

Captain Charles Rourke was leaning against a pillar reading a newspaper when Morgan emerged from immigration and customs. The Captain was wearing a crumpled linen suit of a type favored by many Greeks during the heat of the summer months and which was supposed to help him merge effectively into the background of the crowded concourse.

Professional soldiers in civilian clothes usually manage to recognize each other for what they are. On this occasion Morgan's task was made easy. He had an encyclopedic memory for faces and remembered Rourke's from the front row of a study group—on methods and technology of urban guerrilla warfare—that he'd lectured to in 1969 at Sandhurst.

Ferguson being careful. Not that it mattered. He went to the exchange counter and passed two hundred pounds sterling, for which he received the appropriate rate in drachmas, then walked out of the entrance and hailed a cab.

He'd last visited Athens a few years previously for a NATO conference. He remembered the hotel he'd stayed in at that time. From what he recalled, it would suit his purpose admirably.

"You know the Green Park Hotel in Kristou Street?"

"Sure," the driver said and pulled away.

Behind them, Charley Rourke was already into the back of a black Mercedes and tapping the driver on the shoulder. "That cab up ahead. The green Peugeot estate. Where he goes, we go."

He remembered Morgan now and that course at the Academy. It was really rather amusing turning the tables like this. He leaned back with a smile and lit a cigarette.

* * *

Morgan checked his watch. It had been necessary to advance it two hours, which meant it was now a quarter to five, Athens time.

"Is there still time to catch the hydrofoil to Hydra tonight?" he asked.

"Sure," the driver said. "Summer schedule. They run later, these light nights. The last to Hydra leaves the Piraeus six-thirty."

"How long does it take?"

"Gets in at eight o'clock. It makes a nice run. Plenty to see. Doesn't get dark this time of year till around nine-thirty." He glanced briefly over his shoulder. "You want I should take you to the Piraeus?"

Morgan, aware of the Mercedes behind, shook his head. "No, I'll leave it till tomorrow. The hotel will do fine."

"Hey, for an Englishman you speak good Greek."

It didn't seem politic to mention that it had been gained during three hard years chasing EOKA terrorists in Cyprus.

Morgan said, "I worked in Nicosia for a few years, for a British-owned wine company."

The driver nodded wisely. "Things are better there now. I think Makarios knows what he's doing."

"Let's hope so."

He'd little time to waste, he knew that as he paid off the driver at the Green Park Hotel and the black Mercedes drifted past and pulled in at the curb a few yards away. As Morgan turned and went up the steps to the revolving door, Rourke got out of the car and went after him.

Once inside, Morgan didn't go to the desk. Instead, he crossed to the broad flight of carpeted stairs leading to the mezzanine. Rourke paused for a moment, pretending to examine the daily currency exchange rate on the foyer bulletin board, only going after him when Morgan had moved around the corner of the first landing.

Once on the mezzanine floor, Morgan, who knew exactly where he was going, darted past the souvenir shop and took the narrow back stair which led directly to the twenty-four-hour restaurant on the lower level. He threaded his way between the tables and was leaving by the side entrance of the hotel while Rourke, still on the mezzanine floor, hesitated, not knowing where to go next.

He approached the young lady in the souvenir shop. "My friend just came up ahead of me. He had a brown leather bag and wore a raincoat. I seem to have missed him."

"Oh, yes, sir. He went down the restaurant stairs."

Rourke, seized by a sudden dreadful suspicion, went down them two at a time. By then, of course, Asa Morgan was long gone, already halfway across the park in the square opposite.

Morgan emerged, as he'd expected, by a public taxi rank and got into the one at the head of the queue. "The Piraeus," he told the driver. "I've got to catch the Flying Dolphin for Hydra at six-thirty."

"That's cutting it too fine, Mister," the driver said. "I don't think we can make it."

"Five hundred drachmas says we can," Asa Morgan told him. He reached for the handstrap as the driver grinned, gunned his motor, and shot out into the stream of traffic.

ELEVEN

At Heathrow, it was just three-thirty as Katherine
Riley hurried up to the British Airways check-in
desk followed by a porter with her luggage.

The young clerk examined her ticket. "Sorry, madam, they're boarding now. Too late to pass you
through. Would you like me to see if I can put you
on our seven o'clock flight?"

"Yes," she said. "Please do. I must get to Athens
tonight."

He checked and came back. "Yes, we can do that for
you. You get in rather late, I'm afraid. Half an hour
past midnight, Greek time."

"That doesn't matter," she said. "I'm going on to
the islands. It means I'll get an early start in the
morning."

"Fine, madam. Now if I could have your baggage,
I'll check it through for you."

It was Ferguson who phoned Baker this time, with
the bad news from Athens.

"I've just had Rourke on the line. Asa gave him
the slip and rather easily, from the sound of it."

"Jesus Christ," Baker said, for once totally unable
to contain himself. "Where in the hell do you find
these idiots?"

"A special dispensation from the Almighty, Superintendent. Who are we poor mortals to question his
ways?"

"So—what do we do now, sir?"

"Like Mr. Micawber, sit tight and hope for something to turn up," Ferguson said and put down the
phone.

Morgan made it to the hydrofoil quay at the Piraeus
with ten minutes to spare. It wasn't particularly
crowded, and he paid for his ticket on board and
found a seat by the window.

It was a calm evening, and the Flying Dolphin
was able to operate at maximum speed, straining
high out of the water on her stilt-like legs. And the
scenery was spectacular enough. Salamis with the blue
waters of the Saronic Gulf, the great bulk of the
Island of Aegina and Poros, glowing with brilliant
colors in the evening light.

None of it meant anything to Morgan, even when
he went out to the well deck and leaned on the rail,
staring blindly into space, thinking of only one thing.
John Mikali. And when they met, what then? He had
no weapon. Impossible to risk being caught trying to
bring one in by the security checks at the airport.
There were always his hands, of course. It wouldn't
be the first time. When he looked down at them,
they trembled slightly.

Finally, there was Hydra, bare and austere in the
evening light, like some great stone basilisk, curiously
disappointing until the Flying Dolphin moved into
the harbor and the enchantment of Hydra town itself was revealed.

The house rose in tiers, back into the hills, reached

by a network of twisting cobbled alleys. The evening was just getting going, cheerful crowds moving into the tavernas.

Morgan took a seat at one of the open air tables close to the Monastery of the Dormiton on the waterfront. The waiter who came spoke fair English, so Morgan kept his Greek to himself and ordered a beer.

"You American?" the waiter asked.

"No, Welsh, actually."

"I've never been to Wales. London, yes. I worked in a restaurant on the Kings Road, Chelsea, for one year."

"And that was enough?"

"Too cold," the waiter smiled. "Nice here in the season. Nice and warm." He kissed his fingers. "Plenty of girls. Lots of tourists. You here for a holiday, eh?"

"No," Morgan said. "I'm a journalist. Hoping to interview John Mikali, the concert pianist. He has a villa here, I understand?"

"Sure, down the coast beyond Molos."

"How do I get there?" Morgan asked. "Is there a local bus?"

The waiter smiled. "No cars or trucks on Hydra. It's against the law. The only way you get anywhere is on a mule or your own two feet. A mule is better. In the interior of the island it's rough, mountainous country, and the people there still live like the old days."

"And Mikali?"

His villa is about seven kilometers down the coast from here on a promontory in the pine trees opposite to Dokos. Very beautiful. He uses a motor launch to ferry his supplies and so on."

"Can I hire a boat to take me there?"

The waiter shook his head. "Not if he hasn't invited you."

Morgan tried to look dismayed. "Then what do I do? I'd hate to have come all this way for nothing." He took a one-hundred-drachma note from his wallet and laid it carefully down on the table. "If you could help in any way, I'd be very grateful."

The waiter picked up the note calmly and slipped it casually into his top pocket. "I tell you what. I do you a favor. I get him on the telephone. If he wants to see you, then that's up to him. Okay?"

"That's fine."

"What's your name?"

"Lewis."

"Okay. You stay here. I'll be back in a couple of minutes."

The waiter went inside the taverna to the desk and checked in a small directory, then he lifted the receiver from the wall phone and dialed a number. Mikali answered himself.

"Heh, Mr. Mikali, this is Andrew, the waiter at Niko's," he said in Greek.

"And what can I do for you?"

"There's a man here come in on the hydrofoil from Athens asking how to get to your place. A journalist. He says he was hoping for an interview."

"What is he, an American?"

"No, Welsh, he says. His name is Lewis."

"Welsh?" Mikali managed to sound faintly amused. "That certainly makes a change. Okay, Andrew, I'm in a good mood, but only for an hour, mind you, that's all he's got. I'll send Constantine in for him. You point him to the boat when it comes in."

"Okay, Mr. Mikali."

The waiter returned to Morgan. "You're in luck. He says he'll see you, but only for an hour. He's sending his boatman for you, old Constantine. I'll tell you when they get here."

"That's marvelous," Morgan said. "How long?"

"Long enough for you to have something to eat." The waiter grinned. "The fish I can especially recommend. Fresh in tonight."

Morgan ate well, mainly to fill the time, and found himself enjoying it. He was just finishing when the waiter tapped him on the shoulder and pointed and Morgan saw a white motor launch coming around the point.

"Come on," the waiter said. "I'll take you down and introduce you."

The launch bumped against the harbor wall, and a young boy of eleven or twelve jumped to the wharf with a line. He wore a patched jersey and jeans. The waiter tousled his hair, and the boy gave him a flashing smile.

"This is Nicky, Constantine's grandson, and here is Constantine himself."

Constantine was a small, powerful-looking man with a face tanned to a deep mahogany shade by a lifetime at sea. He wore a seaman's cap, checked shirt, patched trousers, and sea boots.

"Don't be misled by appearances," the waiter whispered. "The old bastard owns two good houses in town." He raised his voice. "This is Mr. Lewis."

Constantine didn't manage a smile. He said in broken English, "We go now, Mister."

He went back into the wheelhouse. "Probably thinks the Devil will get him if he's out after dark," the waiter said. "They're all the same, these old ones. Half the women think they're witches. I'll see you again, Mr. Lewis."

Morgan stepped on board, the boy moved after him, coiling the line, and the motor launch moved out of the harbor past the once heavily fortified battery, with its Venetian guns pointing out to sea as if they still expected the Turks to come.

It was a fine evening, although the coast of the Peloponnese about four miles away was already fading into a kind of purple twilight, and on the Hydrian shore lights gleamed in the windows. The boat surged forward as Constantine boosted power, and Morgan went into the wheelhouse and offered him a cigarette.

"How long?"

"Fifteen—twenty minutes."

Morgan looked out across the evening sea, black as ink as the sun slipped out of sight beyond the bulk of Dokos on the far horizon.

"Nice," he said.

The old man didn't bother to reply. After a while, Morgan gave up any attempt at conversation and went below to the saloon where he found the boy seated at the table reading a sports paper. Morgan looked over his shoulder. The front page featured the famous Liverpool soccer team.

"You like football?" Morgan asked.

The boy smiled delightfully and pointed at the picture. "Liverpool—you like?" His English seemed very limited.

"Well, I'd rather spend the afternoon at Cardiff Arms Park myself, but yes, you have to admit that there must be something in the water in Liverpool."

The boy grinned again, then went to a cupboard, opened it, and produced an expensive Polaroid camera. He pointed it at Morgan, there was a flash, and then the print was ejected at the front.

Morgan said, "There's an expensive toy. Who gave you that?"

"Mr. Mikali," Nicky said. "He nice man."

Morgan picked up the print and stared down as it automatically developed itself, his face peering darkly out at him, the colors deepening.

"Yes," he said slowly. "I suppose he is."

The photo was ready now. Nicky took it from him and held it up. "Good?"

"Yes," Morgan patted him on the head. "Very good."

The phone rang. When Mikali answered it, it was Katherine Riley again.

"I'm still in the international departure lounge at Heathrow," she said. "There's been a delay."

"My poor darling."

"That sounds rather extravagant for you," she said.

"I feel in an extravagant mood."

"Anyway, I'll still be on the first hydrofoil in the morning."

"I'll have Constantine waiting for you. Don't talk to any strange men."

He hung up as he heard the sound of the engine approaching. He picked up a pair of binoculars, opened the French windows, and moved out across

the wide terrace. There was still enough light for
him to see the launch turn in to the bay and move
toward the small jetty where Constantine's old wife,
Anna, was waiting.

There was a light on the end of the jetty. As the
boy tossed the line to his grandmother, Morgan followed him over the rail. Mikali focused the binoculars on him briefly. It was enough.

He returned to the living room where a pine log
fire burned brightly on the hearth. He poured himself a large Courvoisier and ice, then opened a drawer
in the desk, took out a Walther, and quickly fitted a
silencer to the muzzle.

He pushed the weapon into his belt and went
around the room, glass in one hand, opening all the
French windows, pushing back and securing the shutters so that the night wind filled the house with the
scent of flowers from the garden.

Then he turned off all the lights except a reading
lamp on a coffee table by the piano, went and sat
down at the Bluthner and started to play.

Fifty or sixty feet up the steep path from the jetty
they came to a small, rather primitive cottage. A dog
started to bark at Morgan from the porch. The old
woman hushed it, and she and the boy went in. Constantine continued up the path without a word and
Morgan followed him, aware of a terraced garden
fringed with olive trees. There were pots of camellia,
gardenia, and hibiscus, and the warm night air was
perfumed with the scent of jasmine.

He could hear the piano now, a strange, haunting
piece. For a brief moment, he stopped dead in his

tracks. Constantine paused, half-turning, his face
showing no emotion, and Morgan started forward
again.

They went up the steps to the villa. It was a large,
sprawling, one-storied building, constructed of local
stone with green-painted shutters and a pantile roof.
Bougainvillaea grew in profusion everywhere.

There was a double door of ironbound oak. Constantine opened it without ceremony and led the way
in. The inner hall seemed to join two sections of
the house together and was in darkness. A faint light
showed through a door, which stood open at the far
end from where the music sounded clearly. Constantine led the way down to it, motioned Morgan inside,
put down his carryall, and left without a word, closing the front door behind him.

"Come in, Mr. Lewis," Mikali called.

Morgan stepped into the room. It was very long,
simply furnished, with white-painted walls, a floor of
polished brick, the fire burning cheerfully in the
hearth, and Mikali at the Bluthner concert grand.

"Take your coat off, please."

Morgan tossed his trenchcoat onto the nearest
chair and moved forward slowly, like a man in a
dream, throat dry, breathing constricted. The music
seemed to touch the very core of his being.

"You know this piece, Mr. Lewis?"

"Yes," Morgan said thickly. "It's called *Le Pastour*
by Gabriel Grovelez."

Mikali managed to look surprised. "A man of taste
and discernment."

"Not really," Morgan said. "As it happens, it was
one of the pieces my daughter had to learn for her

grade five piano certificate at the Royal College of
Music."

"Yes, I was sorry about that," Mikali said. "I did
try to miss her, Colonel."

Morgan was past any kind of surprise now. He said,
"Yes, I can imagine that. When you murdered Stephanakis in Paris, you let the chauffeur live, the
chambermaid at the Hilton in Berlin and the
chauffeur again in Rio when you killed General
Falção. Who do you think you are—God?"

"Rules of the game. They weren't the target."

"The game?" Morgan said. "And what game would
that be?"

"You should know. You've been playing it long
enough. The most exciting game in the world with
your own life as the ultimate stake. Can you honestly
tell me anything else you've ever done has offered
quite the same kick?"

"You're mad," Morgan said.

Mikali looked faintly surprised. "Why? I used to do
the same things in uniform and they gave me medals
for it. Your own position exactly. When you look in
the mirror it's me you see."

The music changed, some concerto or other now,
full of life and strength.

He said, "The interesting thing is your being here
on your own. What happened to DI5 and the Special
Branch?"

"I wanted you for myself, you bastard."

The music swelled to a crescendo as Morgan went
forward flexing his hands. Mikali said, "Do you like
this? It's Prokofiev's *Fourth Piano Concerto in B flat
major*—for the left hand."

His right hand came up over the top of the piano

holding the Walther. Morgan, his sixth sense bred over thirty years, was already swerving to one side as the Walther coughed once, the bullet plowing a furrow across the top of his left shoulder.

He tore the reading lamp on the coffee table from its socket, plunging the room into shadow. The Walther coughed again, twice, but Morgan was already out through the nearest French window. He ran across the terrace and valuted ten feet into the garden below, landing heavily.

The dog was barking again down in the cottage as he ran toward the cliff edge, through the olive trees, swerving from side to side. Mikali, who had followed him over the terrace without hesitation, went after him.

It was almost totally dark now, the horizon streaked with orange fire as Morgan reached the edge of the cliffs and hesitated, realizing there was nowhere left to run.

For an instant, he was a perfect silhouette against the orange and gold of the evening sky, and Mikali fired again while still running. Morgan cried out as the bullet pushed him backward into space and then he was gone.

Mikali peered down into the gloom below. There was a footstep behind him and Constantine appeared, a shotgun in one hand, a spotlamp in the other.

Mikali took the light from him, switched it on, and played it on the dark swirling waters among the rocks.

"The boy is in bed?" he asked.

"Yes." The old man nodded.

"Good. Doctor Riley will be on the first hydrofoil from Athens in the morning. She'll be expecting you."

Mikali walked back to the terrace. The old man looked down to the dark waters, crossed himself, then turned away and retraced his steps to the cottage.

It was about an hour later that Jean Paul Deville let himself into his Paris apartment. He'd been to dinner, an annual affair attended mainly by colleagues at the criminal bar. Most of the others had elected to continue the evening's entertainment at an establishment in Montmartre much frequented by middle-aged gentlemen in search of excitement. Deville had managed to make his escape gracefully enough.

As he took off his coat, the telephone rang. It was Mikali. He said, "I've been trying for an hour."

"I was out to dinner. Trouble?"

"Our Welsh friend appeared. Knew all about me."

"Good god. How?"

"I haven't the slightest idea. I did establish that he hadn't passed the information on. He was too anxious to have me for himself."

"You've taken care of him?"

"Permanently."

Deville frowned, thinking about it, then made his decision. "Under the circumstances, I think we should get together. If I catch the breakfast plane to Athens, I could be in Hydra by one o'clock, your time. Will that be all right?"

"Fine," Mikali said. "Katherine Riley's arriving in the morning, but no sweat about that."

"Of course not," Deville said. "Let's keep things as normal as possible. I'll be seeing you."

Mikali poured himself another brandy, crossed to the desk, and opened Morgan's file. He found the photo and stared down into the dark, ravaged face for a long moment, then he took it and the rest of the file and threw them on the fire.

He sat down at the piano, flexed his fingers, then started to play *Le Pastour* with enormous feeling and delicacy.

TWELVE

For most of his seventy-two years George Ghika had been a fisherman by profession, living in the same small farm he had been born in, high up in the pine woods above Mikali's place.

All of his four sons had emigrated to America in turn over the years, leaving him only his wife, Maria, to help him work the boat. Not that it mattered. Whatever he liked to pretend, she was as tough as him any day of the week and could handle the boat as well.

Twice a week, for the excitement and a little extra money, they would set out to lay their nets as usual, at night, then turn out the lights and make the four-mile run across the strait to a taverna on the coast of the Peloponnese where they would take on a cargo of untaxed cigarettes, a commodity for which there was considerable demand on Hydra.

On the return journey, once back at the nets, they would carry on fishing. It had always worked perfectly until that night, when Maria switched on the great double sodium lamps in the prow of the boat whose light attracted the fish and saw instead a hand reaching out to her and then a bloodstained face.

"Mother of god, a sea-devil," old George cried and raised an oar to strike.

She pushed him away. "Back, you old fool. Can't you tell a man when you see one? Help me get him in."

Morgan lay in the bottom of the boat while she examined him.

"He's been shot," her husband said.

"Can I not see this for myself? Twice. The flesh is torn across the shoulder and here, in the upper part of the left arm. A bullet has passed straight through."

"What shall we do? Take him to Hydra town to the doctor?"

"To what end?" she said with contempt, for like many old Hydriot peasant women, herbal remedies and potions were a way of life to her. "What can he do that I cannot do better? And there would be the police. It would be necessary to report the affair, and the questions of the cigarettes would arise." Her leathery face creased in a smile. "You, my George, are too old to go to jail."

Morgan opened his eyes and said in Greek, "No police, whatever you do."

She turned and punched her husband in the shoulder. "See, he has spoken, our man from the sea. Let's get him ashore before he dies on us."

They were in a small horseshoe bay, he was aware of that, with a tiny fringe of beach, pine trees flooding down from the mountain above.

The jetty was built of massive stone blocks stretching out into deep water. A strange thing to find in such a deserted spot. He didn't know then that it was over 150 years old, dating from the Greek War of Independence when this bay had held up to twenty Hydriot armed schooners waiting to pounce on any vessel of the Turkish fleet unwary enough to approach that coast.

It had stopped raining, and in the moonlight, Morgan was aware of several ruined buildings as the old man helped him ashore. He swayed a little, curiously light-headed.

Maria put an arm about him, holding him with surprising strength. "Now is not the time to fall down, boy. Now is time for strength."

Someone laughed, and Morgan realized, with a sense of surprise, that it was himself. "Boy, mother?" he said. "I have seen almost fifty years—fifty long, bloody years."

"Then life should no longer surprise you."

There was a movement in the shadows, and old George appeared from one of the buildings leading a mule. It had no stirrups, only a blanket and a traditional wood and leather pack saddle on its back.

"And what do I do with that?" Morgan asked.

"Mount, my son." She pointed up through the pines.

"There on the mountain. There is safety, a warm bed." She stroked his face with the back of one hand. "You will do this for me, eh? This last thing with all your strength so that we may get thee home?"

For some reason he felt close to tears for the first time in years. "Yes, Mam," he found himself saying in Welsh. "Take me home."

The shock of a gunshot wound is such that, for most people, it temporarily freezes the nervous system. It is only later that the pain comes as it came to Morgan, holding on tightly to the wooden saddle as the mule started up the rocky path through the pine trees, old George leading it, Maria walking on the left side, one hand grasping Morgan's belt.

"Are you all right?" she asked in Greek.

"Yes," he said, light-headed now. "I'm indestructible."

The pain was sharp and cruel, like a hot iron. Korea, Aden, Cyprus; old scars opening up instantly so that his body jerked in agony and his hands gripped the wooden pommel of the saddle as if he were hanging on to life itself.

And she knew, and her hand tightened in his belt and the old voice was deeper than anything he had ever known, more insistent, cutting through the pain.

"You will hold now," she said. "You will not let go till I tell thee to."

It was the last thing he heard. Half an hour later when they arrived at the small farmhouse high on the mountain, and George tied the mule and turned to help him down, he was unconscious in the saddle, his hands locked on the pommel so tightly that they had to pry his fingers loose one by one.

Katherine Riley was totally exhausted after the night flight and four hours in an Athens hotel where she hadn't slept for a moment, tossing and turning in the heat, rising early to catch the taxi she had ordered to take her to the Piraeus.

Even the early morning run to Hydra, the sheer beauty of it, had failed to rouse her in any way. She was afraid. What Morgan had suggested was stupid, wicked, simply not possible. She had given her body to Mikali, he had given her a joy in life denied to her ever since her father's death.

Words, only words. No comfort in any of it, she knew that as she disembarked from the Flying Dolphin at Hydra and Constantine came forward to take her suitcase.

She had never felt comfortable with him, had always imagined that he disapproved of her. He seldom spoke, pretending his English to be worse than it was as he did now when they turned out of harbor and she went into the wheelhouse.

"Nicky?" she said. "Isn't he with you?"

He made no reply, simply boosted the controls. "Is he in Athens with his mother?"

They moved out past the point and picked up speed. She gave up then and went and sat in the stern, turned her face up to the morning sun, and closed her burning eyes.

When they moved in toward the jetty, Mikali was waiting beside old Anna and the boy. He wore dark sunglasses, a white sweatshirt, and faded jeans, and waved excitedly, his mouth opening in a smile, showing the good teeth.

She was more afraid than ever, not knowing what she was going to say as he reached out a hand to help her ashore. His smile changed to a look of concern.

"Katherine? What is it?"

She fought to hold back the tears. "I'm so bloody tired. All that time hanging about at Heathrow and then the flight and that terrible little hotel in Athens."

His arms were around her then, and he was smiling again. "Remember what Scott Fitzgerald said? A hot bath and I can go on for hours. That's what you need."

He picked up her suitcase and spoke to Constantine in Greek. As they started up the path to the villa, she said, "What were you telling him?"

"To be back in Hydra for noon. I've got someone coming in from Paris. My French lawyer, Jean Paul Deville. You've heard me speak of him."

"Will he be staying?"

"Probably only tonight. Business, that's all. Some important papers I have to sign." His arm tightened, and he kissed her cheek. "But never mind that. Let's get you into that bath."

In a way, it worked. She lay there, the hot water soaking away every ache, every pain, and he brought her ice-cold champagne and brandy in a crystal goblet.

"It's beautiful," she said. "I've never seen it before."

"Seventeenth-century Venetian. That great, great, great grandfather of mine, the one who was Admiral of the Hydrian fleet, took it off a Turkish ship at the battle of Navarino." He grinned. "Lie back—enjoy it while I make lunch."

"You?" she said.

He turned in the doorway and smiled, spreading his arms wide in that inimitable gesture. "And why not?"

The brandy and the champagne went straight to her head, yet in a way that was new to her. Instead of confusion, a dulling of the senses, there was a sharpening. She saw quite clearly now that this thing that was eating at her must be brought into the open.

She got out of the bath, pulled on a terry cloth robe, went into the bedroom and sat down in front of the dressing table, combing her hair quickly. There was the softest of footfalls, and he appeared in the mirror, standing in the doorway, anonymous in the dark glasses.

"Okay, angel, what is it?"

She sat there, staring at him in the mirror. Strange how easily the words came out.

"Remember my Welsh Colonel Morgan. The one who came to see Lieselott Hoffmann?"

"Sure I do. The guy whose daughter was knocked down by the Cretan after the Cohen shooting."

"How do you know that?"

"You told me."

She remembered then and nodded slowly. "Yes, I shouldn't have done that. It was supposed to be confidential."

He lit a cigarette and moved to the window beside her. "Confidences? Between us?"

"He thinks you're the Cretan," she said.

Mikali stared at her. "He what?"

"He says you were giving a concert at the Albert Hall the night the Cretan shot Cohen. That's on the other side of Kensington Gardens from where he dumped the car."

"This is crazy."

"He says you were at the Cannes film festival when Forlani was murdered."

"So was half of Hollywood."

"And at Frankfurt University when the East German minister, Heine, was shot."

He turned her on the seat, his hands on her shoulders. "I told you that myself. Don't you remember? The first time we met when I gave the Cambridge concert. We were discussing the Hoffmann girl and the circumstances of the killing, and I told you I was in Frankfurt at the time."

It all came flooding back then and she moaned in a kind of release. "Oh, god, so you did. I remember now."

His arms were around her. "He must be out of his mind. Is he going round shooting his mouth off like this to everybody?"

"No," she said. "I asked him if he'd spoken to Baker, the Special Branch man, but he said no. He said it was his affair—nobody else's."

"When did he tell you this?"

"Yesterday morning early—on the telephone."

"And you haven't met him since?"

"No—he said he was going to do some more checking. That he'd keep me posted." The tears came then. "Oh, god, John, he's obsessed, don't you see? I'm so afraid."

"Nothing to be afraid about, angel. Not a single thing."

He led her across to the bed and pulled back the coverlet. "What you need is sleep."

She obeyed him like a child and lay there, her eyes closed, trembling. After a while, the coverlet was pulled back, and he slipped in beside her.

She turned her head blindly into his shoulder as one arm went around her and the other hand unfastened her robe. And then his mouth was on hers, and her arms were around him in a passion fiercer than she had ever known before.

* * *

Deville leaned on the balustrade of the terrace and looked out across the sea to where Dokos drifted in the afternoon heat haze.

Mikali came out through the French windows with a glass in each hand. "You still prefer to ruin good Napoleon with ice cubes, I suppose?"

"But of course." Deville took the glass from him and gestured out across the sea. "This really is very beautiful. You're going to miss it."

Mikali put his glass down on the balustrade and lit a cigarette. "And what's that supposed to mean?"

"It's very simple. You've had it. We both have. If Morgan managed to discover your identity, then eventually so will someone else. Oh, I don't mean next month, or even next year. But certainly the year after." He smiled and lifted his shoulders in a shrug. "Or perhaps next Wednesday."

"And if they got me, whoever it turned out to be," Mikali said. "You think I'd talk?"

"Rubber hoses went out with the Gestapo," Deville told him. "They'd stick a hypodermic in your arm and fill you full of succinylcholine, a rather unpleasant drug which takes you to about as close to dying as a human being can get. The experience is so awful that few people could stand the thought of a second helping." He smiled gently. "I'd sing like a bird, John, and so would the Cretan Lover."

A mile out to sea the hydrofoil passed on its way to Spetsae. Mikali said, "And what would you suggest?"

"Time to go home, my friend!"

"My home is Hydra." Mikali laughed out loud. "If Russia is home to you, old buddy, it doesn't mean a damn thing to me. And if it comes to that, what about

you? You've been away too long. They'll give you a
VIP card to shop in the special section at GUM but
it's hardly Gucci. And when you're queuing up in
Red Square to get a look at Lenin in his mausoleum,
you'll be thinking of Paris and Champs Elysées and
the smell of damp chestnut trees along the boulevards
after a shower."

"Very poetic, but it doesn't alter the fact of the
matter. My old grandmother used to get rheumatism
and knew it would rain within twenty-four hours. I
can smell trouble with equal facility. Time to go,
believe me."

"For you, maybe," Mikali said stubbornly. "Not
for me."

"But what will you do?" Deville was genuinely be-
wildered. "I don't understand."

"Live a day at a time."

"And when that special day arrives, the day they
come for you?"

Mikali was wearing a loose cashmere sweater, which
concealed a Burns and Martin spring holster clipped
to the belt at the small of his back. His right hand
came up holding a Walther.

"Remember my Ceska? That was my London gun.
This is the Hydriot variety. As I told you, I'm always ready."

At that moment, the phone started to ring. He ex-
cused himself and went inside. Deville sat on the
balustrade looking out toward Dokos, savoring his
cognac. Mikali was right, of course. Paris was the only
city, or London on a good day. Moscow meant nothing to him now. He thought of the winter there and
shivered involuntarily. And there was no one—not

really. A cousin or two. No other close relative. But what choice did he have?

Mikali came out through the French windows laughing, a glass in one hand, a bottle of Napoleon brandy in the other.

"Isn't life the damndest thing." His face was ablaze with excitement. "That was my agent. André Previn's just been on to him. It's the last night of the Proms this Saturday. Mary Schroder was to play John Ireland's piano concerto. She's broken her wrist playing tennis, the silly bitch."

"And they want you to take her place?"

"Previn's offered to change the program. Let me play Rachmaninov's Fourth. We've done it together before so it wouldn't take too much rehearsing. Let's see. Today's Thursday. If I catch tonight's plane, I'll be in London tomorrow. That gives me two days to rehearse."

Deville had never seen him so alive. "No, John," he said. "To go back to London now would be the worst possible thing for you."

"The Promenade Concerts, Jean Paul," Mikali said. "The most important series of concerts in the European musical scene. Do you know what it's like on the last night?"

"No, I've never been."

"Then you've missed out on one of life's great experiences. Packed from floor to ceiling, every seat taken and in the arena in front of the stage, the kids who've queued for three days to get in stand shoulder-to-shoulder. Can you imagine what it's like to be asked to play on such a night?"

"Yes," Deville nodded slowly. "I can imagine."

"Oh, no, you can't, old buddy," Mikali said. "Oh, no you can't."

He emptied the brandy glass in one quick swallow and tossed it out into space. It flashed in the sunlight like flame descending, splintered on the rocks below.

Katherine Riley awoke, lay there for a moment trying to remember where she was. She was alone. When she checked her watch it was two-thirty in the afternoon.

She got up and dressed quickly in jeans and a simple white blouse, pulled on a pair of sandals and went in search of Mikali.

There was no sign of him in the living room, but the sound of voices took her out to the terrace, where she found him standing with Deville.

He came to meet her, put an arm about her waist, and kissed her cheek. "Feeling better?"

"I think so."

"Jean Paul, this is the light of my life, Katherine Riley. Be careful what you say, I warn you. She'll psychoanalyze the hell out of you."

"Doctor, a great pleasure." Deville kissed her hand gallantly.

Mikali, unable to contain himself, took both her hands in his. "Bruno's just been on the phone. Previn wants me to substitute for Mary Schroder. The Rachmaninov."

Which for him meant only one concerto, the one he had made especially his own—the Fourth—and she knew that.

"When?" she said.

"Saturday—the last night of the Proms."

"How absolutely marvelous." She flung her arms about his neck in a gesture of spontaneous delight. "But Saturday. That's the day after tomorrow."

"I know. It means catching tonight's flight from Athens if I'm to have enough rehearsal time. Will you mind? After all, you've only just got off the plane."

"Not at all." She glanced at the Frenchman. "And you, Monsieur Deville? Will you come also?"

Mikali said, "No, Jean Paul has to get back to Paris. He only came to get me to sign some papers. He's handling the legal side of a trust that's been endowed by business interests in Paris and London to help young musicians of exceptional talent. They've bought a large country house near Paris. When it's ready, we plan to run master classes."

"We?" she said.

"I've offered my services free. I'm hoping other notable musicians might do the same."

All her earlier fears seemed like some stupid dream. She put an arm around his waist. "I think it's a marvelous idea."

"Fine—now how about something to eat?"

She shook her head. "Actually, I could do with some air. I think I'll take a walk if you don't mind."

"Sure, whatever you like." He kissed her again. "We'll see you later."

He stood on the tiny verandah of the end window and watched her go down through the garden.

"Brilliant," Deville said. "What a performance. You almost had me believing you. How do you do it?"

"Oh, one learns," Mikali said. "Over the years, don't you find? The lies, the deceits. Practice—lots of practice, that's the secret." He smiled. "Now, how about a drink?"

The farmstead of George and Maria Ghika was in a slight depression above the rim of the mountain surrounded by pine trees. To one side a wild and beautiful ravine dropped steeply, still terraced from ancient times, olive trees everywhere.

The farm was a single-storied building with a roof of red pantiles, the walls whitewashed. There was a living room and kitchen combined and two bedrooms. The floors were stone flagged, the walls crudely plastered, but inside it was cool and dark in the summer heat as it was intended to be.

When Morgan went out, he found the old couple sitting on a bench in the sun. Maria was gutting fish while George looked on, smoking his pipe.

"You should not be on your feet," she said in mild reproof.

Morgan was stripped to the waist. His right shoulder and left arm were expertly bandaged with strips of clean linen. He felt old—tired and all used up in a way he hadn't for years.

"Here, sit." George patted the bench beside him. "How do you feel?"

"I'm fifty next month," Morgan said, "and for the first time, I really know it."

Maria laughed out loud. "The old one there can give you twenty-five years, and still tries to get me into bed Saturdays."

George offered him a Greek cigarette and gave him a light. "Last night you said something interesting. You mentioned Mikali. Was he the one who did this to you?"

"Is he a friend of yours?" Morgan asked.

The old man spat and stood up. "Wait here." He went into the house and came back with a pair of Zeiss field glasses.

"Where in the hell did you get those?" Morgan demanded.

"Off a Nazi storm trooper in Crete during the war when I was with EOK. Come, I show you."

He went some little way through the pine trees and Morgan followed. The old man stopped and pointed. "See!"

Below, the ravine spilled down through the pine woods to the bay above which the Mikali villa stood. George focused the field glasses and handed them to Morgan.

"Look, all the way down. The terraces—every stone carried by mule. Built with the sweat of my own ancestors. All stolen by Mikali."

The lines of the ancient terraces jumped sharply into life as Morgan examined them. In spite of the olive trees, the ground was overgrown and obviously not tilled.

He glanced at old George. "John Mikali?"

"His great-grandfather. Is there a difference? A Mikali is a Mikali. Once we of the Ghika clan were substantial people. Once we had respect. But now . . ."

Morgan raised the field glasses to his eyes again, and the garden below the villa came into view, Kate Riley walking down the path to the jetty where young Nicky was fishing with a handline.

"Dear god!" Morgan said.

The old man took the glasses from him and looked for himself. "Ah, yes, I have seen her there before. The American lady."

"Before?" Morgan asked.

"Oh, yes. You know her?"

"I thought I did," Morgan said hoarsely. "Now, I'm not so sure," and before George could stop him he turned and stumbled away down the slope through the pine trees.

It was very hot as Kate moved through the terraces to the garden. The small black dog barked at her as she went past the cottage. Old Anna waved from the kitchen, and then she reached the broad concrete steps and found Nicky fishing.

The water was crystal clear, the motor launch perfectly reflected in it. Nicky turned with a smile and she ran her fingers through his hair.

"Yassou!" she said in greeting, using one of the few Greek words she knew.

He pulled in the line, smiling eagerly. He was already twelve, old enough to have left school. His mother, a widow, worked in an Athens hotel, and he lived with Constantine and his wife for the moment, helping with the boat, learning how to fish. Kate was his special favorite from the beginning. He dogged her footsteps everywhere.

He took a grimy packet from the pocket of his jeans and offered her a piece of his grandmother's Turkish delight. It was so sweet as to usually make her feel slightly sick, but to refuse would have been an insult. She took the smallest piece, popped it into her mouth, and got it down as fast as she could.

She sat on one of the concrete steps. He crouched beside her and produced several Polaroid pictures from his shirt pocket.

"Oh, you're still taking those things, are you?" she said.

He passed them over one by one. There was old Constantine, his grandmother, one of Mikali on the terrace. One of herself sitting in the stern of the boat.

"Good?" he said.

"Very good."

Then he passed her the photo of Asa Morgan he had taken in the saloon the previous night.

She sat there staring at it, and it took several moments for the fact of it to sink in.

"Where did you get this?" she whispered. And then she turned and grabbed him by the arm. "When?" she demanded. "When was he here?" He stared at her uncomprehendingly, and she pointed at the boat and then at the photo. "When?"

His faced cleared. "Last night. From Hydra." He turned and pointed to the villa. "To house."

"But that isn't possible. It isn't possible." Her fingers tightened on his arm. "Where is he?" She waved the photograph at him again. "Where is he?"

"Gone," the boy said. "Gone."

He was a little afraid now, pulled away, and picked up his photos. When he tried to take the one of Morgan from her hand, she backed away. "No," she said, then turned and hurried down the steps, still clutching the photo, and ran along the tiny strip of beach. On the other side of the bay, a track climbed steeply through the pine trees. She followed it without the slightest idea of where she was going, aware of only one thing. Mikali had lied to her.

The track was steep and rocky, fit only for mules; difficult in the light sandals she wore. But she kept on climbing.

Finally, she breasted the ridge and came out on a small plateau.

She sank down on a log, exhausted for the moment. She was still clutching the Polaroid photo of Morgan. She stared at it blankly, then buried her face in her hands.

There was a movement close by. She looked up, and Morgan stepped out of the trees.

For a moment, she actually thought she was going out of her mind. "Asa?" she said. "It is you, isn't it?"

He came at her in a rush, had her over the log, a hand on her throat. "You bitch!" he said. "You bloody, lying whore!"

She felt herself choking, helpless against his strength and then was aware of George Ghika looming over them. He had Morgan by the hair and jerked back his head so sharply that Morgan cried out in pain, releasing his hold on her, and fell back.

Blood began to stain the bandage on his arm. He just lay there looking at her. "You knew all along. You warned him, didn't you? That's why he was expecting me last night."

"What happened?" she said.

"Oh, he put a bullet through me, and I went off the cliff into the sea. I'd be fish bait right now if it hadn't been for this old man and his wife."

"So, he is the Cretan. You were right."

"Are you trying to tell me you didn't know?"

She sat down on the log again, picked up the crumpled Polaroid photo and passed it to him. "Have a look at that, and let me explain about me and John Mikali."

Old George had diplomatically vanished from the scene, turning and walking away when she began to talk. When she was finished, Morgan sat there in silence for a while and she noticed there was sweat on his forehead.

"Do you believe me?"

He got up, sat beside her, and put an arm about her shoulders. "Couple of bloody fools, the pair of us, I dare say."

"Oh, Asa Morgan, I like you." She leaned her head on his shoulder, and his good arm tightened around her.

"Ah, well, that's my Welsh good looks for you, only I'm about twenty years too late, so no nonsense. Now let's go over a few things again. Deville, you said? Jean Paul Deville."

"That's right."

"I bet there's more to him than meets the bloody eye."

He was shaking a little, his face wet with sweat.

"What will you do now?" she said.

"I'm not sure. In other circumstances, I'd like to go down there and settle with him—only the state I'm in at the moment, I feel I might fall down if I breathe too deeply. At least I know where the bastard will be Saturday night. On stage at the Albert Hall."

He was in real pain now, she could see that. She said, "You should be in bed, Asa."

"You say he leaves for Athens this evening, to catch the night flight to London?"

"That's right."

"You'll be going with him, of course."

She sat there, staring at him blankly, hands folded in her lap. "To continue to share his bed, Asa, as if nothing has happened? To keep him warm for you till you get there?" She got to her feet, her face still unnaturally calm. "I should feel sorry for you, I suppose, but I don't. You're as possessed as he is. You deserve each other."

She walked away. When he tried to get up, he found that his legs refused to support him and called hoarsely, "Kate, for god's sake."

"And what on earth could He possibly have to do with it, Asa?" she said without turning around and disappeared into the pine trees.

There was a clatter of hooves behind him and George appeared with the mule, Maria following. The old woman was very angry. She put a hand on Morgan's forehead.

"Fool, there is a fever on thee already. Do you seek death?"

But he had nothing to say now—nothing at all—for it was like being under water, everything happening in slow motion. Between them, Maria and George got him into the saddle and started back up through the pine trees.

By the time they got him to the bed, his fever had risen, and he was shivering. George pulled blankets on, and Maria went to the kitchen and came back with a cup.

"Drink, boy," she ordered.

Morgan got it down. He was thinking of Katherine Riley.

"A great pity that, Mam," he said in Welsh. "A nice girl. But you know how it is?"

And then the darkness swallowed him up.

Mikali and Deville were at the far end of the rear terrace talking when she went in. She watched them for a while from behind a window in the sitting room, then went to the sideboard and poured herself a large gin and tonic. There was a slight movement, and Mikali slipped his arms around her waist.

"A little early for you, isn't it?"

"I'm tired," she said. "That's all."

He kissed her neck and turned her around, and there was concern on his face. "I hate to say it, angel, but you look awful."

"I know," she said. "I've been working like a dog and then the plane trip and last night in Athens." She paused and what came out next was somehow in spite of herself, but once said could not be taken back. "I was thinking. Would you mind very much if I hung on here for a couple of days?"

For a moment he hesitated and then smiled. "Why not? The rest would do you good. But I want you in London, Saturday, without fail. There'll be a seat in a box as close to me as I can get you. I need you there, angel. Something to share. Something to remember."

He held her close and kissed her. Amazing how easy it was, yet after all he was the same man, this man she had given her body to. The Cretan Lover from the beginning. The only difference was that now she knew it.

"If you don't mind, I think I'll go and lie down. I've got a splitting headache."

"Of course."

She went out, and Deville moved in through the French window.

"I think you should kill her."

"Why?" Mikali said calmly. "She knows nothing."

"You love her?"

"I don't know what that word means. I like her—

yes. Her presence, her company. She pleases me in these things more than any other woman I've ever known."

"The seeds of doubt have been planted in her. Who knows when they may germinate?"

"A particularly purple passage, even for you."

He sat down at the Bluthner, and his fingers started to play *Le Pastour* as if entirely of their own volition.

THIRTEEN

Morgan was tramping over the mountain on his way home from the pit again, half-running to beat the thunderstorm that threatened in the black, anvil-shaped clouds that filled the horizon.

The rains came, a downpour of such force that he was soaked to the skin in a moment. And the cold of it seemed to reach inside his brain so that he cried aloud in agony as he went down the hillside to the village below.

She had the door of the little cottage open as he stumbled along the path, her head draped in a black knitted shawl so that he couldn't see her face.

Her arms enfolded him, drawing him into the warmth. "Mam," he said. "I'm so cold. So bloody cold."

He was on his back, head against the pillow, only when she leaned over and the shawl slipped back, it was Katherine Riley who gazed down at him.

"It's all right, Asa. I'm here. Sleep now."

"Yes, Mam," he said, closed his eyes and did as he was told.

Morgan came awake from a dreamless sleep and lay staring up at the wattle and plaster ceiling over his head. He was himself again, his skin cool, the dull persistent ache in his arm and shoulder the only reminder of what he'd been through. It was daylight, sun streaming in through the window.

He could hear singing close at hand, and the dull rhythmic chopping of an ax against wood. Morgan flung back his blankets and got to his feet. He was no longer light-headed. Now there was only the pain and that was good; that would keep him sharp.

George was splitting logs for firewood, Maria was sitting on the bench in the sun, sewing a rent in Morgan's salt-stained jacket. His wallet was on the bench beside her, drying in the sun along with his passport and a row of drachma notes.

She put up a hand and touched his forehead. "So— the fever is gone?" She called to George. "See, old fool, who knows better than the doctor now?"

George leaned on his ax. "She is a witch," he said. "And all the women of her clan before her. This is a known fact."

"So you feel better?" she said.

"Much."

"Good. Many hours have you slept. It was a necessary thing, the potion I gave thee."

He glanced at his Rolex and saw that it was eight o'clock. He felt curiously light-headed as he walked through the pine trees to the ridge. He shaded his eyes, looking down to Mikali's villa in the bay below. Old George appeared at his side.

"They have gone?"

"Both of them."

"And the woman?"

The old man pointed. "See, she comes now."

She emerged from the trees into the clearing two

hundred feet below, following the tract that zigzagged between the old overgrown terraces. She was wearing sunglasses, tee-shirt, and an old cotton skirt, and carried a shoulder bag.

"She has concern for thee, this one, I think," the old man told him in Greek. "Many hours she sat beside thy bed."

Morgan sat down carefully on a log, his eyes never leaving her, and the old man placed a pack of Greek cigarettes and some matches beside him.

"I will tell Maria to make coffee," he said and walked away.

She emerged from the pine trees ten minutes later to find him sitting there on the log smoking. She paused for a moment to look at him, strangely annonymous in the dark glasses.

"So, you're back with us again?"

"That's what they tell me."

She sat down on the grass facing him, her back against a tree, and put the shoulder bag on the ground.

"What have you got in there?" he asked.

"Sandwiches, a bottle of wine. Constantine thinks I like to go walking in the mountains each day."

"And the old woman and the boy?"

"Oh, they're in Hydra at the Mikali town house. This time of the year they sometimes let tourists have a look round. It's something of a museum. Full of relics from the Turkish wars—that sort of thing."

There was an awkwardness between them that this kind of conversation couldn't bridge. He said, "Why did you stay?"

"In spite of myself," she said and removed her sunglasses. Her face was very pale, her eyes haunted. "I told him I was tired. Asked if he minded if I stayed on for a day or two."

"And he agreed?"

"On the understanding that I was in my seat on time at the Albert Hall."

"I see. So, he caught last night's plane? And Deville went with him."

"Last night." She shook her head slowly. "You've lost a day somewhere, Asa. This is Saturday—Saturday morning. They left the night before last."

He sat there staring at her, thunderstruck, unable to take it in. "Are you trying to tell me I've been out for the past thirty hours?"

"Something like that. Oh, you tossed and turned rather a lot, but Maria certainly knew what she was doing. Those herbs of hers are really quite something."

"But that means the concert's tonight." He jumped to his feet and stood there, hand clenched. "Don't you see! The bastard could be on his way again tomorrow."

"He phoned me last night," she said. "Told me he'd been with Previn at the Albert Hall, and that's where he'll be for most of today. Rehearsal for tonight's concert. It's really very simple. All you have to do is ring Baker at Scotland Yard."

There was a lengthy silence. Morgan said, "Yes, I could do that."

"But you won't, will you?"

He sat down on the log again and lit a cigarette.

"Look, let me explain. There's a section of DI5 called Group Four with new powers directly from the Prime Minister himself to coordinate the handling of terrorism, subversion, and so on. It's run by a man called Ferguson. Baker works for him. We go back a long way, Ferguson and me. He's quite a character. Would it surprise you to know he encouraged me in this thing from the beginning? Used me as a blunt instrument. Hoped I might succeed where they'd failed because I had that little extra something working for me—hate!"

"He was certainly right there."

"Yes, only now that I've found him, I want Mikali for myself."

"An eye for an eye. Is that the only way you see it? Blood for blood?"

"And why not? If I accuse him in Greece, they'll laugh at me. He's a national hero. If I let them arrest him in England, they'll give him fifteen years for shooting Cohen, and that's only if they can prove it. All his other killings have been elsewhere, remember. The Germans—the French. They'll all have to wait their turn."

"So?"

"After a while, Black September or the Red Brigade or whatever will hijack a British Airways plane one fine morning. The price for the return of the passengers and crew intact will be Mikali free and on his way to Libya or Cuba or somewhere similar."

"And you want to see him dead?"

"When I'm ready."

"I could get in touch with Baker myself."

He shook his head. "But you won't."

"Why not?"

"Because you owe me, girl." He touched his arm, then his shoulder, and winced. "I should be dead. That I'm not, is no thanks to you. And don't throw Jago at me. That was different and you know it."

She stood up instantly. "All right, Asa. You go to hell in your own way."

"And you?"

"I'll go back to London today. I'll carry on to Cambridge from there. I've had it. You and John Mikali, Asa, deserve each other."

"And you won't phone Baker?"

"No," she said. "Just go and play your bloody violent little games as far away from me as possible."

She walked away very rapidly. Morgan got up and watched her go, then he turned and went back to the farmhouse. Old George, still splitting logs, paused.

"She has gone?"

"Yes. What time is the next hydrofoil to the Piraeus?"

"Ten-thirty. Impossible to catch it now in my boat."

"And the next?"

"An hour after noon."

"Will you take me in?"

"If that is what you want."

Morgan walked to the farmhouse where Maria still sat sewing his jacket.

"My shirt?"

"On the line, drying in the sun. I have washed it for thee." Her eyes squinted up at him from the leathery old face. "But this, even my magic cannot put right."

She gave him his passport. Soaked by its immersion in the sea, it had buckled and twisted in the heat of the sun. When he tried to open it, it came apart in his hands.

"Christ Jesus!" he said in Welsh. "That's all I needed."

"Is that bad, boy?" she asked.

"It could be, mother. It could alter everything. I'll just have to see."

At the villa, Katherine Riley had just finished packing when the phone rang. When she picked it up, Mikali's voice sounded in her ear.

"Heh, you're still there. You should be here already."

"No problem," she said. "I'm leaving with Constantine now. We're using the speed boat. That means I'll catch the ten-thirty hydrofoil to the Piraeus. With any luck I should catch the one-thirty flight, our time." Amazing how calm she felt. "How are things going?"

"Marvelous." His enthusiasm was overflowing now. "Previn's a genius—the best damned conductor I've ever worked with, but it's going to take most of today to get it right, angel. So, if I'm not around when you get in, don't worry. You've got your key. Just make sure you're in that box tonight."

The line went dead. She stood there for a moment, holding the receiver, then replaced it. When she turned, Constantine stood just inside the door watching her. There was something in the face, in the dark eyes, as if he could see right through her. Knew everything. But that was nonsense.

She indicated her two suitcases, and picked up her raincoat. "All right," she said. "I'm ready," and went out of the door ahead of him.

* * *

Deville, sheltering from the rain under a tree on the edge of Hyde Park beside Park Lane, watched Mikali running very fast from the direction of the Serpentine. He wore a black track suit, a single scarlet stripe down each leg. He came to a halt a few yards away and stood, hands on hips, breathing easily.

Deville said, "You never let up, do you?"

"You know what they say," Mikali told him. "Old habits and all that kind of rubbish." He fell in beside him, and they walked toward the road. "So, you couldn't stay away after all? A good thing I reserved an additional seat in Katherine's box."

"She is here?" Deville asked.

"On her way. I spoke to her in Hydra this morning. She was just leaving."

"So?" Deville nodded and went on calmly. "Well then, so that we may understand each other. I have not come to attend your concert, John. I have come for you."

Mikali paused, turning to face him, his hand sliding around to the butt of the Ceska in the Burns and Martin holder under his track suit tunic at the rear.

Deville raised a hand defensively. "No, my dear, dear friend, you mistake me." He produced an envelope. "Tickets for both of us. The night flight to Paris, leaving Heathrow at eleven-fifteen. Ample time for you to make your appearance at the Albert Hall. I understand that on the last night of the Proms, the concerto is played during the first half on the concert."

"And afterward?"

"We arrive in Paris in time to make connections with an Aeroflot flight to Moscow. All taken care of.

There was an item in *Paris Soir* today announcing that you intend to give a series of master classes to the Moscow Conservatoire."

Mikali stood, gazing out across Park Lane, then turned and looked down toward the Serpentine. He took a deep breath, lifted his face to the rain.

"Marvelous," he said. "Early morning in London. Nothing quite like it. Unless you prefer the smell of those damp chestnut trees in Paris." He put a hand on Deville's shoulder. "Sorry, old buddy, but that's the way it is."

Deville shrugged. "You have a whole day in which to change your mind."

"An entire day of rehearsals," Mikali said. "So I've got to get moving. If Previn's there before me he'll insist on making the tea. He always does, and it's lousy."

"You don't mind if I use the apartment?"

"Of course not. I doubt whether I'll have time to get back before the concert, though. If you change your mind about coming, there'll be a ticket waiting at the box office."

They stood at the pavement's edge waiting for the lights to change and he clapped Deville on the shoulder.

"A great night, Jean Paul. The greatest of my life, I think."

As the Trident started its descent to Heathrow in the late afternoon sun, Katherine Riley obeyed the request to fasten her seat belt, then leaned back in her seat.

She was tired—more tired than she had ever been in her life before. Tired, angry, and frustrated. She knew the syndrome well as any practicing psychologist should. Like being in a dark wood in some childhood dream, undecided on which path to take and some nameless evil coming up fast.

She closed her eyes and saw not John Mikali, but Asa Morgan's dark, ravaged face, the pain in the eyes and suddenly knew, with total clarity, that she was wrong.

Morgan had said that she owed him. If that was true, what he was due was her honesty and concern and that could only be expressed in one way.

It was like a shot in the arm, new energy coursing through her. She couldn't wait to get off the plane, was one of the first through to immigration where she presented her passport and asked to be put in touch at once with the nearest Special Branch officer.

It was just after half past two when Captain Charles Rourke got back to his office in the British Embassy at Plutarchu 1 in Athens. His phone rang almost at once. When he picked it up, Benson, one of the Second Secretaries with consular responsibilities, was on the other end.

"Hello, Charles. I asked them on the door to let me know when you came in. I've had a chap kicking his heels here for almost an hour, wanting a temporary passport to get him home. His official one is in pieces."

"Hardly my department, old boy."

"Actually, Charles, I don't like the smell of it at all. He walks in here looking like a tramp and when I examine what's left of his passport, he turns out to be a serving officer if you please *and* a full colonel. Name of Morgan."

But Rourke had already slammed down the telephone and was leaving his office on the run.

Morgan looked awful, the black, silver-streaked hair tousled like a gypsy's, and he badly needed a shave. His linen suit, stained with salt, had shrunk and strained against his shoulders, seams splitting.

"Oh, it's you," he said when Rourke came into the waiting room. "A fine old balls-up you made of it at the airport the other day."

Rourke was horrified at his appearance. "Good god, are you all right?"

"Of course I'm not," Morgan said. "I'm held together by blood, guts, and wire, but that doesn't matter now. What I want is a temporary passport and a seat on the first available plane to London this afternoon."

"Actually, I'm not too sure about that, sir. I'd have to check elsewhere first. I've strict orders where you're concerned."

"Brigadier Ferguson?"

"Yes, sir."

"So, you're DI5? That's encouraging. Maybe those lectures I gave you at the Academy back in '69 did some good after all."

"You remembered me, sir?"

"Of course I did. Never forget a face. Now, you cut along and make your phone call."

"Just a minute, sir." Rourke leaned forward, concern on his face. "Isn't that blood coming through your sleeve?"

"I should imagine so, considering the fact that a certain gentleman tried to inflict bodily injury on me with the aid of a Walther PPK. Maybe a doctor would be in order as well, while you're at it? Only make sure he's one who can keep his mouth shut, boy. I don't want anything keeping me off that plane."

FOURTEEN

It was almost six o'clock when Kim answered the ring at the door of the Cavendish Square flat and found Baker and Morgan standing there.

Ferguson was in the dining room eating alone at one end of an elegant Regency table, a napkin tucked into his collar.

"That smells nice," Morgan said. "What is it?"

"Beef Wellington. For a Ghurka, Kim has a remarkable talent for traditional English cooking. My dear chap, you look awful."

"I'm not as young as I was, that's all."

He went and helped himself to a brandy from the sideboard. Ferguson said to Baker, "No problems, Superintendent?"

"He nearly didn't make it, sir. Fog coming in fast while I was waiting. I should imagine Heathrow will be shut down completely in another couple of hours."

Ferguson took a sip from his glass of claret and leaned back. "Well, Asa?"

"Well, what?"

"Come on now. You quite obviously went to Greece in search of the Cretan Lover. You deliberately gave my man the slip, then turn up four days later with a

couple of gunshot wounds in you and a ruined passport, desperately keen to get back to England as soon
as possible."

"All those tourists," Morgan said. "I just couldn't
take it." He emptied the glass. "Is it all right if I
go now? I could do with a decent night's sleep."

Ferguson nodded to Baker, who opened the sitting
room door. Katherine Riley entered.

"Christ almighty," Morgan said bitterly.

"Don't be stupid, Asa. Doctor Riley has acted entirely in your best interests and under very difficult
circumstances. She's told me everything."

Katherine Riley stood there, very pale, waiting.
Morgan ignored her. "Where is he?"

"Mikali? Busy rehearsing at the Albert Hall with
André Previn. Previn being the perfectionist he is, it
looks as if they'll be there right up till concert time."

"Rather awkward for you."

"Why on earth should it be?" Ferguson poured himself another glass of claret. "We could arrest him on
stage now, but why spoil the musical event of the
season for so many people. Ask the Superintendent."

Morgan turned to Baker, who nodded. "Sealed up
tight, Asa, every entrance guarded. I've got over fifty
men down there now on top of the normal uniformed
personnel usually on duty for crowd control. Mostly
in plain clothes and all of them armed. I've even
got long-hairs from the Ghost Squad queueing for
tickets with the Promenaders."

The phone rang in the hall, and Baker went out.
Ferguson said, "So, as you can see, he isn't getting
anywhere. Let him give his concert. The show, as they
say, must go on. In any case, my dear Asa, Rachmaninov's Fourth is seldom played. To have John

Mikali perform it at the last night of the Proms is a musical event of the first magnitude. I wouldn't miss it for anything."

Katherine Riley turned, went into the sitting room, and slammed the door behind her. Ferguson sighed. "Women really are the most perverse of creatures, aren't they? Why is it the Mikalis that attract them?"

Baker returned with a note. "Apparently this Frenchman, Deville, who visited Mikali at Hydra, is at the flat now. When I contacted French Intelligence about him, they thought I was crazy. He's one of the most celebrated criminal lawyers in Paris. Anyway, they did put him through the computer."

"And?" Ferguson said.

"One interesting point, sir. He was a slave worker for the Nazis during the war. One of thousands shipped to eastern Europe to work in coalmines and so on. Those who survived were returned by the Russians in 1947."

Ferguson smiled softly and turned to Morgan. "And what would that suggest to you, Asa?"

"KGB?"

"Perhaps, but their main task was to infiltrate the French Intelligence system itself in the years after the war. I should have thought Soviet Military Intelligence much more likely. From the sound of him, Deville has style, something I've always found conspicuously lacking in the KGB."

"Even the old Etonian variety?"

"A fair point." Ferguson wiped his chin with a napkin. "But a man like Mikali. It really is quite astonishing. Why, Asa? What is his motive?"

"I haven't the slightest idea. I can tell you where his experience came from, that's all. He joined the

Legion when he was eighteen. Served two years in Algeria as a paratrooper."

"How very romantic of him."

"Excuse me, sir," Baker interrupted. "Might I ask about Deville? Do you want him detained now?"

"A moment, Superintendent." Ferguson turned to Morgan. "I think, Asa, it might be politic at this point if you slipped next door and made your peace with Doctor Riley."

"Which means you don't want me in on this discussion?"

"Exactly."

Baker opened the sitting room door. Morgan hesitated, then passed inside, and the Superintendent closed it behind him.

Katherine Riley stood at the Adam fireplace, her hands on the mantelshelf, staring into the flames. She raised her head and looked at him in the ornate ormolu mirror.

"You've been in hell without a map, Asa. I couldn't leave you there."

"Oh, but you have a way with the words," he said. "I'll give you that. That's what comes of an expensive education."

"Asa—please." There was real pain in her voice now.

"I know," he said harshly. "Passion had you by the throat and wouldn't let go. But who for? Me or him?"

She stood there, staring at him, her face even paler now. When she spoke, her voice was very low.

"We washed you between us the other night, Maria and I. How many times have you been wounded?

Five? Six? And those are only the scars that show. I'm sorry for you."

She walked past him, opened the door, and went into the other room. Ferguson looked up, and Baker turned to face her.

"Can I go now?" she asked.

Ferguson glanced at Morgan standing in the doorway. She leaned forward, her hands on the dining table. "Please!" she demanded urgently. "I can't take much more of this."

Ferguson said, "And where would you go, Doctor Riley?"

"I have the use of a friend's flat in Douro Place. My car's there. I just want to get back to Cambridge as soon as possible."

His face was very calm and his voice surprisingly gentle when he said, "And that *is* what you want to do? You're quite sure?"

"Yes," she said dully.

"Very well." He nodded to Baker. "Put Doctor Riley in a car, Superintendent. Have her taken to this address in Douro Place. We can always contact her in Cambridge if we need her."

She made for the door, and Baker went after her. As she got it open, Ferguson said, "One point, Doctor. Please don't try to leave the country until you receive full security clearance. It really would be most embarrassing to have to stop you."

Kim came in with a covered dish. Ferguson said, "Ah, pudding. I was beginning to think he'd forgotten." He sat down and tucked his napkin into his neck again, and the Ghurka served him. "A rather special cheesecake, soaked in Grand Marnier. Try some, Asa."

"No thanks," Morgan said. "But I'll have another brandy if you don't mind."

"Help yourself. Is it hurting much, your arm?"

"Like hell," Morgan told him, which was true. Yet he deliberately exaggerated the pain in his face as he poured a generous measure of Courvoisier into a shot glass.

As he swallowed, Baker came back. Ferguson said, "No problem?"

"None, sir."

"Good. Mikali's made no attempt to leave?"

"No, sir, I've just phoned our mobile command post in the car park there. The most recent information is that they've just finished rehearsing."

Ferguson glanced at his watch. "Six-fifteen. Let me see now. The concert starts with Debussy. *L'Après-midi d'un faune* followed by Haydn's *Clock* Symphony. That means Mikali will go on around eight-forty-five with the interval at nine-thirty."

"And we arrest him then, sir?"

"After the interval reception would be better, I think. He *is* guest of honor, remember. It would look a little odd if he wasn't there. Let's keep things as normal as possible for as long as we can."

Morgan fingered his arm, an expression of real pain on his face. In spite of that, there was something very close to pleading in his voice when he said to Ferguson, "In all the time we've known each other, I've never begged, Charles, but I'm begging now. Let me go with you."

"I'm sorry, Asa. I understand how you feel, but you've done your job. Your involvement ends here. From now on this is police business."

"All right." Morgan raised a hand. "I know when I'm beaten. Presumably I can go now."

He turned to the door and Baker said, "Wait for me, Asa, I'll run you home."

Morgan went out, and Ferguson said, "Knows when he's beaten indeed. It's when he makes remarks like that that I *really* worry. Take him home. I want 'round-the-clock surveillance of his apartment until this thing is over."

"I wouldn't worry, sir. The state he's in, I'm surprised he managed to walk to the door."

"If you believe that of Asa Morgan, Superintendent," Ferguson said, "then you will indeed believe anything."

When Mikali went into the Green Room at the back of the Albert Hall stage, his shirt was soaked with sweat, and he was trembling with excitement. He had been good, he knew that. The hardest two days of rehearsals he had ever undergone, and the prospect for the concert itself was now quite stunning.

The door opened, and the stage manager came in with a pot of tea, cups, milk, and sugar on an old tin tray.

"Did you try Heathrow?" Mikali demanded as he dried himself with a towel.

"Yes, sir. Both afternoon flights from Athens got in, the last one just before the fog descended."

"Marvelous," Mikali said. "Don't forget to make sure Doctor Riley's ticket is ready at the box office— and Maître Deville's."

As the stage manager opened the door, Previn came in. "Everything all right?"

"It is now," Mikali told him. "Was I good out there?"

"Not bad," Previn grinned. "In places."

"In places?" Mikali laughed out loud. "Maestro, tonight I'm going to give you the performance you've been waiting for all your life." He clapped Previn on the shoulder. "Now, have a decent cup of tea for a change."

When they reached Gresham Place, Baker told the driver to wait, and they went up the steps to the entrance.

Morgan said, "Do you feel like a drink?"

"Don't have the time."

He gave Morgan a cigarette, lit one himself, and they stood there in the porch smoking and staring out at the driving rain.

"Do you ever wonder what it's all about, Harry?"

"Too late for finer feelings, Asa. About twenty-five years too late in your case."

"So what do I do?"

"Go to bed before you fall down."

Another police car drew up on the far side of the street, and Detective Inspector Stewart got out followed by two uniformed constables. They paused at the bottom of the steps.

Baker said, "Colonel Morgan here is about to retire for the night. If he changes his plans, tries to leave these premises for any reason whatever, you will take him into immediate custody. One of you can watch this entrance from the car, the other get round to the courtyard at the rear."

"You'll be relieved in four hours," Stewart told

them. They moved away, and he turned to Baker. "Anything else, sir?"

"No, get in the car, George, we'll be leaving directly."

Morgan said, "Is all this legal, Harry?"

"Ferguson could have had you taken into custody if he'd wanted, until it was over."

"On what charge?"

"Suspicious person would do for a start, suffering from gunshot wounds with no adequate explanation." He tossed his cigarette into the gutter. "Be sensible, Asa. Go to bed."

He went down the steps, got into the rear of the police car beside Stewart, and was driven away. Morgan looked across the street at the other car, waved to the young policeman behind the wheel, then went inside.

Jock Kelso was watching a football match on television when the phone rang. His daughter, Amy, a pretty, dark-haired girl, came in from the kitchen drying her hands on her apron and answered it.

"It's Colonel Morgan, Dad."

Kelso switched off the television and took the receiver from her. "Colonel?"

"Jock. I have a slight problem. A police car parked at my front door and a copper in the rear courtyard to make sure I don't leave. Brigadier Ferguson wants to keep me out of trouble. I was wondering if there was anything you could do about it."

Kelso laughed. "Christ, Colonel, but this gets more like old times by the minute."

Morgan put down the phone, opened the desk

drawer, and took out the Walther PPK. He checked
the magazine carefully, then fitted the Carswell silencer over the muzzle.

He was beginning to feel tired, and that would
never do. He went into the bathroom, opened the
cabinet above the sink, and found a small bottle of
purple capsules. "Belfast bullets" the army called
them because they were designed to get you through
the bad times when rest was impossible. Two every
four hours and you could manage for twenty-four
without sleep. The only trouble was you were like a
corpse for a week afterward.

He swallowed two with the aid of a glass of water,
went back into the sitting room, sat down by the
window, and waited.

It was just after seven-fifteen, and Deville was
making coffee in the kitchen of the flat in Upper
Grosvenor Street when the door bell rang. He poised,
instantly alert, and moved to the kitchen door still
holding the can of coffee beans in one hand, a spoon
in the other.

The bell rang again. Obviously not Mikali. He
would have his key, unless he'd forgotten it, but it
was unlikely that he'd put in an appearance at this
hour so close to the concert. It could, of course, be
Katherine Riley, but it occurred to Deville that she
would be more than likely to have a key of her own.

In the same moment he decided to let it go, a key
rattled in the lock, the door opened, and Ferguson
entered. Deville was aware of Baker standing behind
him, a lock pick in one hand.

Ferguson said, "Thank you, Superintendent. You
can wait downstairs. We shan't be long."

He wore a greatcoat of the type favored by officers of the Household Brigade and his umbrella was damp with rain. He leaned it against a chair.

"Shocking weather for the time of year." He smiled faintly. "You know me, I think."

Deville, familiar with the faces of every important intelligence chief in the Western World for his entire career, nodded gravely. *So it had come,* he thought, *after twenty-five years. The moment that had always been possible. The moment they came through the door for him when least expected.*

There was a golden lion fob on the watch chain that stretched from one pocket of Deville's waistcoat to the other. He touched it casually, feeling for the catch.

Ferguson said, "Is that where you keep it, the cyanide capsule? How very old-fashioned. They used to issue them to us during the war. I always threw mine away. Supposed to be quick, but I was once in the presence of an SS general who took one and didn't stop screaming for the next twenty minutes. Beastly way to go."

He walked to the sideboard, took the stopper out of the whiskey decanter, and sniffed. He nodded his approval and poured himself one.

Deville said, "What would you suggest?"

Ferguson moved to the window and peered down into the rain-filled street. "Well, you could try something desperately heroic like making a run for it, but let's say you managed to make the Soviet Embassy and they shipped you home. I don't think they'd be too pleased with you. You see, at the end of the day, you've failed, and I've always understood they're not too keen on that. Of course, they do have a civilized attitude toward capital punishment. They don't hang people. They send them to the Gulag instead which, if Solzhenitsyn is to be believed, is not a particularly pleasant place. On the other hand, Moscow has always asserted his works to be vicious Western propaganda."

"And the alternative?" Deville asked.

"The French—you are a French citizen, are you not, Maître Deville?—would have the right to demand your extradition and their intelligence people have been highly sensitive about Russian agents since the Sapphire affair in '68 and the suggestion that they had been penetrated by the KGB. You would undoubtedly be handed over to Service Five and they really are very old-fashioned when it comes to squeezing information out of people. They still believe in the power of electricity, I hear, especially when wired to various portions of some unfortunate individual's anatomy."

"And you?" Deville said. "What would you have to offer?"

"Oh, death, of course," Ferguson said cheerfully. "We'll think of something. Car accidents are always good, especially when there's a fire. It makes the identification usually a matter of what's in the pockets."

"And afterwards?"

"Peace, anonymity, a quiet life. Plastic surgery can do wonders."

"In return for the right kind of information?"

Ferguson went to the decanter and poured himself another whiskey, then he turned, sitting on the edge of the table.

"In 1943, when I was with SOE and working with the French underground, I found myself, thanks to an informer, in the hands of the Gestapo in Paris in their old headquarters in the Rue de Saussaies at the back of the Ministry of the Interior. They still believed in rubber hoses then. Very unpleasant."

"You escaped?"

"From a train on the way to Sachsenhausen concentration camp, but it's an old story." He walked to the window and peered down into the street again. "It was simpler then. We knew where we were. What we were fighting for. But now. . . ."

There was a lengthy silence before he said without turning around, "Of course, there's still the cyanide capsule."

"You give me a choice?"

"British sense of fair play, old man. I was a perfect at Winchester, you see."

He turned and found Deville holding out his right hand, the small black capsule in the center of the palm. "I don't think so, thank you very much."

"Excellent." Ferguson took it from him gingerly. "Nasty things." He dropped it on the parquet floor and ground his heel into it.

"What now?" Deville asked.

"Oh, a little good music, I think," Ferguson said. "You'd like that. I hear John Mikali's playing Rachmaninov's Fourth at the Albert Hall tonight. Something of an occasion."

"I'm sure it will be." Deville pulled on his dark overcoat, took his black Homburg from the stand by the door.

"One thing," Ferguson said. "Just to settle my idle curiosity. KGB or GRU?"

"GRU," Deville said. "Colonel Nikolay Ashimov."

The name sounded strange on his tongue. Ferguson

smiled. "Just as I thought. I told Morgan I thought
you had too much style to be KGB. Shall we go?"

He opened the door, standing courteously to one
side, and Deville led the way out.

And at that moment, Katherine Riley, proceeding
in heavy traffic and driving rain along the North Circular Road, swung the wheel of her MGB sports car
into a side street and braked to a halt.

She switched off the engine and sat there for a
moment, aware of the beating of her own heart, hands
gripping the wheel tightly. Finally, the breath went
out of her in a long sigh. There was only one place in
the world she wanted to go to now, and it certainly
wasn't Cambridge.

She started the engine, drove to the end of the
street, and turned back toward central London.

FIFTEEN

In the Green Room behind the stage at the Albert Hall, Mikali stood in front of the mirror and adjusted his white tie. Then he opened his dressing case, removed the false base revealing the Burns and Martin spring holster containing the Ceska. He clipped the holster to his belt at the small of his back, then put on his elegant black tailcoat with a single white carnation in the buttonhole.

On stage, the orchestra was coming into the closing stages of Haydn's *Symphony No 101, in D major*, known to concertgoers the world over as *The Clock*.

He opened the door and went out into the passage. The stage manager was standing at the end of the Bullrun, the sloping gangway that was the artist's entrance to the stage. He moved a little way along until he could see Previn on the conductor's stand and beyond him at stage left, on the very end of the curve, the loggia box that he had reserved for Katherine Riley. There was no sign of her or of Deville.

His disappointment was acute, and he went back into the Green Room at once, found a coin and dialed the flat, using the pay phone on the wall. He allowed the phone to ring for a full minute at the other end, then replaced the receiver and tried again with the same lack of success.

"Come on, Katherine," he said in a low voice. "Where in the hell are you?"

The door opened, and the stage manager looked in. "Ten minutes, Mr. Mikali. Right old crowd out there tonight, I can tell you."

Mikali smiled brightly. "I can't wait."

"Cup of tea, sir?"

"My own weakness, Brian, you know that."

The stage manager went out, and Mikali lit a cigarette and smoked it furiously, pacing up and down. He stopped abruptly, stubbed out the cigarette, and sat at the old upright Chappell piano against the wall, flexed his fingers, and started to run through a series of scales.

The only thing that interested the driver of the police car parked outside Morgan's flat was the color of the small mini van which drew up. Bright yellow. *The Flower Basket—Interflora—24-Hour Delivery Service.*

The driver was wearing a cloth cap and a heavy oilskin coat the color of the van, the collar turned up against the rain. He produced a large gift-wrapped bouquet, ran up the steps, and went inside.

The first thing Morgan saw when he opened the door was the bouquet of flowers, and then the figure in the yellow oilskin coat moved past him into the flat.

He closed the door and turned to discover that it was, in fact, a very attractive young woman, which only became apparent when she took off the cloth cap.

"And who in the hell might you be?" he said as she unbuttoned the oilskin coat.

"Amy Kelso, Colonel. I've grown some since you last saw me, but we haven't time for conversation. Please put the coat and cap on. You'll find a yellow mini van at the entrance. Get in and drive round to Park Street. My father's waiting there in a white Ford Cortina."

"But what about you?" he demanded as he pulled on the oilskin.

"Just leave the mini in Park Street. I'll pick it up within five minutes. Get moving, Colonel, please!"

Morgan hesitated, then pulled on the cloth cap, picked up the carryall, and moved to the door.

"And keep your collar up."

The door closed behind him. Underneath the oilskin she had been wearing a light, town raincoat. Now, her hands went to the hair piled high on top of her head. She withdrew the pins quickly and then combed it down shoulder-length.

A couple of minutes after the mini van had driven away, the driver of the police car saw Amy Kelso emerge from the entrance. She paused, looking out at the rain, then went down the steps and hurried away.

With frank admiration he watched her turn the corner and move out of sight. He would not have been so pleased if he could have seen her reach the yellow mini van in Park Street, slip behind the wheel, and drive away.

When Katherine Riley hurried through the glass portico and went into the foyer at the front of the Albert Hall, the first person she saw was Harry Baker talking to two uniformed police officers. He saw her at once and cut her off in a few quick strides as she made for the box office.

"Now then, Doctor, what's all this?"

"There's a ticket waiting for me."

He shook his head, took her by the elbow, and propelled her firmly outside again. An anonymous-looking van was standing in the small official car park, the Special Branch headquarters for the operation. Ferguson's car was parked beside it. He was seated in the rear with Deville.

The Brigadier opened the door and got out. "What happened to Cambridge?"

"I changed my mind," she said. "I decided I wanted to hear him play again."

"And that's all? No foolish ideas . . . ?"

"Of what, Brigadier? Warning him? And where could he go?"

"True." Ferguson nodded.

She looked beyond him at the Frenchman. "You, too, Monsieur Deville?"

"So it would appear, Mademoiselle."

She looked again at Ferguson. "May I go now?"

"Yes, you can go, Doctor. You deserve your last act if anyone does."

She turned and hurried back to the entrance. Ferguson leaned in the car. "He should be starting at any moment. Would you like to go in now, Maître?"

Deville shook his head. "Not really, Brigadier. You see, strange as it may seem in the circumstances, the piano, as an instrument, has never appealed to me."

In the Green Room, Mikali adjusted his tie in the mirror while Previn waited by the door. There was a knock, and the stage manager looked in.

"Ready, gentlemen."

Previn smiled and held out his hand. "Good luck,
John."

The Albert Hall was packed from floor to ceiling.
Besides the second-tier boxes, the loggia, the balcony,
the stalls, there were fifteen-hundred promenaders,
many in the gallery, the bulk packed into the arena
in front of the stage, standing shoulder-to-shoulder,
crowded against the rail, mainly young people and students in fancy dress, the common tradition on this,
the last night of the Proms.

And when Previn led the way out onto the stage
followed by Mikali, the roar was like nothing Mikali
had ever known, sending the blood racing through
his veins, filling him with excitement and emotion.

He stood there, bowing again and again, and Previn was laughing, applauding also. Then Mikali
turned and glanced up to the loggia box on the end
of the curve just across from the stage and saw Katherine Riley sitting there.

He threaded his way through the orchestra, plucked
the white carnation from his buttonhole, and tossed
it up to her.

She caught the carnation, held it, staring down
at him as if in a dream. With everyone watching her,
she had to do what they expected of her, and yet there
was more to it. She kissed the flower and threw it
back to him. Mikali replaced it in his buttonhole and
blew her a kiss in return. The Promenaders howled
their delight as he went to the piano and sat down.

All noise in the hall faded. There was total si-

lence. Previn, as was commonly the case, preferred
to conduct a concerto from the stage itself and stood
very close to the piano.

He half turned to Mikali, face serious now. The
baton descended and, as the orchestra commenced
to play, Mikali's fingers fused with the keyboard.

Kelso turned the Cortina into Prince Consort
Road and pulled in at the curb. He kept the engine
running and turned to Morgan.

"Anything more I can do, Colonel?"

"Forget you ever saw me if you know what's good
for you."

"That'll be the day," Kelso told him.

Morgan, who was wearing an old trenchcoat and
tweed cap provided by the sergeant major, got out
and leaned down at the window.

"Thanks, Jock. Now, get the hell out of here."

The Cortina drove rapidly way, and Morgan raised
the collar of his coat against the rain and moved
toward the back of the Hall. He paused by the Prince
Consort's statue and looked across at the rear entrance. There were three uniformed police standing
there at the bottom of the steps. In fact, at least one
on duty at every other door he could see, capes
glistening in the rain.

At that moment, a truck came around the corner
and pulled up outside the artists' entrance. It carried the name of one of the best-known breweries in
London on the side panel. As Morgan watched, three
or four porters came out wearing caps and coats
against the rain and started to unload extra crates of
beer while the two policemen on duty at the door
looked on.

Morgan darted across the road and stood in the shadows at the side of the vehicle, waiting for an appropriate moment. The two young policemen had their heads together, laughing. A porter came out, picked up a crate and turned back inside. Morgan, without hesitation, moved around the tailboard, picked up the next crate, hoisted it onto his shoulder and made straight for the door.

There was a burst of laughter from the policemen, but it was already behind him. He passed the stage doorkeeper's office on his left, turned right into the corridor and kept on going, aware of the porter a few yards ahead of him, obviously making for one of the bars.

He came to an open door on his right giving access to a staircase. He moved through quickly, dumped the crate in the shadows, and mounted to the next landing.

He could hear the orchestra very clearly now and the piano, somewhere close at hand, and emerged onto one of the long curved corridors so typical of the Albert Hall. There was a door marked *Exit* opposite. He opened it, stepped inside, and found himself at the head of the gangway leading down to the stairs and the arena at the left-hand side of the stage. And there, at last, was John Mikali.

Mikali, close to the end of the final movement, was waiting, flexing his fingers as the orchestra carried the theme through, breathing deeply, priming himself for the enormous physical effort that would be required in the final moments.

He looked up at André Previn, watching him closely, waiting, and in the same moment saw beyond the conductor the exit door at the top of the gangway open and Asa Morgan step through.

The shock was so enormous that for a moment, he sat there as if turned to stone. Katherine Riley, who had been watching him closely, followed his gaze, but Morgan had already stepped back through the door and disappeared.

My God, Mikali thought. *He's alive. The bastard actually managed to survive and now, he's dared to come for me.* A line from the *Bushido* flashed through his mind. *No deeper loneliness than the Samourai's. None but the tiger's in the jungle perhaps.*

He was not afraid, but filled with a fierce joy at the prospect of facing Morgan again. As Previn nodded sharply, Mikali plunged into the dramatic finale of the concerto, playing as he had never before played.

And at the end, there was a roar from the audience such as he had never heard in his entire musical career. They were all applauding. The orchestra, Previn, the promenaders pressed up against the rail, reaching toward him.

He looked up at the loggia box, saw Katherine Riley standing there, gripping the rail, staring down at him, then Previn had him by the elbow and was pushing him down the Bullrun.

The stage manager was standing outside the Green Room, a glass of champagne in each hand.

"I've never heard anything like it," he said as the noise increased, the promenaders starting to chant Mikali's name.

Mikali swallowed warm champagne and grinned lightly. "Was I good, Maestro, or only in places?"

Previn, obviously greatly moved, toasted him. "My dear friend, occasionally life has its great moments. Tonight was very definitely one of them. I thank you."

Mikali smiled and drank some more champagne, looking beyond him to the end of the passage where it joined the main corridor and thought of Morgan, at large in this old rabbit warren of a building, probably waiting just out there in the shadows.

At that confrontation in the villa at Hydra he'd said he wanted Mikali for himself. No reason to think any different now. Nothing, after all, had changed.

The roaring grew more insistent. Previn said, "Come on, John, if we don't go back they'll invade the stage."

When they emerged again, the crowd began to chant, "Mikali! Mikali!" and flowers started to sail over, university scarves, hats. The entire audience was standing now, applauding. Thanking him for allowing them to share a unique experience.

He nodded, smiling, waving both hands, blowing a kiss up to Katherine Riley. All he could think of was that there was only one way off stage: straight down the Bullrun to the corridor beyond, where Morgan had to be waiting.

And then it occurred to him that that wasn't quite true. He turned and shook hands with the First Violin, moved past him and close to the rail. Below, twelve feet down, was the gangway leading to the arena corridor.

He leaned forward, waving to the front line of promenaders. "You're really too much," he called. "Too beautiful for words. I don't think I can take any more."

He put one foot on the rail and simply dropped from sight, down into the gangway. There were several screams, a sudden uproar, but he landed safely. The gangway door banged and he was gone.

And then there was only laughter and thunderous applause, everyone joining in, even the orchestra, at what must surely have been the most unorthodox departure from the stage by a major artist ever witnessed in the long history of the Royal Albert Hall.

The arena corridor was deserted, but at any moment, people would be pouring out into the corridors at every level of the building, making for the bars during the interval. The third exit door took him out onto the stairs leading to the rear entrance.

Harry Baker was talking to two uniformed policemen in the foyer below. Mikali recognized him instantly, turned, and went back up the stairs.

Could it be that he was wrong? That Morgan had done the sensible thing after all? He hurried along the arena corridor, still deserted, and made for the exit leading to the stage doorkeeper's office and the artists' entrance.

When he reached it, he peered around cautiously and saw two uniformed policemen standing inside out of the rain, something he had never known before in all his experience of the Albert Hall.

It was enough. That sixth sense that had kept him alive for so long now, scenting danger like some jungle animal, told him he was in deep trouble.

He turned and started to hurry back along the arena corridor, a strange, elegant, lonely figure in white tie and black tailcoat. A moment later, André Previn and a whole host of people in evening dress came around the curve up ahead and bore down on him.

In a second he was surrounded by excited admirers. Previn said, "What were you trying to do back there? Break your neck? That was a unique way to leave the stage—even for the last night of the Proms."

"Just trying to add to the tradition in my own small way," Mikali said.

"Well, they're all waiting for you in the Prince Consort Room. The Duchess of Kent, the Greek Ambassador, the Prime Minister. Not done to keep them waiting." Previn laughed. "This is England, you know."

He took Mikali by the elbow and propelled him firmly along the corridor.

The stairway leading up to the Prince Consort Room was jammed with people, and Katherine Riley had to use all her strength to force her way through. She finally reached the glass doors and found her way barred by a uniformed porter.

"Invitation, please, Miss."

"I haven't got one," she said. "But I'm a personal friend of Mr. Mikali's."

"So are a lot of other people tonight, Miss." He gestured down the packed staircase and a group of students started to call, "Mikali! Mikali!"

Beyond, through the glass door, she could see the room crowded with elegantly gowned women, the men in evening dress except for Chief Superintendent Harry Baker in a dark blue suit standing with his back to the door.

She reached beyond the porter and rapped on the glass. As the porter restrained her, Baker turned. He looked at her gravely for a moment, then opened the door.

"It's all right, I'll handle it." He took her by the arm and led her into the corner of the landing. "It's no good, Doctor, he's finished. Nothing there for you anymore."

"I know that," she said.

He stood there, staring down at her for a moment, and then he did a surprising thing. He smoothed her hair gently with one hard and shook his head.

"Women. You're all the same. Never learn, do you?"

He opened the door, stood to one side, and motioned her in.

Edward Heath, the British Prime Minister, was himself a musician of no mean ability, and he shook Mikali's hand enthusiastically.

"Quite extraordinary, Mr. Mikali. A night to remember."

"Why thank you, sir."

Mikali walked on, shepherded by Previn toward the Duchess of Kent, who was as charming and knowledgeable as always.

"I don't think you've recorded Rachmaninov's Fourth together, have you?" she asked.

Previn smiled. "No, ma'am, but I think we may say with certainty that after John's performance tonight that omission should be rectified in the very near future."

Mikali left them talking and moved on shaking dozens of hands. He paused to talk to the Greek Ambassador, not really taking in what he was saying, his eyes moving restlessly around the room, half-expecting to see Morgan's ravaged face staring out at him from the crowd.

Instead, he saw Katherine Riley over by the door standing beside Baker. He smiled wryly, so many things falling into place now, and started toward her. And then, as the crowd parted, he saw Ferguson and Jean Paul Deville standing against the wall drinking champagne.

He hesitated, then walked toward them. "Jean Paul," he said easily.

Deville said, "I think you know Brigadier Ferguson."

Mikali took an elegant gold case from his inside pocket and selected a cigarette. "Only by reputation. You take an excellent photo, Brigadier." He offered the case. "Greek, I'm afraid. I'm very ethnic. They may not be to your liking."

"On the contrary." Ferguson took one and accepted the light.

"And Colonel Morgan of the nine lives? Isn't he joining us?"

"No," Ferguson said. "I wouldn't exactly say he's safely tucked up in bed, but he *is* under what you might call house arrest. For the duration of this evening's events only, naturally. It seemed the sensible thing to do. He did rather want you for himself, you see."

"House arrest, you say?" Mikali laughed out loud. "Why, you've quite made my evening, Brigadier."

The five-minute-warning bell sounded for the start of the second half. Ferguson said, "There's no way out, my dear chap, you do realize that? To use that old-fashioned phrase beloved of the British copper, better to come along quietly."

"But my dear Brigadier, when have I ever done anything quietly?"

The Greek Ambassador tapped him on the shoulder. "We'd be honored if you would join our party in my box for the second half of the concert."

"Delighted, Mr. Ambassador," Mikali said. "I'll only be a few minutes."

He turned back to Ferguson, who was no longer smiling. "Your performance tonight was something I shall long remember, but I should hate it to be your epitaph. Think about that."

He touched Deville on the arm. The Frenchman smiled sadly. "I told you what would happen, John. You wouldn't listen."

"But you were wrong, old buddy." Mikali smiled. "You said it might be next Wednesday, but it's Saturday night."

They went out through the door, and Mikali watched them go, people flooding around him. Baker had disappeared, but Katherine Riley still stood waiting against the wall, still separated from him by the weight of people.

He pushed his way through to her and stood, hands in pockets, the cigarette dangling from the corner of his mouth. And when he smiled, the heart turned over inside her.

"Have you known long?"

"Since Hydra for certain. I found Morgan up in the hills in a bad way, or he found me."

Mikali nodded. "Ah, I see now. If it matters to you at all, his daughter was an accident. I tried to miss her. It just wasn't possible."

"Why, Johnny?" she said.

He leaned against the wall beside her, and for a moment they were isolated from all else. Despite everything she now knew about him, there was total intimacy between them.

"Oh, I don't know," Mikali said. "I was so damned good at it. That was the trouble. But you're the doctor, Doctor. You tell me."

"You had such a great gift in your music," she said. "You showed that tonight. And in the end. . . ."

"Nothing lasts," he said. "Everything passes."

As the Greek Ambassador moved out with his party Mikali took her arm and followed. "You know, they tell me there's several miles of corridors in this old rabbit warren and not a straight line in the place. Everything circular, one curve after another, and Asa Morgan could be waiting round any one of them."

"Hardly," she said. "Brigadier Ferguson had him confined for the night at his flat in Upper Grosvenor Street."

"Well he didn't do too good a job of it. Around twenty minutes ago I saw him standing in the exit door of the gangway just below your box, and he didn't look too friendly. Mind you, I must say it added a certain edge to the final minutes of my performance."

She grabbed his arm, pulling him to a halt. "For god's sake, what are you going to do?"

"Why, join the Greek Ambassador and his party in their box for the second half. The traditional fare. Elgar's *Pomp and Circumstance*, a *Fantasia on British Sea Songs*, and at the end, everybody in the damned place standing up for *Jerusalem* and singing their hearts out. The last night of the Proms, angel. How could I possibly miss that, even for Asa Morgan?"

"What are you talking about?"

She turned from him in horror. She had to find Baker to tell him Morgan was there. As she ran for the exit door she realized that all her attempts to understand the fanaticism of terrorists would fail in the end if she could not understand Morgan's need for revenge.

Mikali kept on walking at the tail of the Ambassador's party, dropping back a pace or two, turning quickly into the next corridor exit they came to, standing in the shadows of the landing, waiting until their footsteps had died away.

There was a brief silence, and then the orchestra started to play Elgar's *Pomp and Circumstance March.*

He said softly, "Right, my friend, let's see if we can find you," and he moved out into the deserted corridor.

SIXTEEN

Harry Baker was talking to a uniformed inspector in the foyer of the rear entrance when Katherine Riley found him. She was obviously considerably distressed and he caught hold of her by the arms.

"Here, what is it?"

"Asa," she said. "He's here—somewhere in the building. Mikali knows. He saw him in the hall just before the interval."

"God almighty!" Baker said. "Where's Mikali now?"

"He joined the Greek Ambassador's party for the second half."

He pushed her down into a seat. "Right, you stay there."

He had the briefest of conversations with the inspector, then disappeared up the stairs on the run.

Ferguson and Deville were back in the rear seat of the Brigadier's limousine in the car park when a police sergeant appeared from the command post van and called him out. After a while, Ferguson got back in the car.

"Trouble?" Deville asked.

"You could say that. It seems Asa Morgan's loose somewhere in the building."

"So, this house arrest you spoke of was obviously not enough to hold him, but then you counted on that, I think?"

Ferguson said, "The Cretan Lover and John Mikali. All going to come out. Bound to. And what would he get? Not a rope, but life imprisonment, this being the enlightened and liberal age it is. Can you imagine what that would do to a man like him?"

"So, you prefer Morgan to play the hangman for you?"

"Asa always has done rather well as a public executioner. Mikali alive is of no direct use to us. You are, and his untimely going would simplify your own position enormously."

"Very neat," Deville said. "Except for one rather important point you appear to have overlooked."

"And what would that be?"

"Don't be too sure your Colonel Morgan will come out ahead of the game. The question of which of them is the better man is arguable, but Morgan is certainly in the worse physical shape. He might end up on his back in there with a bullet between the eyes."

Harry Baker came down the stairs to the rear entrance foyer. As Katherine stood up, he said, "No sign of him in the Greek Ambassador's box. I've checked."

He turned to the inspector and started to talk to him in a low, urgent voice. For the moment, Katherine Riley was forgotten, and she went upstairs

quietly, starting to run when she had turned the
corner and was out of sight.

She paused on the landing below the Prince Consort Room where the reception had been held. She
didn't know which way to go to stop those two from
killing each other.

Faintly, from the direction of the hall, she could
hear the stirring strains of Elgar's *Pomp and Circumstance* and then, quite suddenly, and to her total
astonishment, she heard the sound of a piano accom-
paniment drifting down from above.

There was nowhere to go this time, Mikali knew
that. No way out. The last barricade and standing
there in the shadows, listening to *Pomp and Circumstance* echoing from the hall, he remembered Kasfa,
the smell of burning, the four *fellagha* drifting
toward him as he lay there, propped against the wall,
holding on hard to life, refusing to let go. They'd
been waiting a long time for him. A long time.

"All right, Morgan," he thought. "Come to me."

He went up the dark staircase on his right. He
opened the door at the top cautiously and looked into
the Prince Consort Room where the reception had
been held. It was empty, of course, as he had expected,
the only occupant his other self reflected in the long
mirror at the far end. That darkly elegant creature
that had haunted him for so long.

"Okay, old buddy," he called. "The last time, so
let's get it right."

There was a concert grand in the corner by the
window, a Schiedmayer. As he walked across to it,
he took out the gold case, selected one of the Greek

cigarettes, and lit it. Then he opened the lid of the Schiedmayer and sat down. He took out the Ceska and laid it ready at the end of the keyboard.

"All right, Morgan," he said softly. "Where are you?" and he started to play *Pomp and Circumstance* with great verve, following the distant strains of the orchestra in the hall.

When the footsteps sounded on the stairs it was not Morgan who appeared, but Katherine Riley. She leaned in the doorway to catch her breath, then came forward.

"This is crazy. What are you doing?"

"Trying a little Elgar. I'd forgotten what fun he is."

He was playing quite brilliantly now and very loudly, leaning over the piano, the cigarette hanging from the corner of his mouth.

The sound drifted down the stairwell, along those curving corridors, so that Asa Morgan, waiting in the shadows by the Green Room passageway, turned at once and started up the stairs, his hand on the butt of the Walther in the right-hand pocket of his trenchcoat.

And the sound reached even Baker, standing with the inspector in the rear entrance foyer. He turned and went up the stairs on the run, the inspector and two constables on his heels.

"Please, John, if I ever meant anything to you at all."

"Oh, but you did, angel." Mikali smiled. "Remember that morning in Cambridge on the Backs at the side of the river? That was a set-up because I needed to meet you to make sure Lieselott wasn't a threat to me."

"I know that now."

"Not that it matters. The truth is you were the only woman I ever knew I ever really cared about. Any chance you could explain that to me?"

And then Asa Morgan moved out of the shadows and filled the doorway.

Mikali stopped playing. "You took your damned time about it, didn't you?"

In the distance, the orchestra was into the *Fantasia on British Sea Songs.*

Morgan said, "I'm here now, you bastard, that's all that matters."

"The field of battle is a land of standing corpses," Mikali smiled. "A Chinese military strategist named Wu Ch'i said that rather a long time ago. I'd say it sums you and me up perfectly, Morgan. At the end of the day, there isn't really too much to choose between us."

His hand swept up, holding the Ceska. Katherine Riley screamed, running between them, arms outstretched.

"No, John!"

As Mikali hesitated, started to get up, Morgan dropped to one knee and fired the Walther once, but with total accuracy, striking Mikali in the heart, lifting him back over the piano stool, killing him instantly.

And then, somehow, Baker was there and the three policemen. Morgan stayed by the door holding the Walther against his thigh. Katherine Riley waited, hands at her sides, as Baker crouched over Mikali.

"He could have shot you, Asa," she said, "Only I got in the way. He hesitated because I got in the way."

Baker stood up and turned, holding the Ceska. "No, love, you've got it wrong. He wasn't about to shoot anybody, not with this gun. It's empty. See for yourself. He'd removed the magazine."

The inspector was at the housephone on the wall behind the bar, speaking in a low voice. "Link me with the command vehicle. Brigadier Ferguson."

Katherine Riley went forward and knelt down beside Mikali. His white shirt front was stained with blood, but his face was quite unmarked, eyes closed, and he was smiling slightly.

She brushed the hair away from his forehead, then very carefully removed the white carnation from his lapel. The carnation he had thrown to her in the loggia box. The carnation she had kissed and tossed back to him.

She turned and walked out, brushing past Morgan without a word.

"Kate?" he said and made to go after her.

Baker caught him by the arm. "Let her go, Asa. Just give me the gun."

Morgan handed him the Walther and Baker unloaded it. "Feel any better now? Has it brought Megan back?"

Morgan went and stood over Mikali's body. "Why did he do it?"

"Well, at a guess, Asa, old son, I'd say it goes something like this. You're good, but he knew he was better and he couldn't afford that, not this time. He had nowhere else to go."

"Damn him to hell!" Morgan said.

"It's a point of view. By the way, Asa, have you

read the *Daily Telegraph* today? Got a list of the latest army promotions. You've made it at last. Brigadier. Now you can even tell Ferguson to go to hell if you want to."

But Morgan was no longer listening. He turned and ran out into the corridor. It was deserted except for Katherine Riley disappearing around the curve of the far end.

"Kate?" he cried, and as he started to run, the audience in the hall broke into a storm of applause at the end of the sea songs fantasia.

When he reached the top of the stairs leading down to the main foyer, there was no sign of her. He went down them two at time and straight out through the glass doors. Behind him, orchestra and chorus and the entire audience broke into the glorious strains of *Jerusalem*.

It was raining hard, the road jammed with traffic. As he went down the steps, Ferguson came to meet him, holding an umbrella over his head.

"Congratulations, Asa."

"What you wanted, wasn't it? I knew that from the beginning. We both did. Just the same old bloody game, like always."

"Neatly put."

Morgan gazed around him wildly. "Where is she?"

"Over there." Ferguson nodded across the road. "I'd hurry if I were you, Asa."

But Morgan, darting between the traffic through heavy rain, was too late. As he reached the other side she had already moved past the Albert Memorial and disappeared into the darkness of the park.